THE DELPHI INITIATIVE

A TOMMY DONOVAN NOVEL

WJ LUNDY
AJ POWERS

Edited by
SARA JONES

Illustrated by
AJ POWERS

COPYRIGHT

THE DELPHI INITIATIVE

A TOMMY DONOVAN NOVEL

W.J. Lundy & AJ Powers
V3.30.2020

CHAPTER ONE

O n Washington's south side a three-story stone
building sat in the shadows. A relic of the old
days, the structure was away from the normal hustle of
the Capital. Most senators held private office spaces in
their home districts and only used official meeting spaces
while in session. But Charles Shafer wasn't your typical
senator. He was corrupt and dirty and had plenty to
hide. His history and shady past were no secret in Washington, but still, his colleagues always managed to look
the other way, and his constituents always managed to
keep him in office. Seniority brought power, and when it
came to years in office, nobody had more than Chuck
Shafer.

Of course, even his enemies were more than happy to
take a bit of what he was passing out in return for their
support. Especially at election time when the coffers
were running dry and they just needed a few dollars to
buy those one or two extra points in the polls. Shafer
always knew how to get his name into every special-

interest agenda so that the voters felt he was fighting for them. He was the blue-collar man, the Regular Joe sent to Washington to take on the evil enterprise, and his people loved it.

Senator Charles Shafer knew his way around the swamp he lived in, and he thrived on it. But today he was dealing with a dangerous gator and it wasn't good business to let gators into his public office in the Capitol Building, and that was why he was here. Charles was tired and feeling a bit buzzed from a two-martini lunch that had turned into four, but he forced himself to extinguish the temptation of a nap.

He took a deep breath and spun his chair. From a small refrigerator behind him, he retrieved a can of club soda. He opened it, listened to the fizz, and took a long drink before setting it on the corner of his desk.

There was a subtle knock at the door, and then it slowly opened. He expected to see the face of Sharon Carlisle his secretary, but instead, it was the face he had been ignoring for weeks. Mark Dorsey, the Seattle phenom, the genius behind the predictive artificial intelligence they called the Delphi Initiative.

Mark had been the low bidder and the lead contract holder for a big intelligence project in the Midwest, and now that the facility was close to going online, he had been wagering bets on being put in charge of all of it. Charles waved the young man in. He looked him over and smirked; the kid dressed like a big-city hipster, his beard well-groomed, his trousers two sizes too tight.

How the man became a billionaire dressing like a vagrant amazed the senator. Charles knew the kid's backstory, but it still shocked him. See, unlike the other tech wizards who made millions off the Internet's boom and innovation by inventing things, Mark didn't really make or sell anything; no, he was what the tech giants called a "fixer." He made his money by bundling and compiling existing products. He basically stole technology to slowly eliminate the competition.

If Company A was doing something, Mark took what he needed, paying off engineers, buying thumb drives of data then put up the research capital to allow Company B to do it better. Sure, there was litigation and patent violations, but it was all pinned to Company B. In the meantime, it was Mark Dorsey with the big tech backing who financed all of it, including the lawyers. With billions in the bank, there was no legal challenge that could stop him. Soon companies would settle out of court. Company A went out of business and Company B merged into the hands of the technology giants.

All the prime tech quickly absorbed and drifted into the catalogs of the giants. What was once a company prized application, soon became a widget on a browser toolbar. With Dorsey's help, the tech giants became monopolies, and the little guys vanished. But what do monopolies do when they are king? What do you do when being the best in the industry is not enough? They needed more, they wanted it all. And Mark helped them get it—that was until Mark found something he couldn't resist keeping for himself.

While others in Congress slowly mobilized to push back against big tech and to break up the monopolies, Senator Shafer passed the money around the Senate to make sure nothing ever got done. He quickly learned you don't have to buy everyone; you don't even have to change any minds. Votes were a numbers game, and he only needed just enough to keep a bill from passing, or enough to ensure it passed; the details rarely concerned Shafer anymore. He grinned, thinking about how many votes he'd paid for with the kid's money. Then, looking at his gold Rolex, his grin turned into a full smile, thinking of all the money he had kept for himself.

He stood and waved a hand toward an overstuffed leather chair. "Mark, it's good to see you, my friend. Could I get you a drink?"

The young man rushed in; he was twitchy as always. *Probably a drug thing*, the senator thought, watching the man pace in front of his desk.

"You said it would be up for a vote today."

Shafer frowned and leaned back in his overstuffed chair. "We talked about this; things take time. And something this big takes even more. The committees are demanding more research; they want studies done, they want guarantees."

The young man turned and faced the door, his hands balled into fists, his head twitching. Shafer smiled. *No, it isn't drugs. Probably too much of those frappy-whatever-a-chinos the kids were all into these days.* He shook his head. *Whatever happened to just drinking coffee like a man?*

The senator took a deep breath and exhaled. "Listen, Mark, if it came up today, Delphi wouldn't have the votes. There are just too many unknowns."

The man shook his head and turned back around. "Delphi can save lives. It will save lives."

"I believe that it will—many of us do," Shafer said. He looked at the club soda and wished he'd poured a scotch instead. Dealing with the kid this late in the afternoon was going to be a pain in the ass. He sighed. "There are just too many privacy concerns, too many things to convince people that Delphi won't be used against law-abiding people."

Mark slapped his palm against his forehead. "This again, I cannot believe it's this again." The young man turned and sat in the previously offered chair. "Listen, if people are law-abiding, they have absolutely nothing to worry about. Delphi doesn't care about law-abiding; the protocol only engages on crimes and suspicious activity. It uses metadata to identify threats."

Charles sat up and pointed a finger. "Exactly, but it's that metadata that's got folks concerned. The judicial committee said it might even violate privacy laws." The Senator looked down at a leather briefing case on his desk. He flipped it open to a double-spaced printed page. "This says you are planning to use phone records, banking, travel documents, even social media and utility bills to identify threats, and all without a warrant."

"Yes," Mark said. "That is precisely how Delphi works. No warrant is needed because only the system knows your identity, and the system doesn't care who you talk to or what you talk about. Joke with a friend about robbing a bank, the system doesn't care. Post threats to the bank online, the system doesn't care. But make a threat, buy a gun, and then case out the bank or get a positive facial recognition on the bank's cameras, and the system wakes up—it begins to predict probability. It makes rational decisions, and it moves quickly to save lives. Only after complete calculations will it issue a conclusion to human operators.

"There is still reasonable doubt, sure. Don't put the pieces together, joke but don't plan, and it's like it never happened; Delphi forgets about it. No action is ever taken, nobody will ever know."

Shafer shook his head. "But you are listening to people's conversations, you are tracking what they buy and where they go."

This time, the man shouted. "No! Stop thinking one-dimensionally. You act like some old lady is listening to a police scanner, spying on you."

He paused and reached for the briefing folder, flipping through the printed pages, until finding one with a wiring diagram. He dropped the page on the center of the desk. "This is all existing software. Decades have been spent putting these pieces together. Nobody is listening to how you spend money any more than your bank's fraud department. Nobody is listening to your phone calls, or paying attention to what you watch on TV, or reading your text messages. It's just data, and Delphi isn't a person; it's banks of servers in a basement in St Louis. These are thousands of independent systems. They aren't agents reading your information, so there is no privacy breach. Delphi is a machine, the same as the talking AI in your smartphone. The AI in your phone doesn't tell on you, it doesn't care who you text or if you watch porn, it will never shame you to your friends. Delphi is the same—it just pieces things together. If you have nothing to hide, you are fine, the data will never be acted on. Ever."

"But what happens when Delphi is wrong?" Charles said.

Mark put up his hands. "If the system is wrong, and there is no crime, then who cares? Nobody died. That's what is important, right?"

Charles made a fist with his left hand and put it against his chin. He slowly pursed his lips then sighed. "People are afraid of what the system could do. This is a lot for me to sell, Mark."

"You already took payment. Let's not pretend like this is optional for you anymore. You've spent a lot of our money to ensure that Delphi goes online. And to be frank, Delphi knows a lot about you too, Mister Senator."

Shafer went to speak, but Mark held up a finger, silencing him. "Delphi is already installed. We just need a vote to turn it on, connect with law enforcement. So, tell me, what do we have to do to get those votes?"

Charles turned in his chair so that he was looking out the window. "You are going to have to make people more afraid of a world without Delphi, than they are of a world with it."

Mark stood and rubbed his beard. He nodded. "Easily done, we shall be in touch."

CHAPTER TWO

Tommy Donovan jerked awake, his head off the pillow, the muscles in his neck tensed. He was ready to strike; he just didn't know what at. The pounding of his heart, his head thumping with every beat so hard he could feel it in his eyes. He held his breath, his eyes surveying the room without moving his body, ready to launch himself at some dark shadow. He relaxed, finding they were still alone.

Eighteen months since he'd left Syria and a trail of bodies. He looked up at the ceiling fan slowly rotating above him. So much had changed in that time for him, but one thing was still constant, and that was the war that constantly replayed in his dreams. They weren't always nightmares, but they were always there. Drinking and company tended to dull it, but it was still there. In his mind, he'd heard gunfire, in his mind it was real. Even when he was back here in his island paradise, there were parts of his mind that refused to shut it all down.

He looked down at the cold blue illumination of the

clock's digital numbers. Just after two in the morning. He'd been asleep less than an hour. He reached for the glass of water on the nightstand and took a long sip. Turning back, he saw her still sleeping soundly beside him, Tanya's body outlined by the light linen that covered her. Watching her, he wondered what she meant to him, or really what exactly he meant to her.

She was the only thing stable in his life, and even she was technically paid to keep an eye on him, to keep him on a short leash. There was intimacy there, but was there any emotion, any connection outside of convivence? She was his handler—or was it liaison, as she said she was? He watched her chest rise and fall with each breath and wondered where her professional responsibilities ended and the personal began. Smiling, he laughed thinking about her bosses at the agency and what they would think if they knew she was in his bed. He sat up, swinging his feet to the floor, and rubbed his head.

"Hell, they'd probably give her a medal," he whispered. "They appreciate dedication."

Tommy lifted the glass to his mouth again just as a long volley of gunfire racked the air. His hand shook, and he dropped the glass. It fell to the rug, spilling its contents as it rolled toward the nightstand. His body went rigid on high alert. He turned back to her; she was still asleep.

She didn't hear it? But he did, didn't he?

He held his breath again with his heart beating in his chest. He wasn't going crazy, he thought. Was the gunfire real or was he losing his mind? No, it was real; he not only heard it, he felt it that time. Tommy stood and walked away from the bed, his heart still pounding, the hairs on the back of his neck stiff and tingling while shivers ran down his spine. Cold sweat began to bead on his forehead.

Not here, he thought, this is the Virgin Islands. People here aren't even armed, that's why he lived here. Wearing only boxers, he moved through to the patio door and out onto the street-facing balcony. His small apartment was on Dronnigens Gade, the main street through his new home. Unlike some of the crime-ridden ghettos he'd lived in previously, the main street here was filled with high-end shops and tourist attractions—all the hot spots of Charlotte Amalie. This wasn't a place where you heard gunfire.

He stood at the railing and listened intently. He could hear the tourists walking, their laughs and shouts echoing as they returned to hotels and resorts from closing bars. He gripped the railing and leaned forward, his eyes clenched shut, taking in the humid evening island air. Letting the warmth soothe and shake off the jitters, he breathed in deeply and exhaled.

The gunfire had sounded real to him. Far away, but very real. But it could have been anything, fireworks, a dream. "No," he whispered and shook his head. He knew it was gunfire, every synapse in his brain was snapping and screaming at him to act, every bit of training already identifying the caliber and possible weapons used. They were pistols calibers, but rapid like a submachine gun, probably HK, multiple shooters, two maybe three hundred meters away.

His brain wanted him to prep and respond. Take

cover, grab a go-bag, and leave. He rubbed his forehead and cursed. "What the hell is wrong with me?" It didn't make any sense, not here. He closed his eyes tight again and took in another deep breath. "It had to be a dream."

As Tommy was beginning to clear his thoughts and return to bed, a clap of thunder smacked his ears, and the apartment shook under his feet. He saw the flashes in the western sky roll over French Town. He squatted to his heels, looking over the railing. He watched a black cloud bleed smoke into the distant sky.

"My God," he muttered. "It's the Capital. Who would bomb the Capital?"

The tourist laughter on the streets hushed, then turned to panicked screams. The gunfire was back, and this time it was close and unmistakable. He couldn't pinpoint the source. It seemed to come from all around him. He heard police sirens and more screams. On the apartment block across the street, there was a second explosion. Glass blew out of the first-floor lobby of an upscale apartment building.

He pulled back as he felt his own building rumble from a third explosion. Smoke and fire filled the street below him. Tommy turned back and ducked into the room.

Tanya was standing in front of the bed, looking at him, her eyes wide with fear. Faster than he could speak, he heard shouts and more gunfire from the hallway outside. A man screamed as an extended burst of automatic gunfire rattled in the hallway.

He ran and shoved her toward the small apartment's bathroom. "Go, get in the tub, go."

She'd just vanished into the bathroom as the apartment door burst open. Two men charged through in black police vests, holding black submachine guns. No more time for doubts, his body and brain switched on and allowed his training to take over. Tommy dove back across the bed as the room exploded with gunfire.

The man to the left shouted something then fired again into the wall over Tommy's head. He knew they hadn't seen him in the dark, but more likely heard his body as it crashed to the floor. Tommy dropped and watched the muzzle flashes as he rolled to the bed. He pressed to the cold tile floor, stretched his hand under the mattress and found the Walther PPK taped to the bottom. He pulled it free, blindly returning fire through the box spring in the direction of the men. He heard a muffled grunt. The weapons paused with the yelping, then more gunfire that went wild. There were the sounds of a bolt locking on an empty weapon.

Tommy pushed back from the bed and turned toward the door. The first shooter was against the wall, struggling to bring up his weapon with a gunshot to his right shoulder. The second foe was fumbling with a submachinegun—he took the rest of the Walther PPK's nearly empty magazine to the neck and face. Without hesitation on the final trigger pull, Tommy rushed forward and lunged toward the first shooter. Colliding, he pressed the man against the wall.

He saw a large fighting knife clipped vertically to the man's armor. Tommy dropped the empty pistol and traded it for the man's knife, pulling it free from the vest as the shooter reached for a sidearm with his good hand.

Tommy pushed back and locked the man's gun hand to the wall before driving the blade up and under his chin, twisting the handle as it sank in. He pulled back, releasing the blade, letting it stick as the body hit the floor.

The building's fire alarm was blaring. Lights were strobing in the room, and smoke filled the hallway.

"Tanya," he shouted.

The woman crept from the bathroom, her own service pistol in her hands held at the low ready. When she saw him, her weapon went up and fired three rounds. Tommy flinched then stepped back as a third man dropped dead in the open doorway. She kept her weapon up while Tommy ran to the door and pulled the body into the room, kicking the door closed.

"What the hell is going on?" She paused, her hands still gripping the G19 pistol. Her wide eyes locked on him. He was still in his boxers, his hands and bare chest covered in blood and gore. "My God! Are you all right?"

Tommy clenched his teeth, ignoring the comment, and picked over the dead. They were sterile—no IDs, no badges, yet all dressed as local police. He grabbed a man's jaw; he looked Asian, maybe Hispanic.

"I said are you hurt?" she asked again.

Tommy flinched as more gunfire sounded from outside. "We don't have a lot of time." He stopped his search and looked back at Tanya. He rolled the body to check the back pockets. "Check your phone," he said,

There were footsteps in the hallway. He froze and could see the white light of a flashlight through holes in the broken doorframe. Someone was coming. He exhaled and pressed back to his knees and focused on the door. His pistol was empty. The weapons belonging to the dead men lay just behind him. He looked at the balcony; he could jump, but he wouldn't leave Tanya. He most certainly would break his legs, anyway.

As the sounds in the hall grew closer, Tommy retrieved one of the MP5 submachine guns and moved back to the bed. Tanya held up the phone, shaking her head, on the other end of the room. He put a finger to his lips and pointed back to the bathroom. He stepped around the bed and took a knee as the first figure pressed open the door. He wanted to fire blind, but he couldn't. He had to identify the target. He knew it could be police or a neighbor looking for help. He put the weapon to his shoulder and locked the sights on the shadow as it entered the doorframe.

"Thomas?" the woman said quietly, the word sounding like "thom-us."

He immediately recognized the voice and relaxed his grip on the weapon. A flashlight passed over the bodies on the floor then scanned toward Tommy.

"Freeze," he said before the light could hit his face. "It's me, Donovan."

"Thank God you're okay," the voice responded.

Tommy stammered. He knew her, but why she was here, confused him. Before he could speak, two more men rushed into the room. One tall and Hispanic, the other black and bulking through his tactical vest. They both moved like professionals, but he didn't know them, which concerned him. They scanned the space, ignoring Tommy.

The Hispanic man turned to the female. "Is this him? This the guy the Colonel sent us after?"

The woman nodded. The Hispanic man shone his barrel-mounted light over Tommy then turned back to the woman. "He doesn't look like much; you sure this is him?"

"Trust me, he's plenty enough," the woman said.

The black man moved deeper into the room with a finger to his ear. "We have to go. There is another kill team two blocks up, headed this way."

She nodded and looked at Tommy. "Thomas, we have to move."

He stood his ground and shook his head. He turned around and looked at Tanya, still in her long nightgown, and said, "Get dressed."

As he spoke, he moved to his walk-in closet and pulled on a pair of khaki pants. He snatched a heavy T-shirt and grabbed a pair of boots before moving back into the bedroom. He tossed the items on the bed then grabbed a black canvas field jacket that was folded above a wardrobe. The jacket, which he never wore, had a passport and a few thousand dollars cash sewn into the liner. But these people didn't need to know that.

The woman began to look anxious. "Thomas, in less than five minutes this entire street will be occupied. We have to go."

"You think I'm going out in my skivvies, painted in that clown's blood?" He wiped his chest with a dirty T-shirt. "Sorry, sweetheart, I don't roll like that."

She shook her head. "It won't matter how you *roll*, if you are dead."

He looked up at her with cold eyes. "You said occupied—occupied by who? The police?"

"Does it matter?" one of the men said.

Tommy shot him a cold glare that caused the man to turn and focus on the doorway.

The black man was standing with a finger to his ear. He looked at the woman. "Bad guys three minutes out. If we don't move now, we'll be shooting our way out."

As if to punctuate the warning, gunfire and explosions echoed from outside.

"Any of you want to tell me what the hell is going on?" Tommy said. "Who I just greased?"

The woman nodded and turned toward the door. "Get dressed and meet us downstairs. I'll explain it in the van," she said, and the trio ran back into the hall.

Tanya was dressed now. She had her pistol still in her right hand, her cell phone in her left. Tommy finished with his boots and stood. "Anything from the office?"

She shook her head. "The phones are dead. Who are these people?"

"The ones on the floor or the ones waiting for us outside?"

He moved to one of the dead and took the man's sidearm, a Browning high power. He placed it at the back of his belt and took as many spare mags from the dead as he could get.

"The ones outside," Tanya answered. "Your friends, apparently."

Tommy went to the hallway and checked left and right before stepping into it. "The men I've never seen before. The woman is from an alphabet agency that checks in on me every now and then." He was lying. She wasn't government—at least not with the American government. She worked for an old friend who knew how to get things done. She was a subcontractor of sorts.

Since he'd moved here and Tanya Delgado's employers put him on payroll, he'd been expected to do certain side jobs for them. It was nothing like his days with the Central Intelligence Agency's clandestine Ground Division, but it was still work that required certain levels of deniability. There were just some things that couldn't be done in the light of day, and some things that couldn't ever point back to those responsible. It was for things like that when they called Tommy.

Three times he had been asked to perform a task since he retired to the Island, and all three times it was Natalia who had provided his transportation and papers. She was a provider, they called it, a logistician. She had a network of people who knew how to get things done. Whether it was pulling an asset from war-torn Ukraine or eliminating a known bomb-maker in Damascus. Natalia knew how to get him in and out without anyone knowing.

Whenever he was handed an envelope from the agency, it was Natalia who put the pieces together for him. But because of the probable deniability agreement, Tanya and the agency never knew about her. In fact, even Tommy didn't know how to directly contact her. He'd always gone through his intermediary, a mutual friend in Virginia. His mind began to scramble. Natalia didn't know where he lived, but their mutual friend did.

"Are you cheating on me with another agency, Tommy?" Tanya said, following him into the hall, breaking his thoughts. "Do we not pay you enough to stay exclusive? Is that why you are out doing side jobs?"

He moved to the stairwell and held up, listening. He investigated the hall and found it clear. "I know people that know how to get things done. She is one of them. I might look like Superman, but it takes a network to do the impossible." He stopped and turned to face Tanya. "Hey, you're the spook that has me on retainer. Aren't you supposed to know who she is?"

"I'm not a spook, I'm a messenger," Tanya snapped back. "I don't do anything more than hand you an envelope a couple times a year."

"Yes, and those envelopes ask me to do things, no questions asked. Natalia and her people are one of those questions you shouldn't ask about." Tommy stopped and turned back. He looked her up and down and smiled. "I think you do more for me than hand over envelopes."

CHAPTER THREE

Alexander Winston parked the late-model Range Rover behind the barn and walked up the gravel drive toward the old farmhouse. Douglas, want-to-be cowboy, former Ranger sniper, then Virginia state trooper, turned gun for hire, was on the porch with his head back. The bearded man was rocking in an old chair, a Stetson on his head and a beer in his hand.

"What are you doing drinking? You've got next watch," Winston said.

Douglas shook his head and took another pull on the blue can. "Operation is off. Entire thing is shut down. Guess they picked up that cell at the border."

"Border?" Winston said. "That doesn't sound right. What border?"

The man shook his head and scoffed. "How da hell should I know? They just said border."

For the last week, Winston had been added to this team of knuckleheads. The men weren't DOD—at least not anymore. The team was shaped of all backgrounds and quickly put together to do a risk assessment. Each was supposed to be a specialist in their area—snipers, close quarters battle, demolition. Winston's specialty was infiltration and killing everything in the room. He'd been watching the others, and his impression of any of them being experts was lacking.

Most of the guys were burnouts, let go hard chargers looking for a payday. Sure, in Fallujah or the Korangal Valley, he'd want nobody else watching his six. But here in rural Minnesota, they just weren't the kind of guys he would have selected. The guys were sledgehammers when they really needed scalpels.

He hadn't bothered to get to know the other members of the team. He wasn't interested in their war stories and honestly didn't want them knowing too much about him. It wasn't personal, but in Alexander Winston's business, being well known was a vulnerability, and if he hoped to land a big money contract job post-retirement, anonymity was an asset he was hoping to hold on to.

Winston looked up at the man on the porch and shook his head. No, he didn't like this assignment, but it beat the hell out of the desk he'd been riding for the last three years. Since leaving the Ground Division, or truth be told, since the Ground Division was eliminated from the books, Winston had been bounced around different departments, most having to do with more writing and planning than field action.

From working intelligence at Guantanamo Bay, to

short stints in putting together personal security details with the State Department. When he was called up to red cell this mall in the middle of Minnesota, he took the orders with grace. Well, for the most part; he was volun-told and had no choice, and being less than a year from a pension, saying no wasn't really an option.

He had arrived at the farm a week earlier. There was strong intelligence that an Al-Shabaab cell of Somali terrorists was looking to hit the Mall of America. Someone on the counterterror desk got the bright idea that if they could put together a team of warfighters to survey and develop multiple plans of attack, they might be able to reverse engineer the cell and find the scumbags. Winston laughed at the idea, the absurdity of it. Like always, the college kids in the airconditioned offices at Langley were overthinking shit.

You want to find terrorists, you go to where they live, you root them out, track their phones, track their friends, read their emails. And then once you've done all the homework, you call a man like him, a man like Winston, to move in and kill them. Sitting on a farm, planning an attack on a shopping mall, was a waste of his skills.

"Who gave the abort order?" Winston asked.

The Cowboy drained the rest of his can then reached into a cooler for another. He held it out to Winston, who shook his head no. The man pulled the tab. "That FBI guy, Johnson—"

"Johnston," Winston corrected.

Cowboy shook his head. "Yeah, John *ston*, that's what I said." He grinned. "Anyhow, he was just here. He said they captured the fools at the border, and he dropped off a couple coolers of beer and some steaks and gave us all an attaboy. Said we should celebrate."

Winston smiled from half his mouth and shook his head. "Celebrate what? So... what now? Drink beer and hang out?" Winston said.

Cowboy laughed. "Nah, man. He said a van would be here at 0500 to take us to the airport. Like I said, the operation is off, bro."

Winston moved past the man, onto the stairs, and through the screen door, which was held open with a second cooler. Inside, he could see the sofas and chairs were all empty. He could hear laughing from the back porch. The kitchen table still held the maps of the mall and tactical drawings. On a table was a collection of weapons, most of them junk, but the type and style Johnston said would most likely be available to the terror cell.

Pinned to the wall were photos the team had taken over the last week. They had painstakingly detailed entrances, security doors, cameras. Even the numbers and times police cars parked in the lot. He looked at the work product and gave a half-grin. For a bunch of dirt-bags, they had put together a hell of a package. Maybe the FBI would find a use for it.

Ignoring the noise from the back porch and the savory smells of a barbeque grill, he moved to the first bedroom on the right and picked up his bag. He'd never fully unpacked it, and as he'd always done his entire career, he repacked his bag every morning before he went. He turned and left the house without saying good-bye. Walking down the porch, he saw that Cowboy was now on the phone talking to someone named Cinnamon, promising he'd be home the next day. He laughed and moved back to the Range Rover. He wasn't waiting around for a flight, and nobody was going to miss one vehicle.

CHAPTER FOUR

Jonathon Kershaw lay silent in the tall grass just outside the old house. From inside the home, he could hear shouts of laughter. He used his advance night vision optics to survey the terrain. Finding it empty, he switched to thermals that would pick up on slight variances in temperature. He squinted as he scanned the optic, looking at the structure and counting the red-and-orange blobs. They were all inside, no patrols, nobody on watch. It didn't fit the profile he'd been given. He looked across the grass and saw another of his teams falling into position behind a distant woodshed.

Jonathon had spent most of his life on teams just like this one, most of it on the East Coast as part of an anti-organized-crime task force, then doing drug interdiction on the southern border after that. But this was different; he was in Minnesota, and this wasn't his turf. Hell, it wasn't even his investigation. He'd been sent here blind with very little intel on the guys inside or why it was so urgent they be taken out without the proper planning.

"Four on the first floor, two on the second," he said into a throat mic, keeping his voice low.

"Copy," came the reply from the command helicopter that he knew was flying high overhead, recording the entire event on its FLIR cameras. "You are go for approach."

He paused, unsure if he'd heard the response correctly, and spoke again. "Command, they are still up. The mission plan said to wait for them to be asleep." He took a beat then said, "Request clarification."

The bird in the air was in command of the big picture, but Jonathon still had tactical control on the ground, and the mission brief said they would get into position, hold, survey, and hold again until the tangos were asleep, then hit them hard in the early hours of the morning when they were most likely to be down for the count. Taking them alive if they could, dead if not. A nighttime raid at just after midnight on an armed group that was still up and moving around would pretty much ensure a firefight.

"We have new information; you have to hit them now," came the reply. "You are go for approach."

Fuck, he mouthed to himself, no intel, no floorplan and now this. He closed his eyes and reopened them. He knew the rest of his assault team would be in position all around the building, twenty-four of them divided into fire teams of three. He'd never been with so many men before. Not since his time in the Marines had he had a platoon-sized force to raid a house. They always contingency planned for a full-on assault, and on paper, eight fire teams versus six men were good odds. But no plan survived first contact.

He squeezed his fists together; he felt the presence of the two men beside him. He knew they heard the same order and were having the same doubtful thoughts. He rose to his knee, knowing the others were doing the same. He checked his rifle a final time then stiffened.

"Echo Team, phase lines," he said.

Before he finished the words, he could see in the moonlight his men moving up on the building from the shadows to their pre-determined assault locations. He moved along a front porch and squatted down in a stack with two other teams, his group locked in the middle of nine men that would breach the front door. Nine more would be forming up the same way on the back door. This left two teams to provide overwatch with high-powered rifles and ready to pop choke and smoke into the windows if needed.

"Echo, you are a go," he heard from the command bird.

"Fuck," he whispered. It's a damn Ruby Ridge all over again. They were really doing this the stupid way. "Echo Team, on my count... three, two, one."

There was an explosion as both the front and back doors of the home exploded simultaneously. Flashbangs were launched in with more violent explosions. Before the flash could diminish, he was following his men into the structure. There were more flashes and booms, followed by automatic weapons fire, most from his men, but others from weapons he knew were not friendly.

He entered the house with his carbine up. In predetermined order from days of training, he cut right into a narrow hallway. Others moved up the stairs, as others fought a gun battle in the back of the home. He could hear the boom of sniper rifles outside. Someone called out they were hit. Another man screamed for a medic. Jonathon turned a corner. He knew his teammates were pinned to his back, following close. A bearded man in a white cowboy hat rushed from a room with an 870 shotgun.

"Don't you do it," Jonathon shouted.

A bright flash and pain in his chest let him know he'd been hit. He fell back against the next man in the stack. He leveled his rifle and pulled the trigger, all controlled shots, and the cowboy dropped to the floor with holes punched into his chest.

Jonathon was guided back against the wall, letting the next man in stack take his place. Someone shouted "clear." His teammate moved around him and pulled away at the Velcro on his vest.

"You're good, boss. Your armor took it all. You're one lucky guy."

He heard shouts of "clear" from different areas of the house. He exhaled and investigated the smoke-filled rooms. He couldn't believe they'd hit a farmhouse in the middle of the night with the lights on. How stupid. Whoever asked for this better have a damn good reason.

"Status," he said and received reports from his men. He had two down with light injuries. All tangos were dead. No prisoners.

He walked to the dead cowboy on the floor and knelt beside the body. He was young, early middle-aged, white, bearded. His white George Strait Stetson hat was splattered with blood. Jonathon leaned in and lifted the dead man's shirt sleeve. On his right arm was a 75th Ranger tattoo. He stood and walked back into the entry room of the farmhouse. Men were moving down the stairs, their weapons hanging from slings.

His partner was standing against a wall. Eric Castle, years younger than him but possibly twice as smart, or at least the man thought so. Castle pointed a finger as three men in white jackets walked into the house with cameras and briefcases.

"Damn, tech services didn't take time moving in. The smoke hasn't even cleared." Castle looked at Jonathon's torn vest pulled back. "You hurt?"

Jonathan shook his head. "Plates did their job." He walked into the doorway leading into a large living room. The techs were all over the room, snapping photos. The room was covered with maps and drawings of the Mall of America.

"These guys were the real deal," Castle said. "They were really going to hit the damn mall."

Jonathan shook his head. "Yeah, and we just killed a bunch of people for what they were planning to do, not what they'd done." He looked around at the techs already taking evidence. "We kicked in the doors and we killed them."

CHAPTER FIVE

The midnight-blue minivan drove down deserted side streets. It hit corners fast and headed into the center of the island, leaving the tourist districts behind them. People were standing on their porches and in their yards, looking at the distant fires in the city. The van turned off a street and onto a dirt road that ran through thick trees.

Tommy leaned forward between the seats. "Natalia, where are we going?"

"We have secured transportation off the island, but we have to leave now," Natalia said.

Tanya shook her head and looked at Tommy. "We should go to my office. We'll be safe there."

The black man in the driver's seat laughed. "Your office has been blown to shit."

The second shooter, sitting on a third-row bench seat behind Tommy, put his hands on the back of Tommy's seat and said, "The island isn't safe for you. We have to leave before they lock the place down."

"What do you mean lock it down?" Tommy asked. "What the hell is going on here? Who were those guys?"

Natalia pointed at a turnoff. The driver took the right turn and raced onto a narrow one-lane road going uphill. Looking straight ahead she said, "We don't know who they are." She turned and looked back at him. "Your name came up on a threat report forty-eight hours ago. It identified you directly, using your real name."

Tanya shook her head. "That's impossible. Tommy has been erased. Thomas Donovan doesn't exist; his record is clean."

"Well, one Thomas Donovan living in the big VI has been put on the FBI most wanted for conspiracy to commit violence against the Capital," the Hispanic man behind them said.

"It can't be. I would have been told," Tanya said.

The Hispanic man behind them grunted. "Your boyfriend is a bad man and apparently has some nasty shit planned for tonight."

"What the hell are you talking about?" Tommy asked. "Who were those men?"

Natali turned in her seat so that she could see him. She sighed. "I told you, we don't know who is doing this or why, but it's more than that," she said. "Once O'Connell dispatched us to bring your ass in, people started dying. People like you."

"Who is O'Connell?" Tanya asked.

"He is a friend," Tommy said. "Another one of those questions you don't want answered."

The Hispanic man laughed. "Yeah, I'd say he's a friend. He took a big risk sending us here. Some big people want you dead," he said as the van pulled up next to a small house on the edge of a low-cut field.

Tommy had been there before. They used it as a strip for planes. It was his exit point on the last three ops, and it was also the way O'Connell had gotten him onto the island almost eighteen months ago.

"Why do they want me dead?" Tommy asked. "Can one of you make this easy for me, spell it out?"

"Well obviously, you and your island friends have been planning terror attacks. They need to kill you to stop it all." The big man paused and looked out the window, toward the burning city. "Guess they were too late. Now nothing left but to kill you so you can't talk about it."

Tommy shook his head. "Who the hell is setting me up?"

"And why?" Tanya asked. "What do they think Tommy is going to do?"

The van door opened, and Natalia stepped back. She pointed toward the coastline far behind them. It was glowing, parts of the island city still flashing with explosions. "We don't know, but O'Connell ordered us to get you out; they will kill you for this."

Tommy stepped from the van and froze. "What do you mean? You think I did this? You know I didn't."

Natalia moved away from the van and stood at the edge of the field. The men left the van and closed the doors. One of them walked to a shadowed lump in the field and pulled at a tarp, uncovering an aircraft.

Natalia looked at Tommy. "We have to leave; the

airspace will be closed soon. They will lock down the island, searching for you."

He reached out and grabbed her arm. "What do you mean I did this? Why would they say I did this?" he repeated.

She shot him a cold stare then looked at her arm, and he released it. The tall man entered the aircraft as the second began making pre-flight checks. She glanced down at her watch and said, "The Colonel's friends at the FBI gave him a heads up that there was credible intelligence that there was going to be a terror attack in the US Virgin Islands. It named you directly. They wanted to know if he had a way to reach you."

"Who would do that?" Tanya said.

Natalia grinned and pointed at Tommy. "You're looking at him."

"This is bullshit!" Tommy said, close to losing his temper.

The small plane's engine came to life. Natalia looked at the Hispanic man, now in the pilot's seat, and waved. She looked back at Tommy, and her face softened.

"Yes, we know you didn't have anything to do with it. And when the outside channel showed your name recruiting men for a contract, the Colonel knew someone was trying to frame you."

"All of this, just to get Tommy?" Tanya said. "Why?"

"I said we don't know." Then Natalia nodded. "We hacked their local communications and have been listening in since we landed. It wasn't sophisticated. They were using generic Motorola radios on open channels. They sent multiple teams to attack hotels all over the island. Another team hit the Capital and your office.

"The last team was sent to kill you and take your body. Then they will pull up stakes and vanish. Your body will be discovered by the police and be broadcast on the evening news tonight." She paused and looked at Tommy's bloody hands. "They probably should have sent more to your apartment."

She pointed to the aircraft and urged them aboard.

CHAPTER SIX

H e pushed the overcooked eggs across his plate
with a fork. He wasn't hungry, even if he had
found them palatable. Far past midnight, the diner was
nearly empty. Winston would have preferred a hotel
room, but he was determined to catch the first flight out
of the Minneapolis-Saint Paul Airport down the street,
and that meant he only had a few hours to kill.

He'd purchased his ticket using one of his cleared
TSA profiles and headed straight for a place to burn
time. Even though his personal credentials were clear,
traveling was still one of the places he'd found himself
most vulnerable. Once through the security check and in
amongst the people and unarmed, he always felt naked
and alone. He'd had a long career with the Ground Division and there were at least a dozen people in a half
dozen countries who would love to see him dead or extra-
dited for the work he'd done.

Winston sat in a booth facing the south door, dressed
in dark jeans, a grey sweatshirt, and a dirt-stained red ball

cap. He was as invisible as any other blue-collar worker stopping in for an early breakfast. The diner was long and narrow. A counter stretched the length of the small dining room, booths along the wall, with long windows. There was a cook in the back, and a tired waitress behind the counter wrapped napkins around silverware when she wasn't making rounds filling coffee cups.

Winston looked up from his plate. The only other people in the diner were a young couple two booths down and a uniformed police officer at the very end. There was a TV over the center of the dining counter. The volume was off with subtitles running across the bottom. Some blend of cliché 50s music played over a speaker in the ceiling. Winston sipped at the black coffee, staring at the TV screen, hardly comprehending the stories the local newsman was reading.

Suddenly his mind clicked when a corner box on the screen showed a familiar image—the Mall of America. Scrolling along the bottom of the photo was a thick blue banner. *Breaking News, Terror attempt thwarted against America's largest shopping mall.*

Winston smiled and shook his head. Only a few hours out, and his mission was breaking news. Now interested, he stared at the screen and waited for the usual images of terror suspects' faces to pop up. Instead, a grid of American faces, some in uniform, filled the screen. On first thought, Winston was pissed that they were revealing the identities of his team; they were professionals and exposure would ruin them. But then his brain froze when he read the text at the bottom.

Extremist militia group raided. Six dead in what the

FBI calls the successful takedown of a domestic terror cell, the "Minneapolis Six" cell, feared to be related to the raids in a multi-state takedown.

"Domestic terror cell? What the ..."

Winston felt himself sweating now as a live video feed showed cars with flashing blue lights. In the background was the farmhouse, the porch he'd stood on hours earlier, now surrounded by police. A detective in a long dark coat was giving an impromptu press brief. He wanted to ask the waitress to turn on the volume, but he knew better than to draw attention to himself. He looked up and could see the uniformed officer was elbow deep in a slice of pie, and the loving couple were more interested in each other than the television.

Suddenly he felt confined, something he hadn't felt in a long time. He pulled a twenty from his wallet, placed it on the table, and moved as slowly as his body would allow him for the rear exit. Back in the Range Rover, he opened all the vents and ran the AC on high. He had the satellite radio tuned to network news as he drove toward the airport.

Winston pulled into the long-term parking structure, driving all the way to the roof, and killed the engine.

"What the fuck is going on?" he whispered.

Something was very wrong and, somehow, he'd gotten himself in the center of it. The news anchor on the radio was reporting on the stopped terror attack in Minneapolis, but there were more, in what the FBI and Homeland Security were calling a coordinated effort to stop an assault on America. Cells in San Antonio, Los Angeles, New York, Philadelphia, and Minneapolis. All

cells raided, all put down with no prisoners. The terrorists described as veterans and paramilitaries with grudges
against the government.

He shook his head as he listened and flipped
between networks, all giving the same canned reporting.
There was no mention of the Al-Shabaab Cell of Somali
terrorists that he'd been sent to the center of America to
try to stop. No mention of the state department task force
that he'd been assigned to for the last ninety days. He
reached for his phone, considering calling home. He had
networks of people. He could call the operations desk at
Langley; they would know what was going on. He still
had friends there.

He stared at the display on the smartphone, saw the
missed calls, and froze. They were the ones who had sent
him here. They set up this assignment in the middle of
the country with a bunch of burnouts. Winston had shut
the phone volume off, not wanting to be harassed for
leaving the farm a day early, for not sticking around for
the celebration. He looked at the timestamps of the
missed calls. The last was twenty minutes ago.

He flipped the phone and removed the battery and
SIM card. He needed to get off the grid fast. If they
knew enough to take down the farm, then they probably
knew he was missing, and they had his number; they'd
be tracking him. And even if they didn't have a team
roster, they soon would. His Alias was written on
enough paperwork back at the farmhouse, and—he
paused, looking at the Range Rover's steering wheel—he
was in an agency vehicle. They would know it was
missing.

"Shit," he mumbled. "Why didn't I call a damn Uber?"

He opened the door and walked to the back, retrieving his black duffel bag filled with his personal belongings and gear. He considered for a moment dumping the vehicle in a field, maybe burning it in a back lot. No, leaving it at the airport was the best tradecraft. Obvious so they would quickly find it, but leaving the vehicle here would force the Feds in pursuit to consider he boarded a plane. They would have to check out every lead and split their resources, tracking down flights and destinations.

An hour ago, if he hadn't seen the news report, that would have been the actual case, but there was no way he would fly now. Even if he managed to get in the air, they would pop him as soon as he landed. They would be after him... they might already be on the way.

He tossed the keys in the back and shut the doors. He then walked across the walkway and into the airport. He headed for the departure check-in counters and moved past them before he ducked into a bathroom. It was empty. He took his bag into a stall and closed the door. Quickly, he switched out his clothing and flipped his reversible jacket inside out. He tossed the red ball cap and ran his fingers through his hair. He then broke down his gear and forced as much as he could into a collapsed 5.11 covert backpack that had been stuffed inside the larger black duffel.

He waited in the stall until he heard a group of people enter, then he walked out to the sink, where he washed his hands and combed his hair. An old man in a tweed jacket stood next to him. Winston made casual conversation the way annoying strangers tended to.

"This weather, am I right?" Winston said in a voice with just a hint of southern accent.

The man looked at him and gave a friendly smile. He looked tired from traveling. Winston waited for the old man to leave the restroom then he followed close behind, still talking as if they were together. The man nodding, obviously annoyed at having picked up a new friend.

A lone man in jeans, a grey sweatshirt, red ball cap, with a black duffel bag had entered the restroom. A pair of men, one of them in khaki pants with a sport coat and nondescript backpack had exited. Winston followed the old man toward the security check, being careful to look away from the obviously posted security cameras. When the elderly man turned toward the roped lines. Winston continued walking past them then turned toward the baggage claim, and beyond to a ground transportation sign. Moments later he was outside and in the back of a taxi headed toward the Union Depot Train Station.

CHAPTER SEVEN

C live Jackson tapped his hands on the dash of the 1986 Tahoe to a Linkin Park song, a joint in his mouth and half can of energy drink topped off with Bacardi in his hand. He was amped up; he was excited and ready to crack heads. Everything he'd trained for was coming down to tonight. They were about to light this city on fire. He looked in the mirror—in the back, his best friends, Eric Garcia and Jordan Talbot, were bobbing their heads. They'd been sitting in a used car dealership across from a Cleveland convenience store since they'd gotten the call at just after midnight. It was time to go, time to make a difference.

"Da fuck man—are we doing this or not?" Jordan asked.

"Oh, we are doing it, brother," he said, laughing then taking a long drink from the can. "We are about to set it off."

Jordan was the youngest of the three-man wrecking crew, and he fit right in even though the kid had never served in the military like the rest of the trio. Well, technically, Clive hadn't served either. He'd been discharged in his second week of basic training for what the medical people called associative disorder. It was all bullshit, and he saw no reason for the others to know the truth. And besides, what could they say?

It wasn't like Jordan was any better. The loser had tried three times to join and every time he failed the drug screen. And Garcia—Clive grinned thinking about it—that dickhead managed to make it all the way through training and to a unit in Texas. Then got the boot and did some time for selling drugs to kids at the base school.

He laughed, considering their history. It was all bullshit. They were good people, but the Army just wasn't ready for them. But now the world would see what they were capable of. Thanks to Chris putting them all together, they were going to make history. His phone buzzing on the console pulled him from his thoughts. He lifted it and turned down the volume on the radio.

"It's CJ, talk to me," he said.

He looked in the mirror and could see his friends leaning forward in their seats, anxious for the go order. He shot them a wink as he listened to the man on the other end, Chris Meyer. The dude was cool as hell, and he had loads of bank and connections. He was going to make shit right with the trio. Finance them to do the dirty work that the police and corrupt politicians were afraid to do. By the end of all of this, it would be a changed world and guys like CJ would be there to rule over it.

"Clive, it's me," the voice said. "How's it looking out there?"

CJ rolled down his window and scanned the front of the mom-and-pop convenience store. It was late but, as usual, on this part of town, there were people gathered around the twenty-four-hour entrance. A man smoking a cigarette leaned against a wall to the right of the door. More were gathered near a set of parked cars, listening to music. *But they aren't the target*, he thought, scanning left along the front of the building.

"We got something to shoot at," CJ said. "Something really good."

"Okay, then make it happen. Meet me back at the shop in twenty."

CJ looked at Garcia in the mirror, and the man got out of the Tahoe. He walked two spots over, gave the lot a 360 scan, then opened the trunk of a Malibu and pulled out a canvas bag. The car had been parked there hours earlier by Chris. The trio was instructed to wait until the go signal before grabbing the bag, just in case they were stopped by police. CJ laughed. They were also told not to get high or drunk, but hey, a man's gotta work the way a man works.

Garcia returned to the SUV and passed Jordan a MAC-10 machine pistol with an extended magazine. He then moved to the front and dropped in beside CJ. Garcia closed the door and lowered his window. Then he leaned forward and, with his weapon pointed at the floor, checked the action and gave CJ the thumbs up.

Jordan fumbled with the weapon in the back. He locked the magazine then looked up at the gang members across the street, at least a half dozen men holding court over a bus stop bench just to the left of the store entrance. "Yo, do you all think it's ironic that we are in here getting baked before we kill a bunch of ghetto trash for selling drugs?"

Garcia shook his head. "Nah, it would only be ironic if they were our dealers. Turns out they ain't."

"But yeah, I mean, technically we're a gang same as them. How does it make us any better?"

Clive shook his head. "You are thinking too much. They are criminals, and the cops won't do shit, so now we have to."

"Just like war, baby," Garcia said, his eyes locked on the bus stop.

Grinning now, Clive shook his head. "Hell, yeah, just like war."

Jordan looked out the window then back down at the machine pistol in his hands. "Yeah, I guess, man. Just like war."

Clive started the Tahoe and eased out of the parking spot and into traffic. He let his foot lightly work the pedal as they slowly rolled down the street. They were in the southbound lane, closing on the store on the far side of the street.

"These fuckers ain't the same as us. They hurt people, we help people," Clive said, looking at the men up the street. He tried to keep his voice from breaking as adrenaline raked his heart.

The same group of thugs he'd seen every damn night were sitting on the same bench near a bus stop. But the assholes never got on any bus. No, they harassed old people and trash-talked women and sold drugs. They were bullies, the same as the ones that kicked Clive's ass daily in high school. He could see the group was alone, so hitting an innocent wouldn't be an issue. These scumbags were about to pay a heavy price. The men were standing and yelling about something. One of the men was waving a wad of cash in his hands excitedly. Another standing behind the bench had his head back, laughing.

Clive kept the throttle even, careful not to slow down or speed up as he passed them. Chris had warned them that men might be armed. They had to look like any other car driving down the street. He slowly pulled the wheel, veering into a turn lane to get closer. He checked his speed; exactly seventeen miles per hour, just like they trained. He looked ahead and to the right at the bench. The two men were still laughing but a third was now staring at them.

"Da fuck is he looking at?" Clive whispered.

The man was older than the others. He had been standing back from the group, not participating in the chaos. His eyes didn't show fear but alarm. The man wore a long-sleeve flannel that hung open. He shouted a warning, then reached for a gun that had been hidden under the long shirt.

Clive looked in the center mirror and could see what raised the alarm. Jordan had been leaning into the window and had the stubbed barrel of the MAC-10 extending beyond the door frame. When he looked back to the front, the man in the flannel now held a large pistol at the end of his extended arm. A muzzle flash, then a break in the windshield to Clive's right. He winced with the pain of bits of breaking glass hitting his face. His foot went heavy on the pedal. Garcia leaned out of the passenger window and cursed. The MAC-10 exploded in his hands, firing rounds as fast as the machine pistol could spit them out.

Jordan was doing the same, and the inside of the SUV thundered with the sounds of the weapons. As Clive pounded his foot on the accelerator, he saw the joking men dance backward with impacts from Garcia's and Jordan's machine pistols, but the flannelled shooter was shuffling out of the path of bullets. He side-stepped in front of the SUV, his weapon trained on the windshield. He was peppering rounds across the hood. The windshield was hit again. Clive felt a pain in his shoulder then the wheel pulled away from him. He tried to correct the steering just as the world went dark.

A BLOCK AWAY, ATOP A THREE-STORY PLUMBING supply building, the man known as Raul Chavez watched the chaos unfold through powerful binoculars. He couldn't keep himself from smiling as he saw the Tahoe roll forward and stop against a light pole. Gang members had their arms up, firing blindly into the vehicle that was spewing steam and smoke from the front. He knew the occupants would all be dead.

He watched as a door was opened and a man's body was dragged from the back, only to be kicked and stomped by the surviving gang members. He shook his head. The scene on the ground reminded him of the streets of Cali, Colombia—cartels celebrating the deaths of rival gang members. Now, with the occupants of the Tahoe dead, the fighters had come out of the woodwork to dance over their bodies. "Savages," he mumbled.

He heard the sirens and lowered the binoculars to see flashing blue lights race up the main boulevard. He glanced at his watch. "Two minutes and thirty seconds; impressive response time," he said in perfect English.

Raul was American by birth, born to Colombian immigrants. He had grown up in the States, raised by grandparents after his parents were deported. Raul graduated from school and then college in Florida but soon left to find his roots in Colombia. After reconnecting with his family, he joined the National Police Force. Well educated in America, he quickly moved up the law enforcement chain. Finding the police were no friend to the people, he eventually took a job with La Raza de los Reyes. The Race of Kings had given him the money and the opportunity to truly help the struggling people. Even if it did mean the slaughter of hundreds of others.

With his background and extensive knowledge of police tactics, he again rose up the ranks. Soon the cartel realized he would be of better use as a mole in America. Raul held a dual citizenship, and his education credentials were legitimate. He was positioned inside the Embassy of Colombia on the streets of Washington D.C. From that point on, history was being made. He liaised with American police forces on a major drug interdiction task force, using his vast knowledge of the cartels to take down rivals, while giving safe passage to his own friends in the Raza Reyes. That was when he was introduced to the men of Vortex. Soon he had joined their payroll, earning triple incomes from the Colombian government, the cartel, and the Vortex Corporation.

Today sitting on a rooftop, he grinned with the knowledge that a lifetime of experience and education had brought him to this moment. He was finally waging a war against the United States, a nation that had made his people struggle for a century.

"Yes, a full minute faster than we'd expected," came a low voice from behind, waking him from his reverie. "How'd they do?"

Raul put the optics back to his eyes. With the approaching lights, the victorious side had ended their celebrations and were running up the street. He panned back and could see at least three dead gang members. Pathetic results, considering the firepower he had supplied the boys and the numbers that had been milling around the bench moments earlier. The clowns had obviously exaggerated their military training. The Tahoe was burning now, the vehicle pockmarked in bullet holes. The body pulled from the car lay lifeless near the rear door. He pulled away the binoculars and stored them in a backpack at his feet.

"Three dead—it's possible they wounded more, but not likely." Raul squinted then continued. "Yeah, and looks like our team of *shooters* has been wiped out."

"I'll make the report," said the man behind him.

Raul turned back to see the man in a dark jacket texting the information into a smartphone. The man was Russian, a former spy who had moved to America long after the fall of the Soviet Union. Like many other spies, he was able to sell his talents to the American corporate sector. And Apollo Group, like with many other things, was often the high bidders for talent.

The man had introduced himself as Victor Kesson weeks ago. Raul knew who he was; his own embassy kept a file on the man. Not a criminal, but he was in no way legitimate. The same as Raul, they worked in the shadows providing clandestine services to their clients. Where Raul used his friends south of the border, Victor had many useful assets from Russia. Even though they had the same employer, they intentionally had no relationship in case one was captured.

They were both just wheels in some greater, fast-moving machine. Victor read a reply on his smartphone and then nodded. He looked back at Raul.

"It's locked in. Their names are being leaked to the press; their social media accounts are being edited as we speak. There should be blue suits raiding their safe house within the next half hour."

Raul grinned. Once the call ordering Clive and his group to the car dealership was placed, a second team had staged their apartment with extremist propaganda and weapons. It would be a treasure trove of information for whatever police officer was lucky enough to open that door. Lucky in a sense as that same officer would most likely be dead in a week.

"Some collateral damage would have been nice. A few dead gang members won't spark many tears, but by morning there will be photos of young men with neckties and sweaters sitting in church pews," Victor said. "Our friends at the media will do the grunt work of creating the anger for us. Instead of a drive-by on gang members, it will be *white supremacist gun down youths at bus stop.* We have others standing by to start up social media campaigns for the victims."

Raul nodded. "It's all about the spin."

He laughed, having created the same sort of disinformation campaigns to gain favor for his cause in Colombia. With the right propaganda, the people would praise drug dealers and spit on the police.

The man in the dark jacket reached for a satchel at his feet. "Pack up and move to your assigned sector and wait for further instructions. Stay off the streets. It's about to get really ugly out there."

CHAPTER EIGHT

M ark Dorsey sat in the executive conference room of the Senate Building. The last twenty-four hours had been chaos. Attacks on all continents aimed at Americans. More bloodshed within the borders of the United States. People were panicked, the police were on the run, and the citizens wanted answers. The police still on the job were a step behind, unable to find the attackers. There were no leads, outside of a few early tips that had led to stopping attacks in Minnesota and some small spots out West.

The people wanted a response, and they wanted answers, and Mark Dorsey and Apollo Group had those answers. He only needed the authority to put it into place.

"Is it done?" Mark asked the Russian to his front.

Tall and slender, Victor's hard face concealed his true age. He looked a hard fifty-five but was at least ten years younger. He held his tongue but dipped his chin.

The man grunted then pulled Senator Shafer from a seat and stood him directly in front of Mark.

Charles Shafer shook his head and stepped forward, grabbing Mark by the shoulders. "Tell me you had nothing to do with this, all of this isn't you."

Mark grinned slyly and turned away from the senator, looking back to Victor. "I asked, is it done?"

Victor nodded his head. "Everything is moving along as planned. My men are all in position. The Defense Secretaries will soon be out of the picture."

Mark turned back to Charles. "Is it enough? Will this be enough to force the vote to implement Delphi?"

"You're mad!" Senator Shafer gasped as he took a step back.

Before he could reach the door, Victor hooked a hand under his arm and pressed a stiletto blade against his rib cage, steadying the man. "I am not afraid to run this blade through you, my friend."

"I asked is it enough?" Mark said again. "Will it pass?"

Shafer shook his head. "What did you mean about the Defense Secretaries being out of the picture?"

Victor looked at his watch. He held a finger to the air then smiled. "Just moments ago, a briefcase filled with high explosives detonated in a situation room meeting. Due to the frequency and seriousness of the recent attacks, this was an all-hands meeting. In one shot we sent the might of the US Armed Forces in disarray."

"Why?" Shafer stuttered. "Why would you do that?"

Mark smiled. "Well, you said we need something big —something to make the people fear the world more than they fear Delphi. Senator, you know that if we go big, then the military will eventually step in. You cannot run a coup d'état with the might of the American Military standing by. We just caused a bit of a delaying action."

"You are going to start a damn civil war," Shafer said.

The young man grinned again and stepped closer. "Now, I have done my part. It is time for you to do yours. Get your ass out on that Senate Floor and tell them how important it is that we pass Delphi and get a handle on all of this. Make sure they understand that only Delphi is capable of stopping the killing."

"The FBI, they'll investigate, they'll know it was you."

Mark smiled. "What FBI?"

"It doesn't matter now; you've gone too far." Shafer looked away. "If you killed the defense chiefs, the President will never sign it. Hell—we might not even have a vote. They might evacuate the Capitol building."

Mark put his hands on the senator's shoulders. "You are not paying attention, are you? They have no choice but to vote now, and to vote yes. Delphi will pass by a majority. And it doesn't matter if the President approves or not, once Delphi is online, Apollo Group will control the messaging. We can sell this to the people, all we need is for you to control Congress long enough for us to gain control."

"How is that possible?" Shafer asked.

Mark dipped his chin to Victor, who was now standing against a far wall, screwing a suppressor onto the end of a small-caliber pistol. "Once the vote passes the Senate, there will be a bit of a distraction. Victor's friends will ensure that you all have a nice long recess." He smiled, watching Shaffer's face turn pale. "Oh—don't worry, Senator, you are very safe. This isn't about you."

"No, you can't do this. Please don't."

Mark laughed. "What we can't do is stop it. All of the pieces are in place. Once the vote is final, the Second Civil War will begin. And, Senator, trust me on this, you are going to want to be on our side."

CHAPTER NINE

The Miami warehouse was hot and damp. A desk fan perched on an ancient filing cabinet clicked on every rotation as the blade hit the rusty wire cage. Rain poured outside, only adding to the humidity inside. Tommy sat in a steel folding chair. His back hurt, his eyes burned, and his head ached. He was spent. All he wanted to do was go back to sleep and pretend none of this had happened. The trip here hadn't been the most enjoyable, flying below radar in a thunderstorm and stuffed into the fuselage of a tiny plane built more for cargo and mail delivery than passengers.

The landing was just as hospitable, being more of a controlled crash in a narrow landing field just outside the city. They'd had to walk over a mile through a knee-deep, gator-filled swamp, then to a dirt road before being loaded in the back of a commercial laundry truck. Tommy was at the peak of his frustration and about to ask to be dropped at the next hotel, when the sun came up and they were backed into this building on the south side of the city.

As exhausted as he was, he still couldn't take his eyes off the television. From everything he could see, the country was under attack. The Virgin Island assault wasn't unique. There had been several like it across the country, across the globe even. The screen flashed with updates of attacks from California to New York, everything from attacks on supermarkets and gas stations to larger assaults on power plants and police stations. Anywhere Americans lived, they'd been attacked. But this wasn't an invasion. These weren't attacks from a hostile force or an elaborate terrorist organization. This was domestic terror, or at least it was being reported as such.

Along with the killing, there were also plenty of thwarted attacks as the FBI worked overtime to stop what the media was calling an "American war on decency." Tommy shook his head, wondering where the media came up with this shit. How do they suddenly put labels on everything? How are they always so quick to categorize and pick sides? He listened to a grey-bearded announcer on one of the cable news networks, reporting calls for the President and most of his cabinet to resign, as the names of attacked cities scrolled on a bar below the image. The bloodletting was still in progress, and the talking heads were already making it political.

"You need to let me call in," Tanya said, turning his head from the screen. "I can get us help."

Tommy shook his head no. "You heard Chocolate

and Spicy over there," he said, pointing to a sofa where the two big men who had facilitated his escape were now snoring away. They had been there since shortly after arriving, the men dead on their feet after pulling the operation to extract him from the islands in just the nick of time. They'd stripped their gear and fell hard into the dirty sofa.

Tommy looked hard at Tanya. She wasn't a field agent; she was just a glorified staffer assigned to babysit his ass and deliver messages. To be honest with himself, he didn't even know much about her, but having spent nearly the last year with her, he knew she wasn't an operator. This was over her head. For her to have any chance at all, he needed to get her someplace safe and convince her to stay there. He had to find a way to explain how much danger she was in. "They hit your office along with my apartment. They were planning to kill you and me."

She went to argue with him but before she could, he put up his hand and sighed. "They couldn't afford an alibi; you can confirm where I was, and what I was doing. You call into your office, and they will know we both made it off the island. They'll have a team target us."

"You don't know who did this. They might be as worried as we are."

Tommy shook his head again. "We can't take the chance, we have to hold tight."

The woman wasn't convinced. She shook her head and held firm. "Maybe Natalia could get a message through," she argued. "If the President is really in trouble, they'll need me back in D.C.—they'll need to know what we know."

Tommy frowned. Natalia had left earlier. She said to get breakfast, but he knew the woman would be checking in to back brief Colonel O'Connell on what had happened. He looked at Tanya and could see the desperation on her face. She wasn't like him; she had a life back home, a life away from all of this. Even an apartment in the Capital, and officially, she was part of the White House Intelligence Team. She was right. If the President was in trouble, they would need the information she had.

He smiled and nodded. "Maybe. We'll ask her, we can figure something out."

A large brick of a phone with a fat blue display on its side vibrated on the table beside him, and Tommy reached for it. Natalia had placed it there before she left and told him she would check in with him every hour. He looked at his watch; she was running late. He knew what the phone was. The technical name was Genii, and he'd seen them used before on operations in Europe.

The plug-in piggyback device disabled the phone's microphone and GPS. Instead of transmitting voice transmission, it sent binary information in packets of data as sound that could only be unpacked and decrypted by the matched receiver's phone. The GPS receiver would bounce and send random locations from hundreds to even thousands of miles away.

The system worked well, but it wasn't foolproof. Even with high-level encryption, the geeks at the National Security Agency would eventually be able to grab the packets of data over the grid, piece it back together, and listen to the recording. But until then, most eavesdropping systems would think the phone call was nothing more than a fax machine or a dial-up ATM modem.

He looked at the display flashing UNKNOWN and flipped it open. He pressed it to his ear without speaking.

"Before you say anything, know that this line is only nominal. They won't know where you live, but we have to assume it's being put on the shelf, so watch where you leave your keys."

Even though the voice had been over modulated to sound almost robotic, Tommy immediately knew it was his old friend and now benefactor, retired Air Force Colonel James O'Connell, owner and CEO of one of the largest military contractors in the nation. Since Tommy had started his second career as an off-the-books paramilitary, the Colonel had become a provider of clandestine assistance. Not out of charity, of course. The Colonel had set Tommy up with a very expensive and very discreet account that was careful to bill the government and reimburse O'Connell Transportation for all at cost, plus contract.

Tommy grinned, listening to the modulated yet friendly voice; the Colonel knew his tradecraft. What the man was saying was the line was secure, couldn't be traced, but probably recorded, so stay away from key words on the very remote chance that someone would record the analog tones and convert them back to digital to be encoded and later indexed to pull up the call. Without positive search data, the call would just vanish into one of millions being recorded at the very moment.

"I understand," he whispered, hearing his own voice in the same broken tones.

"I talked with our mutual friend. The situation is understood. I'm looking to get you out of there as soon as possible, but it's going to take some time and rubber. The all-non-essential-air-travel order is in place. The airports are closed."

"What's happening?" Tommy asked.

There was a long pause. He knew the Colonel was probably trying to find a way to say it in a way that would confuse the NSA bots. He eventually sighed and just came out with it. "If you have been watching the news, there have been attacks from coast to coast and overseas."

"Who is doing it?" Tommy said. He really wanted to ask how he was involved and why he was being dragged into it, but at this point he didn't dare.

"We don't know, but the attackers are all current or former military, no known or only very loose affiliations to each other."

"Yeah, like me. What the fuck?" Tommy didn't really expect an answer and was already cursing himself for losing his temper.

There was a long pause. "War, chaos, all of it—this seems to have been by design," the man said, no longer avoiding key words. "There are victims, and we know who the targets are, but we don't know why. Someone is trying to shut you and everyone like you down."

"I don't understand," Tommy said, but already the answers were buzzing in his head. Someone wanted to get him out of the way, make him a wanted man, or make him dead. But why the others? Tommy had heard a news story about some halfwit assholes killing people at shopping malls and convenience stores. His mind took

another beat then came back; the rest were added intentionally to cloud the waters. The other attacks the ones
stopped, and the ones where the perpetrators were killed
were the real targets.

"You still there?"

He heard the voice and put his focus back on the
phone. "I'm here, just trying to figure this all out. The
Syrians couldn't have put this together, and the French
wouldn't have the balls. This isn't about me."

"It looks like someone is organizing a coup d'état
against the current administration."

"All this to take out a President?" Tommy laughed.
"They have to know the military won't stand for it."

"The Secretary of Defense is dead. As are most of
the Joint Chiefs."

"How is that possible?"

"This is not being reported yet, but they are calling it
an insider attack. There was an explosion in a defense
council meeting. They said a Marine officer, an aide,
brought in a case of HMX, it went off just as they were
briefing the Secretary of Defense on the Navy Yard
attack."

"That's not possible. You can't get HMX past the
sniffers at the doors. You just can't."

"I'm sorry, but they insist that's what happened.
They have video of the guard bringing the case through
an underground garage and into the meeting. With
everything else that's going on, they were distracted."

"You know that's bullshit, right? If it was, in fact,
HMX in a case, all the evidence would be vaporized. It

would be impossible to know where it came from, and if they were that distracted how did they manage to close an investigation in record time? Whoever filed this report is lying—in fact, they are probably in on it."

"You know what, right now none of that matters. We just need to get you out of there. Somewhere safe. We can figure out the rest later."

"No, I'm coming in. I need to get to Washington."

"You can't. The city is in lockdown. You'd never get in, and we don't even know what's going on yet."

"I have a friend that needs to check in," Tommy said. He was growing exhausted from the conversation.

"I'm aware of the situation. And I have to say, her situation is no better than yours. She was reported dead about twelve hours ago."

"Dead with no body, obviously."

"Even better—guess who the prime suspect is?"

Tommy sighed. "They work fast, don't they?"

"Listen to me and listen close; take your friend and get off the grid. You know the protocol—G plus six, no more than five, you got it?"

"G plus six for five," Tommy said, making a mental note of the numbers. "I understand."

"God speed, Tommy." And the line went dead.

He sat silently for a minute. Then he took a pen and wrote the characters G, 6, 5 on the inside of his wrist. The exercise was more for muscle memory. He'd have the digits stored in his brain once he'd looked at it a dozen times. He was going dark, and they would be on the run.

The contact protocol was unique to Tommy and the Colonel, something they'd come up with over a scotch years ago. Their previous arrangement was 3, A, 6, 10... Tuesday at 0700 for ten minutes.

Now, the omission of the first number told him his check-in would be daily instead of a defined day of the week. G was the seventh letter of the alphabet, plus six was thirteen. His contact time would be at 1300 daily, and he would leave his phone on for no more than five minutes to avoid detection.

He looked over at Tanya, who shot him an inquisitive look. Her face edged from anxious to the angry. Tommy knew that she wanted answers, and he wanted to give them to her, but he wasn't sure how to do it.

Before he could speak, the back door opened, and Natalia walked in. She was carrying a pair of black backpacks and a leather satchel. She dropped the packs by the door then moved to the table. Tommy eyed the bags; he could tell they weren't anything she'd gone out and grabbed especially for them. They were safe house mission packs, probably kept in the vault and would be topped off with traditional get-out-of-Dodge essentials.

She tossed a set of car keys on the metal tabletop. "There is a blue SUV out back."

Tommy looked down at the keys with the Jeep logo on the tag, and then up at the woman. "I take it we are leaving then?"

Natalia shook her head. "Only you two. And you should do it quick. We are okay for the moment, but shit is about to cut loose at the seams. I saw a lot of cops on the interstate." The woman pointed toward the back-packs. "Grabbed you some extra clothes for the bags, thrift store shit, nothing fancy. There is cash in the satchel, along with your new identity papers."

Tanya stood from the table. "Wait—exactly what the hell is going on? What do you mean 'new papers'?"

Grinning, Natalia looked at the woman and then back at Tommy. "It was my understanding that you spoke to the Colonel."

Tommy nodded.

"And she doesn't know?"

"Know what?" Tanya scowled.

Natalia laughed and shook her head. "Well, for starters, hunny, you're dead. Your boyfriend here killed you last night just before he shot up half the island."

Tommy put a palm over his eyes while Tanya shook her head.

"I need a phone," she demanded

"Bad idea. Being dead is good for you right now; it means nobody is out there trying to kill you yet. I would say that you've lucked out." Natalia softened her tone. "But the ruse won't last for long. They will soon know you escaped the island and, depending on who did this, they may know about the aircraft headed to Miami during the assault. Even if they don't, we should assume that they do. You two need to get out of here."

Tanya still shook her head but had turned back to the others; Tommy could see she was in shock. He asked Natalia, "Where do we go?"

"No, I don't want to know that," Natalia answered

sternly. "The Colonel was explicit that we don't talk about that. Just grab your packs and go, and please make it quick. I have places to be myself." She went to step away then looked back at Tommy. "If you need me again, contact the Colonel. He will know how to find me."

CHAPTER TEN

Colonel James O'Connell ended the call and unplugged the Genii devices from the side of the contract-free mobile phone. He placed the phone in a top drawer of his desk then rotated his chair and placed the Genii in his shirt pocket. It would normally go in the wall safe, but with Tommy stateside, he wanted the device close in case he needed it. He looked at a shelf on the far side of the room. At the top of it was a photo of his wife and son.

After his family had died, James Junior in a faraway war and his wife of cancer, he'd been alone and had resigned himself to a lonely and boring death. Even with a successful business, he found little spark in his life. Well, that was until Tommy reignited a fire inside him, and even if he was just living vicariously through the young man, it made him feel like he was a part of something greater than just a job. And as misplaced as it might be, working with Tommy brought him a connection to his son.

Before he could close the desk drawer, there was a buzzing sound from the kitchen's intercom. He paused and listened intently. James lived alone in a large home on the west side of Great Falls in the Washington DC area. Even though alone, a housekeeper was on the grounds during most of the day. He looked at his watch. He knew Maria would be working today; she was probably in the kitchen, wondering what he wanted for breakfast. He could hear her speaking. The woman tended to shout down the hall even though she knew the old man couldn't hear her. He ignored the shouts and soon heard the footfalls in the hallway outside his door. There was a soft knock.

"Mr. O'Connell, there is a gentleman at the gate for you," she said. "It's Cole Wallace," she continued before O'Connell could ask who it was.

James tightened his brow. Cole was his contact at the FBI. He'd been a family friend since high school, where they played on the same football team before James had chosen the Air Force Academy and Cole, the University of Michigan.

He tried to think of why Cole would be at his driveway gate and why he hadn't called first. Cole had tipped him off to Tommy's dilemma, and they'd agreed to keep their distance until things had cooled off.

"Please, Maria, let him in," James said, closing the desk drawer and standing.

He moved close to a window that overlooked his front yard and driveway and watched as a black Chevy Suburban moved up the blacktop. He passed to a coat rack and put on his jacket as he continued toward the kitchen. Normally, guests would arrive at the front door, but Cole always made his way up the back steps and into the rear of the home. James moved through wide alcove decorated with family photos and stepped into the spacious kitchen. Maria had already set a tray of white mugs and a coffee pot on a granite island. James thanked her as she left the room.

He heard the back door open and Cole's shoes clicking on the stone tile floors. The man passed through the entryway and shook his head as he entered the kitchen.

"James, we've got problems. I need you to grab your things so I can get you out of here."

James laughed and shook his head. He moved to the serving set and poured a cup of coffee. "Please, have a coffee and tell me what's on your mind."

Cole's jaw tightened. He looked back over his shoulder nervously then checked the time on his wrist-watch. "Seriously, James, you have about five minutes to pack a bag, and we need to get the hell out of here. If you want to skip the bag, that works even better—but either way, we need to be moving."

The old man took a step back. "What's happening? Is this about my young friend in the islands?"

"I don't know that, not yet," Cole said. "But that list, the one I showed you" —the FBI man coughed nervously — "the one with your island friend's name. Well, your name is on it now... and not only you; there are a lot of friendly names on it."

"I'm on a burn list?" James laughed. "That's ridiculous. Who the hell would want an old man like me killed off? I'm damn near retired."

"It's not just you, James, it's your company—most of your board of directors, and plenty of those just like you."

"Wait a second, the FBI is targeting defense contractors? The Military Industrial Complex? Do you know how stupid that sounds?"

Cole looked at his watch again. "Can we please talk about this in the car?"

The Colonel shrugged and looked at a clock on the wall. "Well, if you insist on taking a drive, I could use some air. Maybe we could hit the diner on Walker Road. Maria ain't a bad cook, but I could use some variety."

Cole rubbed his brow, then stiffened. He reached for a phone that buzzed in his jacket pocket. "This is Wallace," he answered, holding a finger to James. He grunted and nodded as if the speaker on the other end of the line could see. "Yes sir, I understand. I'm on my way back to your office now."

Another beat. "Where am I? Just at the pharmacy up the street; this damn cold has been bugging, me. Thanks, I appreciate that. See you in twenty." Cole disconnected the call and placed it back in his jacket. He looked at James hard. "No more fucking around. We've got to move now. If they see me here, I'm as dead as you are."

Suddenly feeling the seriousness of it all, James followed his friend out the back door, grabbing his wallet and car keys from a small shelf as he passed it. He moved out of the house and climbed into the Suburban. James hadn't previously noticed that Cole had left the big vehicle running, and before he could say a word, the truck was in reverse and rapidly backing out of the drive-way. Once they were in the road, Cole slammed back into drive and cut away.

James sighed, latching his belt. They'd gone less than two blocks when he said, "You're serious about all of this, aren't you?"

"Shit!" Cole cut the wheel hard to the right and drove partway up a neighbor's driveway. He hit the brakes, slamming James forward in his seat. The old man looked at his friend and could see that the lawman's eyes were fixed on his side mirror. James did the same and watched as a procession of police cars rolled past them. Cole waited for the last one to pass before re-entering the road.

James began to think about the past twenty-four hours. The reports across the globe directed against Americans. The arrests and the deaths of terrorists reported on the news. It all pointed to one thing; para-military groups were revolting against the United States. He shook his head, thinking about Tommy, and then himself. But they weren't. If he and Tommy were being set up, then others could be also. He looked at Cole, who was white knuckle driving with his eyes darting from the mirrors and to the road ahead.

"Who is doing this?" James asked. "Why does the FBI have a burn list?"

"It's not a damn burn list, and it's not originating at the FBI. Why does everything always have to be Holly-wood with your old ass?"

"If it's not a burn list, then enlighten me," James said. "And for the record, you're two months older than I am."

"The list came down from Justice, but I don't think the Attorney General had anything to do with it."

"Why is that?" James asked.

"Because he has been missing for the last seventy-two hours. The Assistant AG is also gone. This has rolled way down the chain. But it's being enforced with an iron fist. Everything we got is being put in the field to act on it immediately. They are seriously saying anyone identified is responsible for the attacks or an imminent threat."

"So, what the—they go out and arrest a bunch of old guys? The public isn't going to buy this. Even my lawyers will destroy this in court."

Cole sighed. "The directive was target anyone on the list. There was an emphasis in the instructions that the targets were dangerous, and that making a live arrest was not the priority. They are publishing in the belief that the list is responsible for the planning and mass murder of American citizens."

"It's madness."

Cole shook his head. "I know, and I think I made your list, right along with you. My boss has called me back to his office exactly two times in the last thirty years. Both times for a promotion, and I don't think anyone is getting promoted today. Something is big is happening, and they are knocking off anyone that can stand in their way."

"Why?" James asked again.

Cole took his eyes off the road for just a moment and locked them with James. "You heard what they said about the President; someone is cutting the head off the snake, and we need to find out why."

CHAPTER ELEVEN

Alexander Winston exited the yellow cab and paid the driver in cash. He was on Route 66, traveling the east side of Amarillo, Texas. He walked down the busy street with his face turned away from the traffic, his eyes down toward the sidewalk. He was wearing dark jeans, a black sweatshirt, and a dark-green ball cap. He looked like any other blue-collar worker just finishing a shift. Like his cover profile, Winston was tired and needed a room, and he knew just the one.

From the airport in Minneapolis, he'd played a full-on game of cat and mouse. Something he'd done plenty of times in Europe and the Middle East but never back home in the United States. He hopped a few cabs to a bus station, then took a greyhound to Kansas City, then rented a car and drove to Oklahoma City, where he then took a final train to Amarillo. It was a lot of effort, but he needed his pursuers off his track before he dug into the cache.

He was burnt-out and feeling the fatigue from the

evasion run, but he was certain he'd cleared his back trail. He'd been careful, every purchase being made with unnamed pre-paid credit cards from his burn deck. He carried a stack of plastic in a pocket of his rucksack for emergencies. He used each card only once then tossed it, regardless of the remaining balance. If anyone was after him, they would have been slipped in Kansas City; Winston was certain of that.

He kept walking as he closed his eyes. But why the hell were they after him? What was it all about, and why had he and those men been targeted? Winston shook off the thoughts—not the time nor place to be letting his mind wander.

He passed by a small chain hotel with a nearly full parking lot. Ahead, he saw a flickering streetlight. On the far side of the street was a minimart and just across from it was a traditional motor lodge where you could park your car right in front of your room. The place had a low black fence all the way around it. Low class by any standards and that was exactly what Winston was looking for. But finding this place was no accident. He'd been here one time before. He hefted his bag to his shoulder and moved through the gate toward the small lobby.

He scanned the nearly empty parking lot filled with old cars and spotted a red pickup truck backed up to a room near the lobby. The truck's tailgate was down, and two men were sitting on it with beer cans in hand. One was wearing an orange road worker's vest, the other a dirty gray T-shirt. A third man was in the open door of the hotel room, smoking a cigarette. Winston walked past them, the men not even lifting their heads to acknowledge him. He walked through an open door and into the lobby.

There was a fan blowing hot air. Flies buzzed and walked across the counter. The clerk at the reception desk barely made eye contact when Winston approached and asked for a street-facing, ground-floor room near the far corner if it was available.

"Corner rooms are usually bigger," he joked.

The clerk grunted as if he couldn't care less about the reasoning for the room preference. The man looked at his ancient monotone computer screen, clicking an even older keyboard with a single finger, slowly scrolling through lines of text, grunting every time the cursor moved.

Winston had found this place by accident on a trip to Phoenix, nearly a decade ago. Back then, he'd gambled that the owners would stay in business longer than he did and that this place would hold its old-world charm for as long as he needed it. The check-in software was old and custom made, it wasn't connected to the Internet, and the hotel didn't have a website. The Route 66 Motor Lodge was exactly what a man on the run needed.

Winston recognized and remembered the clerk from his last stay. It was a curse that he could memorize a face at a glance. Even the faces he wanted to forget were stored forever. And he knew from his previous trip here that the clerk was the grown son of the owners, and he also knew the man was gaming him. The parking lot was empty, they weren't booked up, and he doubted they were even at ten percent capacity in this shit hole. But without a doubt, the man would claim they were at their peak rates to squeeze an extra buck out of him.

He stepped away from the check-in counter and scratched at the back of his head as he listened to the man click and clack on the keyboard. He heard the clerk grunt and then stop clacking.

"Well, I got something upstairs facing the street, nice view if that works for you?"

This time it was Winston who grunted. "I'd really like the first-floor corner. Corners are bigger, and I get claustrophobic, ya know? And I'm afraid of heights," he added for class.

"Hmmm," the man put on as he looked back at his spreadsheet, still scrolling. "Well, looks like that room just opened up. I'll call housekeeping and see if it's ready—but it'll cost ya. Ground floor is extra, and we're nearly booked, so I can't give you the discount."

"That's fine," Winston said, trying to contain a smirk, having fully expected the ruse. He turned to look out the window facing the street.

"Now, how long will you be staying?" the clerk asked.

Winston smiled from one side of his mouth. Not bothering to turn back toward the clerk, he said, "One week," knowing he'd be gone the next day, if not sooner.

"Oh—a week, perfect. Yup, I can get you on the ground floor, far corner, but rates go up on the weekends. And what card will you be putting this on?"

"Cash."

The man stopped clacking on his keyboard. "Cash?"

"Cash," Winston repeated. "I can pay the week's rate and any security deposit up front."

Winston knew that cash went directly to the man's heart. His room would be off the books now, and no reason for his parents to ever know about this transaction.

The man smiled and went back to the terminal. "Then cash it is, my friend."

Winston looked from the window and back to the pickup truck. The drinking men were outside now. A fourth man had shown up, and they were unloading black duffel bags from the back of the truck. The bags were curious; it could be luggage, but they were all the same. But maybe they were from the same crew, and that was normal. The clerk caught Winston's gaze and said, "Don't worry about them. Road construction workers just trying to make it back home to Oklahoma. With all that's going on, work has been halted for a bit."

Nodding, Winston said, "Oklahoma, aye?"

He was curious why Oklahoma boys would be doing road construction in Texas, but he always found it better to keep suspicions to himself. It's not good to make memorable comments or ask a question that could be repeated later. He held his tongue and let the clerk do the talking. Sometimes it was better to pick up information rather than pull it out.

"Yeah, they said they were working a crew down by Arizona. They would normally fly home, but you know with the airports closed and all." The man cursed under his breath. "You know, with all that's going on, it's making it really hard for folks to get home. Everything is grounded. That's why I'm booked, or expecting to be, at least. All the airport traffic is moving down Route 66. The airlines dropped off a busload of stranded passengers earlier just down the street. I'm guessing I'll get the next load of stranded, myself."

Winston smiled. "Oh, I'm sure the airlines will drop someone here eventually."

He looked back at the truck. It wasn't a rental. If the men had planned to fly but got stranded, it couldn't have been owned by one of them. Maybe the company loaned it, but then there were no markings identifying it as a construction vehicle. The clerk spoke again, and he shifted his attention back.

"Well, yeah. Naturally, I got to save rooms for the airlines. Can't have folks stranded without a place to sleep, you know."

"Naturally," Winston said. "It's very thoughtful of you."

The man smiled at that and turned. He retrieved a printed page and a registration card and placed them on the counter. He reached under the counter and retrieved a room key attached to a small block of wood. "I got you in 67, corner room just like you wanted." He set the key next to the paperwork. "The pool is open until ten, and the pizza joint down the road delivers until midnight." The man pointed to the paperwork. "Cash up front will be four fifty for the week, and another fifty deposit."

Winston reached into a shirt pocket and flipped out five hundred-dollar bills from a folded stack. He laid them on the counter then took the pen and filled out the registration card and signed the invoice then pushed them to the clerk.

The man lifted the card and squinted at the hand-written text. He looked Winston in the face and said, "Thank you, Mr. Anderson." The clerk tore off a yellow slip of paper from a receipt pad and handed it over. "You have a good night, call if you need anything."

JUSTIN SANDERSON SAT ON THE BACK OF THE tailgate, holding a beer can on top of his right knee. They'd been tasked here for hours, watching this hotel for suspects moving away from OKC. Another team was up the street and two more were further west all along old Route 66. He wasn't a cop, he wasn't military—hell, technically he wasn't even government.

He was contract security of sorts. He wasn't the legit store-bought badge-and-uniform type that the casinos hired, but more the shock troop of the industry kind of guy. When an agency or private sector payer needed something done in a hurry without any strings attached, they called Vortex, and Vortex called Justin.

He shook his head. Still, the shit he was doing right now was the oddest thing he'd ever done in his career. Hunting down and killing criminals inside the United States was technically against the law. But somehow, for some reason, that is exactly what he was tasked with and had the highest assurance that it was being sanctioned by the US Government.

Freelance security work wasn't all bad. He'd spent most of his field time guarding State Department assets as they traveled the world. After that, he got pretty good at supporting the FBI or some other three letter agency when they picked up an international criminal on an extradition order. It was on one of those trips that he found out about the big bucks independent contractors could make. There was more money in private security than what the agencies could pay. So, when he got an offer, he jumped and signed on with Vortex Corp.

Vortex didn't care so much about the employer; they were more focused on the billing. Under VC, more than once, Justin found himself doing work on the wrong side of the law, especially the last five years doing short but very lucrative gigs in Central and South America.

Just like the name implied, the Vortex was great at making details disappear, but the work was hard. Lately that had him traveling where the FBI and DEA couldn't go, helping sort things for the highest bidders. Mostly south of the border, sometimes working for the Federales, sometimes for the cartels. As often as the employers were legitimate, they were just as often shady. But even as crazy as that work was, this was odd; he'd never thought he'd be working American streets without a badge. Justin frowned. The terrorist strikes had the country on the ropes, and according to management, the President had signed several classified executive orders, allowing teams like his to mobilize here at home.

He put the beer can to his lips and took a long drink. It wasn't good beer in the can; it was piss warm domestic, and he was feeling ill from drinking so damn much of it.

Justin turned and watched the lone man on foot enter the lobby. A light jacket and nothing but a backpack, he carried himself well and, to Justin's trained eye, he looked like trouble. It was the first traffic they'd had into the hotel since dinner time, and the man being on foot was even more interesting than the retired couple that checked in earlier.

He looked away as the man turned in his direction. He was tall, a bit over six-foot, blonde, blue eyes. He was lean and athletic, his hair long but well groomed, which was odd for being on foot only carrying a single backpack. Didn't fit the hitchhiker image. He could be military or even law enforcement.

Putting a hand to his collar, he spoke into a tiny microphone. "Any P.I.D.?" He waited on the word from the tech that Vortex Corp had provided.

A response came back through his earpiece. "Negative on positive identification."

This was a fruitless hunt. He'd rather be out knocking on doors, but as more and more targets scattered like roaches with the lights on, passive observation points like this one were established for the hunter-killer teams. Roadblocks were working too, but the men working those were more the grunts of the industry, several of them even brought in from south of the border. Nothing more than tough guys with a gun and just about as useful. He shook his head again. "The President must be desperate to bring in foreigners to do police work," he said to himself.

"Check the book," he said while looking at the man in the doorway so it appeared he was having a conversation.

Justin was talking to his tech man inside the room. He knew the man would be poring over images and running any photos he'd taken of the man through a facial recognition database. On top of that, he would be snapping real time images of the man from a camera they'd planted earlier in the lobby. Apollo Group, the sponsor for this hunt, had provided them with top-of-the-line tech, and as fast as the photos could be taken, they would be scanned against a massive database of targets.

Justin's hunter-killer team was assigned to the Southwest region, as most of their assigned targets were suspected to be in Texas, New Mexico, and Arizona—and all of them were assumed to be armed, dangerous, and on the run. A second task force was in Oklahoma and another in Denver, and even more in the East. They were running a tight net to track down and arrest the terrorists responsible for the last three days of domestic attacks.

"He's looking away; can't get a good grab on the live feed, but the stills I snapped as he entered are coming in now. Checking the database for matches..."

Justin squinted and dared a look back to the lobby and watched the man turn away and face the clerk.

"No go, boss. The guy's face is either not in the database, or he is not on the list."

"He sure looks the type, though, don't he?" Justin said. "This boy is either a cop or a grunt, I can feel it."

This time it was the man in the doorway who nodded, Carl, one of his shooters, an ex-SWAT cop from California. "He looks like a killer, for sure. Guess he just isn't one of our killers."

"Got 'em!" The tech's excited voice came back over the radio.

"Who is he?" Justin asked, his senses now perked.

"Unknown, name isn't on our list—wait, got him... that's odd; he isn't our region. This guy is national. No name. The identity is sealed. Wait one—Oh, shit, boss, he's a Mark Six."

"A Six? Are you sure?" Justin said, his voice showing as much anxiety as excitement.

Same as when Justin traveled and hunted drug king-pins, the targets were divided into mark types. It was a thing the company did. A Mark One was just a civilian wanted for some reason, maybe they were a financer, chemist, bombmaker, or a lawyer with ties... simpletons. A Mark Two through Four were your harder types of criminals; the elevation of the number corresponded with the risk level of apprehension. Most of the list, as it was being called, was made up of Four and below.

Now, a Five was where things started getting tricky. A Mark Five was former military or law enforcement with specialized training to earn them a special level of respect when trying to take them down. As of this morn-ing, when Justin scanned the list for the Southwest region, there were only ten Mark Fives known to be in the three-state area. But there were no Mark Sixes. They were the unicorn of all bad guys. The Mark Sixes were just there. You didn't hunt them; you just happened upon them or they found you, and when you got on their bad side, you didn't live to tell about it. The Mark Six was a classification reserved for especially dangerous types—special forces, paramilitaries, agency guys. They were the ones momma had warned him about.

"Positive, ran the face again and it's hitting 59% on a known Mark Six."

"Only 59%," Justin said.

"That's right, but it makes sense, as in the base photo the man has a beard. Our boy in the lobby is clean-shaven."

Justin put his head down and scratched at his scalp. When he looked back up, he could see that the lone man was walking toward them on the sidewalk. Justin crushed the can in his hand and shouted to the hotel room, "Hey Freddy, beer me."

A hoot came from the room. Justin nodded to the stranger as he walked past him, the man's eyes hardly drifting. Justin attempted to size him up. He looked like anyone else. Nothing pegged him as anything more than a regular Joe America. *What made this guy a Mark Six?* He watched the man reach the end of the hotel and enter the corner room.

"I called it in. Command is sending the other team our way; they said to take him down."

Justin raised his brows. "Take him down? Are you sure?"

"That's what they said, take him down."

"What in the hell did this guy do to earn a kill order?" Justin said.

CHAPTER TWELVE

The rain let up just after midnight, but the traffic headed north was constant. The radio nonstop reported acts of violence across the country. Airports had been shut down and curfews were being put in place in large cities. There were rumors that the President had been removed from Capital and was governing from Air Force One. Like during a hurricane, people were fleeing the coast and cities, running for the heartland of the nation.

Tanya was in the seat next to him, asleep. He'd checked the go bags provided by Natalia at the last stop. Just as Tommy had thought, they were standard agency-provided gear bags, just the essentials. A few meals in shrink wrap, basic first aid kit, a half dozen magazines of ammo, and a SIG P320 fitted with a threaded suppressor. The identification cards she issued were only decent but would pass most cursory inspections. According to the documents, they were a married couple—Allen and Josephine Hanson of Starbuck, Minnesota. When

Tommy dug through the glove box at their last stop, he was impressed to see that Natalia had matched the ID cards to the vehicle registration card.

Ahead of him was a row of bright-red brake lights, and he slowed then came to a stop. Tanya stirred in the passenger seat and looked up. "Where are we?"

Tommy stared at a road sign and pointed. They were three miles south of the Georgia border. "Looks like state police have a roadblock set up. Radio said something about interstate traffic being blocked for residents."

Tanya followed his finger to the sign. Her eyebrows arched, and she looked at Tommy, confused. "If the state border is closed, how are we supposed to cross?"

"The border isn't closed. They are just trying to keep Florida residents from leaving." Pointing at the pair of driver's licenses in the console, Tommy said, "Lucky for us, we are from Minnesota. Remember, my love?"

Tanya shook her head and scowled. "Of all places, Minnesota. You don't actually intend on driving all the way there, do you?"

He laughed. "No, we are not going to Minnesota, but I think it's best if, for now, you don't know any more than that."

"Why?" she asked him, her face now hard. "Are you planning to ditch me?"

Tommy grinned. "My darling bride, if I had planned to ditch you, I'd already be gone." His eyes hardened and fixed on the van ahead of them. "Now what the hell is this?"

The column of vehicles crawled ahead, but Tommy could now see the front of the column and the start of the barricades. There were only two patrol cars blocking the northbound lane. Four uniformed officers paced between cars, looking into windows with flashlights. Some cars moved through, some pulled off to the side, and others turned around.

"Something's not right," Tommy whispered. His tone had gone hard, and his eyes were straight ahead.

Tanya leaned forward, trying to get a better view when Tommy stretched out his right hand, cautioning her. "The police cars' logos don't match, and they aren't state police. The officers aren't the same; I see at least two different uniforms."

"What does that mean?"

Tommy shrugged. "It could mean nothing."

He clenched his jaw and moved into the right lane. The traffic moved up one at a time as a uniformed officer waved cars through. When there was only one vehicle ahead of them, the officer approached the van to their front and tapped the glass. Tanya started to say something, but Tommy held up a finger, silencing her. He rolled closer to the rear bumper of the van, and the officer turned the bright light in his direction.

He pressed the brake and placed the car in park. Looking to the right, he saw a cluster of armed men in black utility uniforms resting against an unmarked, dark-blue response vehicle. Behind them were more vehicles pulled off the shoulder.

"Something isn't right here," Tommy whispered again.

His hand dropped to the space between the center console and his right thigh. He pushed the grip of the suppressed SIG down so that it was hidden. Then he brought both hands up to the steering wheel as he watched the officer approach.

That man's hand was spinning, giving the universal signal to lower the window. He looked ahead, where a pair of men had already surrounded the van to his front, shining their lights in the windows. Tommy pressed the control button and let the window glide down. He looked up then shielded his face and closed his dominant eye from the officer's mag light. He knew the man was trying to blind and diminish his night vision. Looking under the light, he could see the man's badge and name. Thompson, from the Valdosta Police Department.

The man leaned forward and investigated the vehicle, his light passing over the back seats. "Where you folks headed?"

"Starbuck," Tommy said, trying to force a smile.

The officer pursed his lips and then took the light off the back seat then focused it back on Tommy. "Starbuck? Not familiar with that. You have any identification?"

"Minnesota. The wife and I are headed home from a second honeymoon," Tommy said, handing over his newly minted driver's license. "So what's this all about?"

The officer lowered the light to examine the card and nodded. "Lockdown. You've probably heard of the troubles on the news. Georgia governor is closing the border." The man smiled, relaxing a bit. "But don't worry, folks, we'll let you all through, but we're turning back Florida residents—for now, at least, but even that is going hour by hour."

Tommy frowned, accepting the ID card as it was

passed back. "This something we can expect the entire drive home?"

The officer looked toward the dark-clad men on the shoulder then leaned in close to the window. "If I were you, I'd keep your tank full and not waste any time getting your bride back home."

The man looked up as the van ahead of them was cleared and pulled away. He slapped a hand on the roof of the Jeep then leaned in again and said, "Avoid Atlanta. It's not hitting the news, but riots are bad there." Without another word, he stepped back from the vehicle and waved Tommy forward.

Tommy eased the Jeep back into gear then moved past the cluster of black-clad officers. They had several detainees on the ground with hands cuffed behind their backs. Further up, a silver sedan was pulled over, a woman and children inside, with a man behind the car being frisked.

"What is happening?" Tanya gasped as she made eye contact with the children in the back of the sedan.

Tommy slowed as they rolled past several of the men in black walking on the shoulder of the road. They were suited up in full body armor, with baklavas over their faces and carrying carbines across their chests.

Without turning his head, Tommy said, "Do you recognize those people, the uniforms or the department?"

Tanya looked at the men as they drove past. She shook her head. "FBI maybe?"

"No. The uniforms are sanitized, no patches, no yellow banners labeling them as law enforcement. And FBI, or even the marshals, couldn't put this many people together this fast. And why do they have their faces covered like a third-world hit squad?"

"Security contractors then?" she said. "Something like this takes a lot of resources. They have to get help somewhere."

He frowned, trying not to stare at the shakedowns. "Yeah, maybe."

Tommy kept his eyes on the road in the bumper-to-bumper traffic. Every few miles there was another scene of a stopped motorist being searched by the men in black. A police helicopter flew low over the procession, illuminating the vehicles with a floodlight. Tommy followed the van until they reached the first exit then left the freeway and entered a county road, headed west toward Alabama. The traffic let up and there were no more signs of the men in black.

In the early morning hours, the wet pavement reflected the headlights. Tommy guided the Jeep past homes with lit porches and cars in the driveways.

"Where are we going?" Tanya asked him.

Tommy shrugged and pointed at the compass on the dash. "We'll head west until I can find us a safe spot to hole up and wait for the Colonel's call."

Driving through a yellow flashing stoplight, he pulled into a small gas station. They still had over a half tank of gas but heeded the warning to stay topped off and pulled up to a pump. He removed the pistol from between the seat and the console, sliding it into an over-sized inside pocket on his jacket.

"I have to use the bathroom," Tanya said.

He turned off the car and investigated the shop

through the large glass windows. It was well lit, with a female clerk behind the counter and a young man drinking a soda as he looked over a magazine rack. He nodded to her. "Okay, let's go together then."

Tommy leading the way, they stepped out and approached the store. He held the door and allowed her to go in first, a ringing bell announcing their presence. Neither the kid at the magazine rack nor the clerk acknowledged them. There was a sign pointing to a restroom at the back of the store. Tommy pointed toward it then worked his way to the counter. A young girl chomping gum looked up at him. He opened his wallet and placed a twenty-dollar bill on the counter.

"Can you set me up on that pump out there?" he said.

Just as she pulled the bill toward her, she moved to the side and Tommy spotted a small camera on the shelf behind her. He cursed under his breath. It wasn't a closed circuit; it was one of the mass-produced Internet cameras that loaded data directly to the cloud. He dipped his chin and turned away.

"You are coming from the freeway?" the boy said from the magazine rack.

Tommy turned toward him, keeping his back to the camera. He nodded his head. "Yeah, crazy up that way. Any idea what it's all about?"

Before the young man could answer, the girl behind the counter said, "My cousin Rodney is on the fire department. He says a bunch of people are trying to start a war."

"Muslims," the boy said. "They always starting shit."

"Nuh-uh." The girl shook her head. "Rodney says it's domestic terrorists."

"What?" Tommy asked.

The boy laughed, stepping away from the counter. "Like the firebomb on our police department? It's ISIS, man, they hate us."

Tommy tightened his brow then looked to his side as he saw Tanya leave the restroom. He looked back at the boy. "Firebombed?"

"Yeah someone drove by there this morning and set the front of the building on fire. Cops say it was some good ol' boys, but that just doesn't make sense to me. We ain't that kind of town out here." He shrugged. "You ask me, we've gotten soft and been asking for terrorists to hit." The boy lifted the front of his shirt, exposing the handle of a revolver. "That's why I am standing watch tonight. Too many crazy folks on the road."

Smiling and holding up his hands, Tommy said, "Well, I'll just leave you all to it then."

He waited for Tanya to fall in beside him then they exited the building. He moved quickly to the pump and began filling the car as Tanya opened the back and rifled through one of the backpacks. Lights lit up the parking area from behind, and Tommy shielded his eyes as a dark-gray Chevy Tahoe pulled around them and parked in a spot on the side of the store.

The driver exited. Tall and slender, he was wearing the black utility uniform Tommy had seen on the officers at the roadblock, but his face was uncovered, and he wasn't wearing armor. The man stepped out and moved to the back of the vehicle, lighting a cigarette.

He stood there until a second man, bulkier in the shoulders, with his sleeves rolled but in the same uniform, joined him. Even though Tommy was the only car at the station, the men seemed to have little interest in him.

Tommy got the meter to $18.50 before the tank hit full. He heard the back door close and Tanya returned to the cab with a bag of granola and a bottle of water. He replaced the pump handle and watched the men move from the Tahoe and enter the store. One went to the counter as the other moved directly to the boy at the magazine rack. Tommy kept his eyes focused on the building before switching them to the Tahoe. Virginia plates, no government markings, no light bar or anything to identify it as law enforcement.

"Tommy, let's go," Tanya said, buckling her seatbelt and showing concern on her face. "I know you're curious, but it's best we just get clear of them."

Tommy frowned, looking back to the store. The young woman behind the counter was now backed against the wall as the bulky man had the kid shoved against the magazine rack. As the boy stepped back, his shirt tightened, exposing the grip of the handgun. The man in black pushed on the kid's right shoulder then reached in and snatched the revolver. He was laughing as he waved it to the second man still standing by the counter. Then he turned back and pointed the handgun toward the young man's face.

"Tommy, forget about it," she said. "It's not for us to deal with."

Tommy shook his head and tossed the keys on the

seat. "Go ahead and get it running. I have change coming back to me."

"No, Tommy—"

He closed the door and walked around the front of the SUV, moving toward the entrance. He pushed open the door, and the bell chime announced him. The young man was all the way against the rack now with his hands held up. The tall man at the counter turned toward him as the second man kept the gun on the kid.

The man at the counter glared at Tommy and said, "Store is closed," in a thick Spanish accent.

Tommy frowned and pointed his left hand at a neon 24-hour sign glowing in the window.

"Don't give a shit what it says, amigo. I said the store is closed."

Nodding, Tommy shrugged. "I got change coming to me from the pump. You know how it is with these pre-pays."

This time is was bulky that spoke. Slapping the kid from the rack and onto the floor, he turned the snub-nosed revolver on Tommy then took a step forward. Tommy shook his head and raised his hands. "It's fine, you all can keep my change. I don't want any trouble."

"Who are you? Show me some identification," the bulky man said.

Keeping his hands up, Tommy flashed his thumb back toward the gas pumps. "It's in the car." He squinted and looked at the man with the gun, and in a shaky voice said, "Are you cops? I don't see any badges."

This time the man's face hardened, and he took a step forward. Tommy held his hands higher. Flinching away, he took a half step back. The man fell for the trap and lunged at Tommy, thinking he had the upper hand over a defenseless patron. When the man lunged in, Tommy stepped hard to the right and delivered a striking knife hand down to the side of the man's neck. Not enough to do any real damage, it sent a shockwave down the arm holding the pistol. Tommy pushed the arm up with his left hand, and grabbing under the wrist, he twisted down. The bulky man released the gun and turned away. Tommy delivered a knee to the man's kidney, collapsing him to the ground.

When Tommy turned toward the second man, he had the Sig from his jacket pocket, leveled on the stunned man's chest. "Move and I'll kill you."

The tall man gulped and nodded his head. Tommy looked down at the writhing man on the ground. He stepped hard on the back of his neck, causing the man to stop moving. He used his free hand to remove an S&W pistol from the man's drop holster. He then grabbed a pair of handcuffs from a pouch on the man's duty belt. He slid them to the kid. "Lock him up. Hands behind his back."

The kid nodded his head in response and scrambled across the floor, doing as he was told. When the big man tried to resist and cursed in Spanish, Tommy exerted more pressure to the back of the man's neck. With Bulky secured, he told the tall one to hold his hands high and turn around. Tommy disarmed him, then let the kid apply the handcuffs. Then Tommy pulled him away from the counter and front tripped him so that he fell next to his partner.

"You know who these men are?" Tommy asked.

The boy shook his head. "No sir, I ain't never seen them before. But guys like them been coming in here all day."

Tommy stepped over one of the men and removed his wallet. He tossed it to the counter and grabbed the second wallet. He flipped the first open and saw an ID and plastic credential card for Vortex. He looked closer and could see that it had been issued less than a week ago. Checking the second wallet, he found the same thing. No driver's license or other personally identifiable information. He shook his head and placed them both in his jacket pocket. He then retrieved the revolver from the floor and placed it on the counter.

"Call the police, tell them you had an attempted robbery," Tommy said.

The girl shook her head. "Cops won't come. It was on the news earlier; all the cops have been ordered to only work city limits." She paused then looked over the counter. "These guys are supposed to be watching over the highways and county roads."

Rubbing his jaw, Tommy pointed at the open sign. "Turn that off, go home, and call your cousin Rodney. No matter what these guys tell you, they are not cops. You aren't safe with them unlocked. Don't trust anyone unless you know them." Tommy reached into the driver's pocket and removed the man's car keys. "Now go, and don't worry about coming back for these two."

Tommy stepped over the men and left the building. He caught a shocked expression from Tanya as he walked by the SUV and moved to the Tahoe. He opened the back hatch and saw the men's kits laid out. Two sets of body armor, a pair of carbine rifles, a plastic ammo box, and a large kit bag. It took him two trips to transfer it all to his vehicle. Then he started the Tahoe and parked behind the store so it was hidden from the road. When he moved back to the front, he could see that the open sign was off and the store lights were out. The kids were moving toward a small sedan.

Tommy closed the hatch of the Jeep and the got in the back seat. "Tanya, I need you to drive now."

"You mean you want me to be your getaway driver," she said.

Tommy pointed toward the small sedan just beginning to back up. "You could go with them, if you prefer. I'm tired of arguing about it."

Without waiting for her to move, he reached over the back seat and removed the black gear bag and unzipped it. By the time he was digging inside, Tanya had the Cherokee back on the county road. "Would you really let me leave with those kids?" Tanya asked.

He looked up at her, smiling. "Would you really leave me on our honeymoon?" He pulled a leather mission pouch from the bag. "What do we have here?" he said, flipping open the binder.

There was a signed six-month Vortex contract for an Ernesto Garcia of Fort Wayne, Indiana, and two cashed checks for ten thousand dollars each. Looking at the contract closer, it said he was to be assigned to the Southeast division of enforcement control. He read the line to Tanya. "Ever heard of it?"

She shook her head. "Where are we going?"

"Next main road head north, before going west again."

"We aren't going to Minnesota, are we?" she said, looking at him in the mirror.

Tommy leaned back against the bench seat. "No, we need to get to Montgomery before the sun comes up."

"What's in Montgomery?"

Tommy sighed. "You'll see when we get there."

CHAPTER THIRTEEN

P resident Frederick "Mac" MacLeod sat behind his desk in the Oval Office, staring at a portrait of Abraham Lincoln. He was waiting on word from his Vice President, who was held up at the Senate in emergency debates. The country was in chaos, every region showing civil unrest from riots, to outright murders in the streets.

There was too much confusion, protests calling for peace were crossing the lines with criminal riots. Active shooter calls had popped up across the country, alongside bombings and bank robberies. Police were serving criminal search warrants on suspects but, instead, were finding armed civilians ready to protect their property. Society was in full breakdown. State governors were recalling the National Guard to poor effect. Most of the guardsmen who reported for duty left and took their weapons with them shortly after being given assignments.

The boys in uniform had no stomach for fighting

friends in their own neighborhoods, choosing their families and local communities over their nation. Some soldiers fled under the leadership of their unit commanders. One unit from a small town in upstate Massachusetts entirely refused the governor's orders to march on rioters in Boston. Instead, they turned around and went home. Reports said they had barricaded their own small town. There were similar reports of police officers doing the same thing in communities across the nation. Highway exits and roads leading in and out of small communities were being blocked and defended.

At the first signs of the crisis, Mac had managed to get word out to his military commanders. The last order given was to hold strong, recall everyone into their bases, and secure until they received further instructions. The one thing the President didn't want was a full-scale battle between the military and civilian lawlessness.

But that was before the attack on the Joint Chiefs had taken out his military leadership with a single strike. He still held the loyalty of the armed forces, but his time to respond was fading. The military wanted revenge, and it was getting close to them going after it on their own if Mac couldn't find them a target. He looked at the clock on the wall and slammed his hand down on his desk. "Where in the hell is Chris? I need to know what's going on out there."

The door opened and a thick-chested black man on his security team moved in. He stepped aside and allowed Tyler Spence, the Acting Director of the Central Intelligence Agency and now his recently appointed head of security, to enter. With the Secret Service compromised after the attack on the Joint Chiefs, Spence had been called in by special favor. He was now running the show for the President's personal security detachment, not replacing the Secret Service but working closely with them.

Mac nodded to the Secret Service man, and the man pulled back out, securing the door. Ever since the attack on the Joint Chiefs, the White House had been in lockdown with all visitors, regardless of their level, being searched and escorted. Tyler moved into the room and stopped at a sideboard to pour himself a cup of coffee while the others in the room watched him nervously. They had all been questioned in detail by the President, and all of them had come up short on answers or solutions to the current situation.

On the sofa to the President's front were Charles Carson, his Chief of Staff, and General Allen Cartwright, the acting Secretary of Defense. Charles cleared his throat and stood. He walked to the sideboard, standing near Tyler, and poured a glass of water. "Sir, if I may," he said, looking at the President.

Mac sighed and put up his hands, showing his palms. "What does it matter? Yes, you may, Charles."

"It's time to go, Mr. President," the man said. "We should evacuate."

Shaking his head, Mac said, "And go where? You think we should just surrender the White House to these terrorists? You want to give up the Capital to mob violence?"

Charles nodded and rubbed his chin. "It's a bit more complicated than that, sir."

"Is it then?" Mac looked at a large flat-screen television screen in the corner of the room. The volume was off, but they could see street fighting in the center of the Capital with the nation's monuments as a backdrop. In another shot, people were being pushed up against the White House security fencing. And in another scene, a running gun battle at the Reagan National Airport with bodies lying dead in the terminal. "You don't think I know that it's complicated?"

Charles turned to Tyler. "I assume you prepared a brief. Are you ready to present it or not?"

Tyler nodded and sipped at his coffee then moved across the small room to a laptop already positioned on a black walnut pedestal that had been brought in just for this purpose. It was unusual to hold this sort of briefing in the Oval Office, but under the circumstances, it was the most secure space in the White House. Not because of its proximity, but precisely because it was unusual.

Anyone with knowledge of the President's movements would expect him to be in the situation room, and with the security breach, that was out of the question. Tyler's key to the President's security now was to stay unpredictable. If Mac insisted on staying here, then the President would stay in this room. Tyler opened the laptop, and as he entered his credentials, the CIA logo appeared on the flat-screen television across the room.

Tyler took another sip of his coffee before setting it on the table. "Sir, as you can see from looking outside, the

Capital police have become strategically ineffective. Many are refusing to fire on civilians, many others have left their posts. We estimate we will lose the fences within twenty-four hours without using deadly force."

The CIA man paused and looked down at his hand-written notes and sighed. "Contracted security elements are being brought in to support rural areas and highway patrol elements. The contractors will primarily be used to beef up lapses where police lines are failing or where the police have refused to operate."

"Contracted? Contracted by who?" the President asked.

Tyler pursed his lips and nodded. "That is an interesting question. When I investigated it, they pinned it on Homeland Security, but I know that isn't the case. I called down the street and asked the director himself, and he said the order came from State. He doesn't know who placed the contract."

"Bullshit." Mac slapped a palm on the desk. "Nelson wouldn't give that order without running it past me."

Charles coughed and said, "Keith Nelson is a back-stabber—always has been." The man paused, walking away from the wall and standing closer to the President's desk. "You should have fired Secretary Nelson months ago. He will do whatever he is told if he thinks it'll set him up in the end."

The President scowled and shook his head slowly. "How sure are you on this, Spence?"

"Near one hundred percent, I am afraid. The order was placed by State."

Charles interrupted. "So, who did they hire then?"

Scratching at the stubble on his chin then looking up from his notes, Spence said, "They are one of our defense contractors. You probably know of them as Vortex Corporation."

"Aww, hell no, not Vortex," General Cartwright responded. "Vortex are low-rent fake cops, a bunch of thugs headquartered out of Virginia." The uniformed man grumbled. "And they are not Department of Defense. We pulled all our agreements with them after the disaster in Cairo. They rarely even work inside the United States anymore."

Spencer sighed and looked at General Cartwright, who waved a hand for him to continue. "Somehow it wasn't noticed. There were lots of new hires, and lots of old disgraced Vortex agents being placed back on the books over the last few months," Tyler said. "It was a lot of money, but most of the recruits went in under old Justice and State contracts for Central America, so it didn't raise any alarms. The line item said they were staffing up to aid in the election security in Venezuela. So, the orders made sense—no red flags, no alarms."

"How many people?" the Chief of Staff asked.

"Ten thousand," Tyler said.

"*Ten thousand!* Is that usual for State to place a contract for that many men?" Mac asked.

Tyler shook his head. "It's not common, but by itself, it is not unusual, either. We've shifted away from military to contractor-based agreements when working overseas. A contract this big does happen from time to time. And the elections would be something that requires a large number. Vortex is private security. They are funded under traditional continuing resolutions and private investors, and there are several reasons they could ramp up without any new resolutions.

"They are used for short-term security contingencies. Summits, the Olympics, to provide security after an earthquake, or sometimes, like in Cairo, to overthrow a dictatorship." Tyler looked at the General, who frowned in response.

"But ten thousand men?" The President sighed, looking down at his hands before looking back up. "That's a small army, and you say they are now being used to quell the riots? And tell me again who the opposition is?" Mac said. "I don't know if these people in the streets are with me or against me."

Charles cleared his throat and interrupted again. "And that is where it gets complicated; we really don't know either, and it certainly isn't the same everywhere." Charles crossed the room and sat in a high-backed chair.

Tyler hit a key on the laptop and a long list of names and time-stamped locations popped up on the monitor. "What we know at this point, is yesterday we were hit in thirty-six spots across the nation and in areas overseas of national importance. In every site Americans were targeted. The initial reports blamed the attacks on American militants. In every corner of the nation, fingers are being pointed at different groups—everyone from local police departments, white supremacists, to Antifa activists, and, in one case, even a set of rival street gangs. There is no common thread except for mass violence and chaos."

"It's all bullshit," Charles broke in. "You say militants in association with hate groups, but we know exactly who they are blaming." The Chief of Staff pointed a hand at the names and looked at the President.

"We both know a lot of the men who are on the terror watch list that was published this morning by that new intelligence think tank in St. Louis. Some of them are good people, and professionals. Hell, one of the suspects was a disabled veteran in a wheelchair. The report said he boarded a Metro bus and fired on the passengers before detonating a suicide vest. They said he blew up with ISIS literature. Are you kidding me? Whoever is publishing these reports is a damn liar."

Tyler went to speak, when Mac held up a hand and looked to General Cartwright. "Is that your opinion as well?"

The General dipped his chin. "I have to agree. I also know some of these individuals personally. Of course, a single man could snap, even a few together could do something—but to this level of coordination without anyone knowing? And multiple groups across political spectrums?" The General shook his head. "I read the report on the prevented attack in Minnesota. The accused were all men known to the US Army. Several of them were recently discharged, some with families. Spouses indicated they were all currently employed on government contracts. Those aren't people that go out and shoot up a shopping mall."

Tyler spoke again. "Yes, and don't forget they were all killed in an early morning raid, no witnesses left to say otherwise, and it is becoming a trend."

"You think the FBI was in on it?" Mac asked

Tyler shook his head. "At this point, we don't know what to think. But there are a lot of people dead, no witnesses, no prisoners to interrogate." He pointed to the monitor. "This list and these attacks don't make sense. It's so random; no objective is met in these attacks. It's just chaos, it's violence for the sake of violence—there is no purpose to it."

Tyler hit a key, and a picture of a burning government building filled the screen. "This was one of our overseas locations. The perpetrator was named as one Thomas Donovan." Tyler paused and looked at the President for recognition that he immediately received.

The President shook his head and looked at Charles. "Get Tanya Delgado on the phone."

Tyler frowned. "She is reported as missing, presumed dead. The entire field office is gone."

"Impossible," Mac said. He knew the woman personally and had dispatched her himself to run that office. "Thomas would have no reason to do that, and to coordinate with what? A mall attack in Minnesota? A bus stop in Philly?"

Tyler nodded in agreement and said, "It doesn't make any sense, and no one is claiming responsibility. There have been no demands. There is nothing to win here. The only thing putting them together is the proximity on the clock."

"Then why?" Mac asked. "Are we looking at a second Civil War here?"

Tyler flipped to a new slide with more lists of attacks. At the top were police stations, hospitals, and at the bottom, a nuclear plant in California. He stopped and pointed. "The nuke plant was hit last night. They have the plant stable for the moment, but the crews are not making any promises. The accused perpetrators were all paramilitaries with close affiliations to the agency. More than that, I knew the men personally. They were good men; in fact, they are the kind of men I would call for help right now if they weren't listed as deceased." Tyler ended the presentation, letting the TV go back to the news broadcast. "We can't stop this until we know where it's all coming from."

"There has to be something we can do," Mac said again.

"It's Shafer," the Chief of Staff said, pointing at the television that now had switched to an image of the Speaker of the House standing with Senator Charles Shafer. "He has been pushing this Delphi plan of his for months, and it's been rejected every time because of security concerns. Now, suddenly, this guy is on every station that will listen, praising it as the only thing that can quell the violence. The same people that called it dangerous a week ago are now declaring it a magic pill to solve all of our problems today."

Mac frowned and shook his head. "Delphi is just a gimmick. Even if they did get it in, it's useless without an enforcement piece. The Department of Justice ruled it unconstitutional. A poll of police chiefs declared they wouldn't support it. Many said they would actively fight it. Hell, you said yourself police and National Guard are walking off the job. What good is Delphi with no one to enforce it?"

"Shit—it's Vortex." Tyler shook his head. "We should have known."

The Chief of Staff moved closer. "Known what?"

"Delphi is owned by Apollo Group, the same parent company of Vortex. And it's not just that," Tyler continued. "There's more with the contracts; they were formed in Central and South America. It made sense, as they were being hired to secure the Venezuelan election."

"But?" the President asked.

Tyler sighed. "A lot of them had requested travel visas to come to the States for some training course in Virginia before they were sent out to the field. A lot of these guys aren't Americans. They would have no qualms with enforcing Delphi on our population."

"That's madness," Charles said. "Mr. President, you can't go public with a theory like this."

Tyler sighed. "No, the President is right, they need an enforcement measure to make Delphi work, and local police won't do it, and the Guard won't disarm and arrest people because a program told them to. The National Guard only takes orders from the President or their governors."

"It's a waste of time, even with Vortex standing by," Mac said. "It'll never pass; Delphi is dead on the floor."

Charles shook his head. "Sir, it already passed the House, and they are calling an emergency session in the Senate as we speak."

"It doesn't matter; I will never sign it," Mac said, balling his fist. "I can't."

Charles frowned and dipped his chin. "And that's another problem. Over half the country thinks Delphi will quickly root out and identify the terrorists and stop the violence cold. We've lost the media war on this one." He paused and rubbed his temples. "The media are destroying you in the public opinion poll, asking why you would oppose something that can stop the violence. They are calling for you to resign immediately."

The phone rang, and Mac saw the name of the Vice President on the display. He pressed a button, activating the speaker. "It's about time, Chris. What the hell is going on over there?"

"Mister President, I talked with the Speaker and the Majority Leader; they are ready to work out a compromise."

"Compromise on what?" Mac said.

"Sir, the United State Security and Monitoring Enhancement Act is about to pass the Senate."

"You're talking about the Delphi Initiative," Mac replied.

The Vice President paused then said, "Yes, sir. They will send it over by courier. They are asking you to sign the passed bill and to make a brief public statement in support of it. Once it goes live, they say we'll have what we need to put down the attacks."

"And where in the hell is the compromise?" the President asked.

"Sir, they said if you do this, they will allow you to retain some of your powers and allow you to stay in office until the crisis ends. Then they will ask you to resign."

"You're joking. They seriously expect me to resign?"

"Sir, they are talking about having you removed by force if you oppose the Bill."

This time Mac laughed. "You're talking about a coup d'état."

"Yes, sir, and they think they have the public's backing to do it. If you refuse, we are looking at a Constitutional crisis like we have never seen; they want you removed."

Mac took a deep breath and leaned back in his chair. He rubbed his forehead and then leaned forward over the speaker. "Listen closely, Chris. Tell them I'll agree to their terms."

"Mister President, are you sure?" Chris said.

"Tell them I agree to all of it, then I need you to get back to your family. We'll have transportation meet you at the residence and get you someplace secure."

"Mister President, I don't understand."

"Just do what I said, tell them I agree, have them send over the Bill." Mac pressed the button and ended the call. He looked at Tyler. "Can they do it? Can they take the White House?"

Tyler lowered his head and looked toward the windows. "There are crowds on the gate. The Capital police can't control them. Unless you want blood on your hands, the gates will fall. We can't hold this position if the gates fall, and we won't be able to evacuate without mass causalities. I don't think you want images of our security forces killing protestors on the evening news."

Mac hardened his jaw and said, "Well, in that case, I guess it's time to get the hell out of Dodge."

Tyler nodded. "Yes sir, the helicopter is ready. I have Camp David prepped. We can lock it down and secure you there. It's isolated. If they want a fight, then that is where we should have it."

Mac stiffened his lip then looked at General Cartwright. "I need you to get to Fort Bragg, take control of the troops, let the branches know what's going on. We might have lost the Capital but we sure as hell won't surrender the nation to these people."

CHAPTER FOURTEEN

W inston closed the door and secured the deadbolt then dropped his backpack to the floor. Looking back to the window, peering through the curtains, he saw the men in the work truck now gathered around the tailgate. The man who had been sitting high in the back was looking in his direction as he spoke to the others. He knew he'd been made and that he didn't have much time. Winston walked to the back closet and opened the door, feeling along the back wall until he found a tiny bit of exposed Kevlar thread he'd planted there nearly a decade ago.

As he pulled on the thread, it cut downward through the painted sheetrock. It went down three feet before moving horizontally and then back to the vertical, and then horizontal to meet the starting point. He grabbed at the top corner and pulled out the square piece of wall, exposing a large black garment bag. Quickly, he snatched it from the exposed cavity and dumped it on the bed.

Unzipping the bag and flipping it open, he began

removing the contents. A slim black tactical plate carrier, two bundles of cash wrapped tightly in cellophane, a Glock 18 Machine pistol equipped with a flip-out stock and a trio of loaded 31-round magazines in a freezer bag. A second freezer bag contained several now-useless flip phones and expired credit cards. He set the items aside and flipped over the bag, opening pockets and removing an MP5, suppressor, and another stack of magazines.

Winston walked back to the window and could see that a second vehicle had arrived, and the occupants were now talking with the man, surrounding the truck. He went back to the bed and pulled the plate carrier down over his jacket. Reaching into the bag, he filled the magazine pouches sewn onto the chest. The Glock had a holster mounted vertically on the top, and the MP5 was set up with a D-Ring to clip to his shoulder. He loaded and charged his weapons before grabbing his backpack and moving back to the opened panel in the closet.

He turned on the TV, walked to the shower and turned it on, then closed the bathroom door. Back in the closet, he listened for a moment then front kicked through the opposite wall, creating an opening into the other room. He looked inside and found it empty. Winston tossed his bag through the hole, closed the closet door and did his best to replace the square cutout behind him as he passed through.

Moving through the room, he exited into a rear parking lot. There were only four cars visible and no people. If he stole a car, he would have to drive past the men waiting for him to get to the vehicle gate. Inevitably they would fire on him and eventually chase him down.

Behind the lot was a tall wooden fence; he could jump it, but then he would be back on the street, on foot, and exposed. Nope, ambush was the only way.

He looked at his watch. The sun was going down and was to his back. He knew the men in the front would probably be stacking up on his room. He gripped the MP5, exhaled, and moved along the back side of the building. His path was clear as he moved around to the corner of his room with the suppressed barrel of the MP5 up. He waited, listening. He could hear the soft slaps of boots on pavement and the clacking of equipment belts. He knew just around the corner the men were lined up and ready to breach his corner hotel room. They would be to the left of the door, avoiding the large glass window placed on the right.

He waited for the sound of a forced entry, when he heard more metallic clicks. They were attempting to pick his door. He steeled his mind, checked his weapon a last time, and rounded the corner. His head immediately flashed the number six. Three were directly to his front, fanned out and covering the door, a fourth on his knees, working the locks with a pick set. Two men stood behind him, crouching with shotguns ready to make entry. Those men took the first rounds to the shoulders, then the security team and the lockpicker. The rest of the men were stacked up along the hotel's exterior wall. They hadn't seen him move around the corner, and the sounds of the suppressed MP5 shocked them, as they hadn't been expecting the fight being brought to them so suddenly as they waited for the door to be opened.

Winston squared his armor plates to face the front

and fired the MP5 in rhythmic bursts, putting rounds into the neck and face of each man in sequence, the bodies falling as the rounds impacted. In seconds, the breach team of six men were down on the ground and bleeding out.

He moved closer, kicking at the bodies. The dead men were all dressed in the civilian clothes, the men in front with shotguns, the follow-up four with short-barreled carbines. He was surprised by the lack of body armor. Had they been in armor and helmets, his job wouldn't have been so easy. A hasty scan quickly determined they weren't law enforcement. The weapons and equipment were wrong, and the tactics were lackluster. This was a thrown together posse if he'd ever seen one. These men weren't used to working together and hadn't taken the time to suit up.

Moving beyond the dead, he continued toward the pickup truck. He heard a noise coming from the room, and he rounded the corner, leading the way with his weapon's barrel. A twenty-something man sat at a desk, his eyes glued to a laptop screen. The image on the screen was fixed on the hotel door. The man was clicking keys in frustration, speaking into a headset. "Hey, your image is frozen, let me see if I can get you more bandwidth."

The lock picker must have been wearing a camera, which was now trained on the door.

"It's not frozen; your guy is dead," Winston said, taking another step inside.

The man's body went rigid, and his head turned to

face Winston. "He's here," he gasped. "He's in the room right now."

"Maybe I wasn't clear—they are all dead." Winston frowned and stepped closer, pointing the MP5 at the man's face. "Who are you working for?"

The man shook his head no. But didn't say another word.

"Last chance before I shoot you in the face. Who are you working for?"

The young man reached out and closed the laptop. He took the headset and placed it on the desk, crossing his arms across his chest. "I ain't saying shit."

"Dumb—I don't have time for this." Winston shrugged and pulled the trigger twice, hitting the man in the face.

He shoved the body out of the way and retrieved the laptop. Then he grabbed a wallet and a pair of car keys off the corner of the desk and put it all into a laptop bag he found on the floor. Going through the man's pockets, he pulled out a cell phone and unlocked it with the dead man's thumb. He scrolled through the last set of messages, finding nothing of use. He tossed the phone on the body and moved back outside.

Looking right, he was surprised to see that the men still lying dead in front of his hotel room hadn't been noticed. Not a single person had come out to see what was happening, and traffic hadn't even slowed down to see why six grown men were lying on a sidewalk.

In the back of the truck, Winston discovered a pair of long, black Pelican cases. He slammed the tailgate shut and walked to the cab. Taking another scan of the lot, he opened the door and removed his backpack. After taking out the key he found on the desk, he put the laptop bag inside his backpack then placed it on the bench seat.

The key was a perfect fit for the ignition, and he fired up the truck. Winston looked behind him a last time before dropping the truck into gear and moving back onto Route 60 and headed east. They knew he was here now, and they would be swarming on this location. His only hope was to throw them off. He'd been going south-west to find a place to lie low, but now that option was shot. He would have to move straight for his objective now.

He'd need to change vehicles, get into something old and unmarked. He unclipped the MP5 from his vest and placed it on the seat beside him. Looking at his watch he grunted—he was exhausted and was really looking forward to a shower and a nap. But now that was behind him; he needed a place where he could hole up and examine the laptop. He looked in the mirror, checking the road as he stopped at a red light, still surprised to see a lack of response. There was no way they had gone unnoticed by now. The hotel clerk had to have reported it to the police.

Shaking off his concern, he reached to the glove box and opened it. The compartment was nearly empty except for a small vinyl registration and insurance pouch. He pulled it to him and flipped the booklet open. Allison Family Ranch was stamped on the title, and on the insurance card. Winston knew the name; it was a large corporate farm in the area. He tossed the booklet back into the glove box and pulled away. They weren't construction workers, but he already knew that; the truck was prob-ably stolen. Not cops, not military. Who the hell were they?

Continuing east, Winston stayed in the right lane running parallel to railroad tracks and followed Route 60 past the airport, then out of the city. As he entered the desert, the sun set behind him, leaving him in darkness. The gas gauge read a nearly full tank. He drove another few miles and stopped at a convince store in a small town, loading up on food and water, then continued east for another hour. He saw a set of steel pole buildings just after two a.m. and pulled into a wide gravel lot then drove around to the back. He wanted to get more miles on the gunfight, but it was risky being the only vehicle on the road.

Winston cut the engine and turned on the radio. He cycled through the dial, finding an AM news station. He sat, listening to the reports. It was the first time in almost twenty-four hours he'd been alone and able to focus on the events. What in the previous day he thought were targeted attacks in specific areas, he soon discovered were more widespread. Nothing was left untouched, and the Capital was in chaos as the government fought for control.

How things could have gone to hell so quickly stunned him. There was a report of a massive attack from an army base in Germany. American tourists in Italy had been murdered on a passenger train, resorts in Mexico attacked by armed gunmen. Another report came out about a terrorist attack at Reagan National Airport and another at Chicago O'Hare.

Reporters didn't know who was responsible or why. Nobody was taking credit for the attacks. Even the usual suspects were backing off, afraid to have so much blood on their hands. The media was begging to call the day of violence the "Big Shot," the day of the first coordinated attacks, and what they assumed had motivated the follow-up attacks and uprisings by groups across the nation.

These more localized attacks had been focused on grocery stores and food distribution centers. Gas stations and sporting goods stores were being looted. Most of the conflicts had happened in the East and in big cities, but no place had been spared. He shook his head; it didn't make sense. What do they want? It wasn't a civil war or terrorism. It was just violence, and as far as he could tell, there was no organized response from the government. The President had gone quiet and Congress was proposing drastic law changes to give law enforcement more power to crack down on extremist groups.

Winston cut the radio, having heard enough. He sat quietly watching the structure then grabbed his back-pack and MP5. He stepped out of the truck and worked his way around the back of the vehicle, keeping his eyes on the building. Opening the trunk, he pulled one of the Pelican cases toward him and undid the latches. Inside was an off-the-shelf, scoped Remington 700 with several box magazines packed in foam. He snapped it closed and pulled the second box, finding empty foam cutouts. From the design, he could tell M4 rifles had been placed there. He closed the case and pushed it back into the truck and put his eyes back on the building.

A low light glowed over a pedestrian door. To the right of that were two large overhead doors. There was an empty set of parking spots and sign indicating the compound was an agricultural supply store. Winston approached the door and found it locked. A closed sign hung in the window, and a number was listed for emergency deliveries. Not wanting to break the glass or risk an alarm, he walked around the perimeter of the building. On a side window, he found a mounted box style air conditioner protruding from it.

He pressed on the air conditioner unit and felt it give slightly. He grabbed it on the sides and tugged, pulling it free from the window casing. He carried it to a shadow alongside the wall and dropped it. Moving back to the window, he looked inside, giving his eyes time to adjust to the low light.

Winston removed his backpack then pulled himself through the window behind it. He found himself in a small paper-cluttered office. The room was hot and humid, and Winston considered unlocking the door and going back outside to reinstall the AC unit. He pushed off the idea and instead closed and latched the window.

Turning on his flashlight, he surveyed the space. It was a manager's office. There were old pictures on the desk and a tractor calendar on the wall. He stopped at a handwritten cardboard sign on the service counter. DUE TO NATIONAL EMERGENCY, CLOSED UNTIL FURTHER NOTICE. Winston walked slowly across the room and waited by the door. He pushed it open and stepped into a larger storefront, where another sign on the wall again indicated that they were closed until further notice.

He walked past a counter and down a hallway that led into a massive grain bay. There were several utility pickup trucks backed up to a loading dock. On the dock were pallets of seed waiting to be loaded. A whiteboard listed prices and a clipboard attached to a pole had order numbers listed down it.

Winston continued through the bay, to another office at the back. This one was covered in dust and grime. Large canvas work coats hung on hooks, lockers were on the back wall, and in the center of the room was a wooden table. There were dirty coffee cups on the table, and an empty pot on top of a filing cabinet in the corner. He moved around to the back of the table and set down his pack and MP5.

He pulled up a chair and sat heavily, closing his tired eyes for just a moment. He concentrated and listened intently, memorizing the sounds of his environment. Analyzing every creak and crack of the building, the hum of all the equipment. He knew he was alone; the building was secure. He opened the pack and removed the laptop. It was a custom build, steel cased with a green rubberized skin. Apollo Group was stamped on the top of the laptop shell. He paused, staring at the logo. Apollo was well known, but their tech wasn't traditionally built for the average man on the street. They were advanced, sold to the government or top-tier developers.

Winston was familiar with their ruggedized equipment designed for military use. But it wasn't the only thing Apollo Group did. They were also known for high-end electronics and software development. They served military and commercial clients top-grade items. Biting at his lower lip, he started to reconsider the men he'd put down at the hotel. "Who the hell were they?"

He opened the laptop lid and saw that it hadn't powered down. It was still on the same frozen image of the hotel door. He could see that the Wi-Fi connection had dropped. The tech in the hotel must have been running the machine from a mobile hotspot on the tech's phone. It was good that it didn't have its own cellular connection, but he cursed himself for not checking it out sooner. If the laptop had been connected, they could easily vector in on his position.

He opened the settings and quickly placed the device in airplane mode, not wanting to take any chances on being tracked. Winston slowly tabbed through all the open windows. There was one that contained several images of him in the hotel lobby. Next to them was a comparison photo of himself that he barely recognized. The photo was a decade old. There was no identifying name, only a number: 11069. Many of the added biography details about him were incorrect, some harvested from official covers he'd used in the past, others just flat wrong. He scrolled through the details of his file. This was a high-level intelligence dump. These were official details, not things gathered from social media or from having him followed. Whoever built this record was connected. His eyes went back to the Apollo Group logo. This wasn't a criminal hit; these guys are working for the feds.

He tabbed down. The next window was a large spreadsheet, on which the number identification was highlighted. In the next column was a kill order. All active records were identified by number only. Some records had been marked "completed." In those fields, a name was listed in a neighboring column.

Winston stared at the table, trying to make sense of it. He opened a search box and typed the name of Douglas Nelson, the cowboy from the safe house in Minnesota. He sighed, seeing the man's name in red next to a date column. Winston clicked an arrow, sorting the column by date. All the team members from that date were listed as killed during a mission raid. Scrolling up, he stopped, and his jaw dropped. The first to die was Federal Agent Johnston. He was the FBI contact lead, the man who had set up the entire countersurveillance mission on the Minnesota Mall.

From everything Winston knew, Mike Johnston was a good FBI man and a straight shooter. Why would they kill him? He opened the search bar again and typed in the name Frederick Owens, his direct supervisor at the Agency. The name popped up in red. Killed yesterday morning in Memphis, Tennessee, while resisting arrest. Fred Owens was a desk jockey. He hadn't been operational in half a decade—what would he have to resist?

Winston's hand began to shake as he slowly scrolled his way down the list, seeing many names in red. Hundreds had already been purged, and hundreds more were being hunted. Many of the fields were by number only, but all the dead had names revealed. He went back to his number and saw a threat level box. On a scale of one to six, Winston was noted as a Mark Six. He went to the arrow and sorted off the threat column.

Less than a dozen entries populated the screen,

several numbers indicating they were active targets. One name in red popped out at him. Thomas Donovan, killed in St. Thomas in an attempted terrorist attack two days ago. He'd seen Tommy just over a year ago; he knew he wasn't operational and certainly not a terrorist. Scrolling through the last of the Mark Six list, Winston froze, seeing names of several Ground Division Operators. Hagan, Gentry, Carlson, Meyer, Kidd, all listed as dead, all killed in acts of crimes. Winston felt bile rise in his throat, and his stomach began to wretch. The Ground Division had been inactive for years, and most of the team members had retired.

Winston stared at the screen a few moments longer then closed the laptop, leaving it on the table. He felt the grief in his chest slowly turn to anger. An hour ago, all Alexander Winston wanted to do was escape, to make it to a hole and hide in it. He wanted to figure out what was going on and why. That emotion was gone now, replaced by rage. Someone was killing men like him. They were killing his brothers. He closed his eyes tightly and slowly opened them. He no longer cared about the why. It didn't matter anymore. He was no longer running. He would hunt and kill every one of them.

CHAPTER FIFTEEN

J ames O'Connell turned off the gas burner on the stove and removed the screaming kettle. "Who the hell drinks tea? This is America, why don't you have coffee in here?" he called out, pouring water into a porcelain cup.

They had been on the run since the previous day, hiding mostly in parking garages until way past midnight, when Cole took a chance on this place. They cleared the small home together, then spent the rest of the morning and early afternoon sleeping.

Frowning, Cole moved around him and grabbed the kettle as soon as it was placed down and filled his own cup. "This was the best I could do on no notice." He turned and walked out of the small kitchen and into the living room of the tiny Alexandria safe house. "You should be grateful I even knew about this place, or we'd be sleeping in the car."

Looking around the small L-shaped kitchen, James

walked into the sparsely furnished living room. "What is this place, anyway? Nobody actually lives here, do they?"

Cole shook his head. "We had a witness holed up here for about six months. Trial just ended last month, and they sent her off to who knows where." He paused for a second then said, "Probably sent her home, I guess. Anyway, I just happened to remember the address and figured this safe house might still be vacant."

James dunked a tea bag into the liquid and looked up at his old friend. "A safe house, huh? So, what did the broad do? Murder? Bank robber?"

Shaking his head and leaning back into a well-worn easy chair, Cole frowned and said, "She didn't do anything, really. Some banker she worked for was into some shady offshore stuff. The prosecutor's office thought she might make a credible witness, so we picked her up and held on to her for a while. We planted thoughts in the banker's head that she had evidence and was ready to testify against him. Turns out she didn't know shit, but the banker didn't know that, so he spilled the beans. The banker ended up taking a plea deal, and she had nothing for us, so we cut her loose."

"So—you just ruined some innocent woman's life and left her unemployed, based on the threat of her testifying against her boss." James laughed. "And then you just threw her back out in the wild. And people think defense contractors are evil."

Cole shrugged, blowing at the top of the cup before taking a sip. "I don't know, man. When you put it like that, it does sound messed up."

James leaned forward and placed his cup on a small coffee table. "So, what are we doing here?"

"I don't know." Cole furrowed his brow. "That's the God's honest truth, James. Over thirty years with the Bureau and I really don't know." He sighed, looking down at his shoes. "What happened with the kid?"

James looked at him, his jaw hard.

"Seriously," Cole said disappointed. "You going to even pretend like you don't trust me, after all of this?"

Shaking his head James said, "No, it's not that. I was just thinking to myself. I have no idea how the kid is." He reached into his jacket pocket and removed the phone and Genii device. "You know they shot up half that island trying to frame him for it."

The FBI man rubbed his forehead. "I don't know the details. There were so many damn reports coming in last night. I meant to pull details on his case, but they pushed me off to things in the District, and then I—"

"Then you saw my name," James said.

Cole dipped his chin and pointed at the phone., "Is that how you're talking to him?"

James shrugged, placing the Genii prongs into the charging port of the burner phone.

"You know that's not secure, right?" Cole said. "NSA cracked that shit months ago."

"Partially cracked," James corrected. "They can read the message if they find it. But as of now, we've only had one conversation. And he's on the move."

"No," Cole said opening his palm. "Hand it over, I can't risk it."

James laughed. "Come take it from me, old man. I

told the kid I would call every day at 1:00 p.m. and it's 1:00 p.m. Who knows how long he has been out there waiting on me?"

He watched as Cole closed his eyes and put his head back in defeat. He looked at the screen as it powered up then at his watch. Five minutes to one, close enough. He entered a number from memory and placed the receiver to his ear. Tommy picked up on the third ring.

"Are you safe?" James asked.

"Safe, not comfortable." Tommy's voice came back modulated.

"Listen, I'm in the wind. Not sure what has happened, but it looks like I'm on your roster now."

"Who is doing it?" Tommy asked.

James looked across the room at Cole, who still had his eyes closed, but James knew the lawman would be intently listening in. "I don't know, but it's coming from someplace high. Very high."

"How high?"

Cole opened his eyes and looked across the room at James, shaking his head.

Smirking, James said, "Sky's the limit, son. Listen, keep doing what you are doing. Stay out of the way, okay?"

"No," Tommy said, "I want in the game, coach. Give me something to go on."

"You're not listening," James said. "I'm on the outside, I've been exposed. I have nothing."

Cole stood up, holding a finger to his lips. From outside came the sounds of a car door closing. The FBI man made a slicing motion at his throat and drew his service pistol.

"I've got to go, we have company," James said, disconnecting the call.

Cole looked at him then pointed to a back bedroom. "Get in the closet."

"Screw you, you get in the closet," James said.

The Colonel moved against a wall on the far side of the entrance door while Cole stepped to the other side with his pistol up.

They heard a muffled voice outside the door then a scratching sound. The house had a cipher-type lock on the front door, a stainless-steel box with eight numbered buttons. There was a similar lock on the door to the garage, where Cole had parked their SUV. That lock, and the one like it on the back of the house had been conveniently disabled. Only the front door still worked. An audible click and a motorized sound pulled the dead-bolt back into the door housing.

Cole brought up his pistol in a weaver's stance as James leaned back and away, ready to lunge at any attacker that got past his friend. If things totally went to hell, he would throw his weight at the door, knocking any attacker off balance. The knob turned and the door pushed open, letting in the light. James watched as his friend's eyes went wide and his stance softened.

"Jacobson—what the hell?" Cole gasped as he holstered his weapon and stepped forward as a blood-covered man fell into his arms. James stepped forward and looked out onto the empty stoop. A black sedan was in the driveway, the yard was empty, the neighborhood quiet. He closed and bolted the door. Looking back into the room, Cole had already dragged the injured man into the living room.

The man was lying on the sofa, his face pale and to the side. His eyes were heavy with dark circles under them. In his bloody right hand, he clutched a set of car keys. Cole was pulling the man's jacket open, exposing a baby-blue shirt with a crumpled red towel soaked in blood over the man's right chest.

Cole looked back at James. "There is a first aid kit in the bathroom."

James nodded his head and hurried for the bathroom. He opened the vanity and found a large, black vinyl bag. Back in the living room and kneeling by the sofa, he opened the kit and found it to be closer to a first-rate trauma pack. The FBI may have skimped on coffee, but they went all out on medical supplies.

He dug through the kit and grabbed packages of sealed pressure dressing. He opened one and placed it on the man's chest then tore the top off the second but left it in the packaging. He removed a pair of scissors and handed them to Cole, who quickly went to work cutting away the man's clothing. Two inches below the man's collar bone was a dark, black hole oozing thick blood.

Cole pulled him up and felt the man's back. "It went through."

"Lift him up," James said.

From the pack the Colonel removed a small box of QuikClot bandages and ripped it open, spilling several of the sealed envelopes onto the couch. He looked at the injured man. His eyes were open, his mouth agape and drooling. James peeled back the paper wrapping and passed the Combat Gauze to Cole. "Stuff it in. It's going to hurt like hell."

"I know how it works," Cole said.

James put his hands on the man's shoulders, steadying him as he convulsed. Cole worked in the gauze then grabbed the adhesive pressure dressing and held it over the exit wound. He looked at James and nodded. The Colonel pursed his lips and opened the second QuikClot Combat Gauze and forced it into the man's entry wound. The man shuddered but had no fight left in him. James held the dressing against the wound. He dried the skin with a corner of the towel and applied the second adhesive pressure dressing. He stood and double-checked Cole's work, then helped lay the man on his side.

Back in the bag, James found a fluid set and started an IV. "Who is he?" James asked as he worked.

"Arthur Jacobsen," Cole said. He had alcohol swabs, cleaning blood from the man's chest in back. "He works in the Maryland office."

"Not anymore," the man gasped between labored breaths.

Cole moved around to the man's head and helped cradle it against the sofa with a pillow as James finished with the IV bag. "Just rest, Arthur. We're going to get you some help, okay?"

The man reached out and grabbed Cole's wrist. "No, you can't—you can't call anyone, you can't take me anywhere."

Cole nodded softly, took the man's hand, and placed it back on the sofa. "Who did this?"

The wounded man closed his eyes, taking pained breaths. "I don't know who they were, never seen them before. They came into the office this morning and said they were closing us down. They had paperwork." He took a deep breath and exhaled. "Kevin called it in. Downtown said it was all legit, that we should pack up and leave.

"We asked for some authorization from upstairs and that's when they hit on us." He paused for a beat then closed his eyes tight. "Kathy took it right off—they shot her at the receptionist's desk. I was able to draw on them and return fire." The man paused again, his face twisting up. "I was hit I don't know when. I fell back. Kevin pulled me out of the office. Got me to the car."

"Where is Kevin?" Cole asked.

The man tried to shake his head; he closed his eyes tighter. "I'm the only one that got out." The man coughed. "We tried to get away, but there were more of them outside." He opened his eyes and looked at the senior FBI man. "They were in cop cars, Cole, but they weren't police. They were coming for us. Not to take us away—they were there to kill us."

James moved away from the man and sat on the coffee table. He looked down and said, "How did you get away?"

"It was Kevin," Jacobsen said. "He pushed me behind the wheel and told me to drive." The man took a long breath. "He slapped the car, he told me to drive, said he was jumping in the back."

"You left him?" James asked.

Attempting to shake his head again, the man gasped. "No, I watched him go down. He's dead." The man's jaw quivered. "They're all dead."

"It's okay, Art. You're okay now. We'll take care of you," Cole said.

The man closed his eyes. "I'm sorry I came here. I didn't know anyone would be here."

"It's okay," Cole said. "Just rest."

The pair sat, silently watching the man until his breathing became rhythmic. James stood and walked to the kitchen then washed his blood-covered hands in the sink. He moved, aside toweling off, and Cole replaced him at the faucet.

"We can't stay here," James said, looking into the living room at the injured man. "Too many of your people know about this place, and he could have been followed."

Cole bit at his lips. "I'll give you the keys to the Suburban—you go. I'll stay with him."

James shook his head. "No, we're not splitting up." He paused, walked to the kitchen window, and pulled back a heavy curtain. The yard was empty, the neighborhood still ominously quiet. There was no traffic on the street. Cars were in driveways, curtains drawn, and garage doors closed. He shook his head again. "Nobody is coming after this kid," James said. He pulled back from the window. "If what you say is true, they'll be too busy hunting hard targets than to come after us."

"You got more medical time than me," Cole said,

pointing toward the living room. "Is he going to be all right?"

James shrugged. "I don't know. He needs a proper doctor. We bought him some time. If the bleeding stops, we'll have even more."

The lawman nodded. "We wait till dark then we move."

Dipping his chin in agreement James said, "I know a place we can go."

CHAPTER SIXTEEN

"What did he say?"

Tommy powered off the phone and removed the Genii device, placing the pieces into his shirt pocket. "He's exposed. They're after him now."

"The Colonel?" Tanya said. "Why would they go after him? Do they know he helped you?"

"I don't know, he had to kill the call," Tommy answered.

She looked at him. "What do you mean he killed the call?"

Tommy put his hands on the steering wheel. They were parked on an exit ramp off US-231, just south of Montgomery, Alabama. They had stopped to sleep, but Tommy remained awake the entire night. Nobody had passed through; they were virtually alone on a normally busy highway. "He just said they had company and hung up."

She looked out of the passenger window. Then back

at him. "You said we were going to Montgomery. How much further?"

Tommy reached down and started the car. "It's close. We're not getting back on the highway."

He eased the vehicle into gear and continued off the exit ramp, then he took a right onto a broken blacktop road that quickly turned to gravel. They were in rural countryside. Tanya reached to the dash and turned on the radio. The scanner moved past several stations, stopping on one giving an emergency alert tone. They had heard it earlier; every station that hadn't gone altogether down was playing it. Like in Florida, the Alabama stations were now also announcing curfews and warnings to stay off the streets and highways. Telling residents that they would not be allowed to leave the state.

She flipped the band to AM. She looked at Tommy, and he nodded his approval. She spun the dial to a frequency they'd found earlier, a man preaching extremism from some satellite location. He claimed to be in a van, or an RV. Said he was beaming the signal remote to his home tower. Who knew what the truth was, or if the guy was even for real? At first, Tommy took it as the typical conspiracy stuff. As the night went on, he began to wonder if his message was really that crazy at all. Maybe this was the opening days of a new war.

He found himself buying into the man's rants as he drove, and Tanya slept in the seat beside him. Just before dawn he'd had enough. He flipped it off to allow his head to clear before he made the phone call to James. Now the man was back on in the early afternoon, and Tommy was eager for updates.

The man's weary voice came through, fatigued and tired. He'd probably gotten as little sleep as Tommy, but the energy of the message was still there. Tommy relaxed his grip on the wheel and focused on the voice as he drove.

"I'm on the move, and I'll keep broadcasting until they shut me down. I managed to get out of the city. But don't worry, folks, I am still streaming signals back to the house. I will stay live as long as I can. If you're receiving this, my broadcast tower is still up. But don't worry; if they take it down, I have another.

"Eventually they'll get it, you know they will. But don't worry, friends. You know the Mad Jack has connections, and if they take down one station, we'll stream to another. Radio free Alabama will not be shut down.

"Seriously folks, stay away from the cities. If you're out in the sticks, stay there and be ready. They have the cities locked down. Nobody goes in or out. The curfews are being enforced. Trust no police that you are not personally familiar with. We've received reports that local precincts have been completely shut down, the personnel replaced by outsiders. They call themselves the New Regional Authority. Do not trust them. They wear black-on-black uniforms. They have no badges and unmarked police cars. They are not your friends.

"If you are one of the unfortunate souls trapped in the city, stand too—we will be organizing, and we will come for you. Be ready, but until then lay low, don't cause problems for yourself, blend in, and take notes. If they try to take you, you will have to fight. There are no camps, they are not doing roundups.

"This is it, people, this is the big one. Don't believe the lies, they are promising a miracle fix, they say everything will be okay in a day or two, they say they'll bring those responsible to justice.

"Well, listen to me, ladies and gentlemen. They are the ones responsible. While you stay in your home, following instructions, they are tracking down and killing anyone they fear, anyone they think will fight back. They are killing your neighbors, your brothers and sisters. This is a national culling.

"This is it, ladies and gentlemen, this is the big one, this is the civil war they have been asking for."

"He's nuts, right?" Tanya said. "These AM guys always sound like this, don't they?"

Tommy kept his eyes on the road, looking for the hidden turnoff. "I'm not sure what to believe. You saw those guys at the gas station, and the others at the roadblock. Who are they?"

"But the government doesn't just kill people. This has to be someone else." Tanya looked hard at him. "How could they act so fast? It's been less than forty-eight hours and they are stretched from Miami to Alabama. People are in hiding and the radios are already offline."

"Like the man said, this is the civil war they wanted, they've been planning it." He grunted. "We saw the signs; they told us it was coming." Tommy found the road and slowed the car, turning onto a narrow gravel driveway. Weeds grew high on the sides and down the middle. He drove up it a hundred yards then stopped at a closed cattle gate.

"Tanya, who do you think those people were at the

station? The ones at the roadblocks? Who were those men on the island?"

She shook her head. "I don't know, but there has to be an explanation. This can't be what they are saying it is." She pointed at the radio then turned it off. "It's not war."

He kept his hands on the wheel, looking at the gate, then nodded. "Yeah, we're going to figure this out."

She swallowed hard and sighed as she looked at the locked gate. "Where are we?"

Staring into the distance, Tommy said, "In the Ground Division we called this place home, others called it the Ranch."

"You lived here?"

He smiled and shook his head no. "It was nothing like that; it was more like a headquarters, a base of operations and a place to recoup or train for things that couldn't be done in the open."

"So—a CIA headquarters in the backwoods of Alabama?" Tanya said skeptically.

Nodding, he said, "That's what made it perfect. It's in the middle of nowhere yet still close enough. We worked out of agency-owned safe houses all over the country: in Baltimore, San Diego, New York. But the *home* here in the boonies was always the real HQ."

She looked at him. "Then why are we here? It can't be safe."

"That's the thing, this might be the safest place in the country right now. Nobody knows about it."

"If it was your home base how could nobody know?"

"Seriously? I thought you did your homework on the

Ground Division before you became my handler. I thought you were read in on all of this?" Tommy looked at her and winked. "We were the most clandestine of off-the-record services, the phantoms of paramilitary forces. You don't think we could keep a secret?"

He looked at her expression and could see that she wasn't amused. He nodded and continued. "My old boss set this place up right after the Ground Division teams were authorized. He used funds from the black budget."

"Black budget?" she asked.

He looked at her. "Like those yellow envelopes you pass me every six months. The money that congress approves without really knowing where it comes from or where it ends up. Every year the media has a story about how this agency or that agency has millions of missing cash. Defense Department can't account for a hundred million here, State Department lost a hundred million there. Well, it's not missing; they just can't say what they spent it on. In our case, we had a respectable facilities budget. We could have had nice buildings with all the included gizmos in the Capital. Top-of-the-line setups. Instead, Tyler paid cash for this place and a few hundred acres and made leases on a half dozen other safe houses to cover it up. The *home* was never put on any inventory list."

"Who is Tyler?"

Tommy grinned. "Tyler Spence, my old boss."

"Tyler Spence, the frigging Assistant Director of the Central Intelligence Agency?"

He smiled and dipped his chin.

She looked at him suspiciously. "He's a personal

friend of the President. He's my damn boss. Why didn't you tell me you knew Director Spence?"

Tommy shrugged. "I thought you knew. Didn't you think it was odd that the President put me on retainer? That he even knew who I was?"

"Odd yes, but I didn't think Tyler Spence was your friend. He never talked about you, not once. Everything to do with you always came from the clandestine services branch."

"I'm out of the loop," Tommy said, shaking his head. "Besides, I'm not sure we are even friends. He was my boss once, but we were never that tight. He was a couple pay grades above me."

"So, if this place is off the government books then Tyler owns it?" she said, moving on.

"Yeah, that's another funny story. Tyler doesn't own it. If Tyler owned the place, it would be connected to him, and crooked as hell if he used company money to buy himself a ranch. No, the owner, if he is even still alive, is Marcus Wahl, a retired Marine."

This time it was Tanya who shook her head no. "And let me guess—he lives up this road."

Tommy smiled again. "I'm kind of hoping so. Hey, slide over and drive through, would ya?"

He unlatched the door and walked to the cattle gate. At the end was a heavy length of chain with a combination lock. He worked the combination to a number stored deep in his memory then tugged down on the lock, and it clicked open. Tommy pushed the gate open and waved Tanya through before closing the gate shut and relocking it.

He stopped on the drive and examined the hard-packed gravel and weeds. Same as it had been all those years ago, the crushed stone and red soil made it nearly impossible to tell the last time the drive had been used. To the right of an entrance was a concrete pad lined with a short knee wall. A pair of knocked over trash cans lay inside, overgrown with weeds. Tommy moved back to the car and, this time, sat on the passenger seat.

Tanya eased off the brake and followed the drive up and through the thick clusters of longleaf pine trees. Through the dark shadows, the trees opened to wide pasture where, at the end, sat an old farmhouse, the sides a rough wood that looked like it hadn't been painted in a decade. To the back of the property was a large barn. Tanya was looking at the building with disappointment when Tommy grinned and told her to stay on the road. She looked at the end of the gravel drive and said, "What road?"

Tommy pointed toward another cluster of trees. At the corner of the tree line, as the car drove closer, the road revealed itself in the high grass and into the natural rolling terrain. If she hadn't been looking, she would never have noticed the path. She wound the car along the drive and onto the next lane, through another forest of pines. Here the trees didn't open into a clearing. Instead, the road moved into a cluster of buildings covered by the canopy of large pines. She stopped the car and put it into park.

"What is this? A Boy Scout camp?" she asked.

Tommy laughed. "Actually, I think it used to be."

He opened the door and walked around the front of

the car and sat on the hood. There was no point in knocking on a door or risk walking the property and getting himself shot. If Marcus was still here running the place, he would have known Tommy had arrived as soon as he parked in front of the cattle gate. The entire place was wired with sensors and cameras.

Tanya exited the vehicle and walked around to stand beside him. "What are you doing?"

Tommy held up a finger. "It'll just be a minute or two."

"A minute or two for what?"

He heard the crunching of pine needles somewhere behind them in the shadows, and Tommy smiled. He dipped his head in the direction of the tree line and said, "Tanya, meet Marcus."

She turned behind them and spotted the man, dressed in woodland camo and a ski mask. He was holding a rifle in their direction. Tanya raised her hands and stiffened. "Uh, Tommy?"

"Tommy?" the man with the rifle said. "Donovan, that you?"

Tommy turned and looked back. "Marcus, you never could sneak up on anyone."

The man lowered his rifle and rushed forward, grabbing Tommy by the shoulders. "Jesus, son, they said you were dead!"

"Who said?" Tommy asked.

The old Marine pointed toward the structure to their front and the door opened. Two men dressed in flannel shirts and tan cargo pants stepped out. The pair held rifles at the low ready. Both men oversized, both heavily bearded, one tall and black, the other white and as a wide as a bear. Tommy squinted, quickly identifying the duo with a broad smile.

"You know these guys?" Tanya asked.

Tommy stood and moved to the porch. "Hell yeah, I know these guys. They are Grounders."

The men moved quickly down the path and soon had Tommy flanked as the trio exchanged hugs. Tommy looked back at Tanya. "Hagan and Sol were both Grounders back in the day." He stopped and turned to the wide man with long black hair and a beard just beginning to show silver. "What are you guys doing here?"

Marcus came up behind them with Tanya. "Not here, Tommy. They might have eyes in the sky. We need to get inside." He pointed to the house. "Hagan, get them settled. I'll move the car to the barn."

Hagan nodded and pointed, shaking his head. "Damn, Tommy, it's good to see you, brother." He turned and walked toward the building with Tommy following close behind.

"What are you doing here, Hagan? I almost expected to find the place empty, instead I find Wahl and both of you," Tommy said, following the men onto a roughed-in plank porch and through a steel entry door. They passed into a spacious square room sparsely furnished with large brown sofas arranged in a square. There was a large wood stove against a wall and tables lined against the outer walls. At the far back of the room was a long kitchen that would fit in any restaurant. On the west wall hung a series of matching doors.

Tommy stopped and looked around then shook his head. "Marcus hasn't changed a thing in this place, has he?"

Hagan laughed. "Nah, the old man made some changes, you just can't see them from here." He moved back, leaning against a countertop, and pointed to a long row of doors. "The team rooms are all the same. Yours is probably just the way you left it. Armory is intact, but Marcus built himself a little apartment back in the old kill house." He paused and turned in a 360 and shrugged. "But, yeah, the front office is very much the same as we left it a decade ago."

Tanya leaned in. "A decade ago?"

Hagan looked at the woman suspiciously, then to Tommy, who nodded. "Yeah," Hagan said. "Operations here ceased just over ten years ago. This place sort of went idle after that." He held up a finger, wanting to change the subject, then pointed at the kitchen. "You want a beer?"

Raising his eyebrows Tommy asked, "Seriously? Beer?" He shook his head. "I thought that was Spence's golden rule: *No booze at the Ranch.*"

Nodding, Hagan said, "Yeah, that's another change Marcus made. Turns out once Spence mothballed the Ranch, Marcus turned the beer light back on."

Tommy moved across the room and dropped into one of the sofas. "Well, in that case, I'd love a beer." He looked left and right, seeing the dust on the furniture. "Not many visitors, I take it?"

Hagan laughed. "No, the old man doesn't come up

here often, just for maintenance. He lives out of the apartment."

The door opened behind them and Marcus entered the room, barring the door behind him. He leaned his rifle against the wall and then reset the security sensors. He turned back to the room just as Solomon tossed a beer from the kitchen, which Tommy caught one-handed.

"Whoa, boys, don't be getting into the old man's stash."

Tanya stepped in angrily. "I don't mean to interrupt the frat party, but what the hell is going on?"

The men all stood silently and turned to Tanya. Tommy cleared his throat and pointed the now open can at her. "Boys, this here is Tanya. Tanya, meet Marcus Wahl, Matt Hagan, and Solomon Kidd, some of my old fraternity brothers from the University of Hard Knocks."

Marcus grinned. "Son, did you go and get yourself married?"

Tanya scowled and looked hard at the Marine. "I'm Tanya Delgado with the Agency."

"Damn, boy, you married a spook? Never figured you to hook up with an agency spy." Marcus howled moving to another sofa and sitting, then patting the seat next to him for Tanya. "Come sit by me, girl."

Tommy laughed. "No, she's my handler. I've been freelancing."

"Nice, had no idea you were still on the payroll," Hagan said, making his way to the sofas with a beer of his own, dropping into one across from Tommy. "Nice to meet ya, Miss Delgado. Please, have a seat."

She shook her head sternly. "I'll sit when I know what's happening out there."

Solomon moved from the back with his arms full of beer cans. He set them on the table in the center of the square then dropped back into the last open sofa. "Shit, girl, you're with the agency." He laughed, opening a can. "You tell *us* what the hell is going on."

"We don't know anything." Tommy grunted. "We were overseas when whatever this was kicked off. Seems you already know the story." He shook his head. "I was pulled out by some friends just as it all when down over there. They got me out, but just barely."

"Yeah, I heard you were dead and gone overseas, bro," Hagan said before taking a sip. "News had it that you are a notorious terrorist, killed gunning down women and children in paradise."

"Bullshit," Tommy said. "What about you? What's your story?"

Hagan scowled and shrugged. "Allegedly popped a nuke plant out on the West Coast."

"Popped a fucking what?" Tommy gasped.

Hagan nodded. "I don't know all the details, because I wasn't there..." He took a long pull on the can, draining it, then reached for a fresh one on the table. "Night before last I was home in Ohio, lying in bed, watching TV, when my motion sensors chirped. I thought it might have been a deer or something. Yard sensors alarmed then the first-level doors breached. TV auto flipped to the closed-circuit cameras. Ten fools lined up in black. The crew they hired hit hard and fast. They were good but not professionals. Still pro or not, there were too many for me to fight. If I had to guess, they were common criminals, not law enforcement." He laughed smugly. "And the fools didn't do their homework—didn't know who they were messing with.

"My second story is basically a hardened safe room. They got stalled hard and bottlenecked at the steel door to my stairway. The rookies stacked up and prepared to breach, when I popped a claymore embedded in the ceiling. From there on, it was all automated protocols—"

"Wait," Tanya interrupted. "You had a claymore in your ceiling?"

Solomon laughed, holding up his can in a toast to Hagan. "Doesn't everyone? I mean, every self-respecting sapper I know has at least one claymore in the ceiling."

She shook her head and reached for a can, then moved to sit next to Marcus. "And what the hell are automated protocols?"

Hagan shrugged and relaxed back into the sofa. "You know, basic stuff like, all the yard lights kick on, sirens blare. Oh, and a fifty-gallon drum of jet fuel in the attic ignites. All while I roll out of a crawl space tunnel."

Tanya shook her head. "Fifty gallons of jet fuel?"

"Give or take," Hagan said. "I made it out into a drainage tube that let out on the far side of a county road and made it to my hide site. Next morning, I saw the news reports about me leading an attack on a nuke plant two thousand miles away. Apparently, I'm dead." Hagan held up the can, looked at it, then took a sip. "Doesn't suck as bad as I thought it would."

She shook her head and looked at Solomon. "And what about you?"

The big black man frowned. "I was just having dinner. Heard a noise downstairs." He paused and took a long drink. "I've been renting a small space over Rabbi Simeon's garage. I heard something—a scream maybe. I went downstairs to check, and they were already going at Rabbi Simeon. I did what I could..."

"You killed them?" Tommy asked.

Solomon nodded slowly and drained the rest of his can. "I killed all of them. But they cut deep on Simeon and his family." He shook his head slowly. "I waited for the police to arrive, but when the showed up, they tried to arrest me. Someone had placed a 911 call identifying me as one of the killers.

"And why the hell not?" He shook his head. "I was covered in blood. I looked like a damn killer." He stopped and stared down at the table. "I bugged out through the back. I was talking to my lawyer about turning myself in when I heard about you all on the radio. I knew this was the only place I could go." He paused again and looked Tommy in the eyes. "I'm a wanted man. They think I killed the only father I ever knew. The Simeon family took me in when I was a boy, they treated me like I was one of their own."

Tommy clenched his fist. "We'll make whoever did this pay."

Tanya shook her head. "Who the hell do you guys think you are? Obviously, this is far bigger than any of you can comprehend." She went to stand but when she could see that all of them were looking down, she dropped back into her seat. "We need to get back to Washington so I can report it."

"No can-do, Miss," Marcus grunted. "I've had limited contacts with some friends up that way. Highways are closed, the city is in lockdown. Best thing we can do right now is stay put."

"Lockdown?" Tanya repeated, "They've locked down the Capital?"

The old Marine shrugged. "President has even left town. There was a shooting on the Senate Floor. They decided enough was enough and evacuated the city. They are rolling out continuity plans. The President flew out on his helicopter and that's that."

"What do you mean 'continuity plans'?" Tanya asked.

"Moving important people to safe places, bunkers, out-of-the-way hotels, things like that," he said. "Vice President and his family are sheltering at a Navy Base north of Chicago."

"Then who is running the government?" she asked.

The old man leaned forward and placed his empty on the table. "Officially, the President is still in charge, but scuttlebutt has it that Senator Shafer and some others are calling the shots now. Media doesn't know anything, and nobody is talking."

"Shafer?" Hagan grumbled. "How do I know that name?"

"He's a senator now, used to be in the House, big player and a right-hand man to the majority leader," Marcus said. "A lot of people say nothing gets passed without a nod from Shafer."

Tanya raised her brows in suspicion. "He is one of many, how is that possible?"

Marcus grinned. "Money. Shafer has a lot of it, and he knows how to get more."

"So, he can be bought," Tommy said. "But what's your real take on him? Would he do something like this?"

Marcus slowly nodded his head. "He's as crooked as a barrel of fishhooks." He stopped and pursed his lips "But an all-out mutiny? I don't know. He would open the door to it, but I don't think he'd have the balls to go through with something like that. If I had to render a guess, I'd say he hitched his wagon to the wrong people."

Tommy leaned forward and set his empty can on the table. He could see the other men were all back with heavy eyes. He nodded. "As much as I want to act quickly on this, I really need some sleep. I've been going all most two days straight."

Marcus quickly got to his feet and pulled a big ring of keys from his pocket. He fished through them and unlatched one and passed it to Tommy. "Your team room is just the way you left it. You go and get some rest; I have the watch until you all are ready to relive me."

CHAPTER SEVENTEEN

There was a maroon Chevy Malibu parked in the first bay of the safe house's two-car garage. James walked around it to the back and popped the trunk. There was a small tool kit in the back. He opened the bag, finding a jack and a pair of road flares with nothing else. He sighed and lifted a bag of gear he'd salvaged from the safe house and dropped it in. Then he went to Cole's Suburban and removed his tactical bag and gear from the back, cross-loading it into the Malibu.

He turned when he heard the door that led to the house open. Cole was walking out, escorting a visibly pale, and wounded FBI man. Arthur had slept through the night. The bleeding had stopped, but he still had a gunshot wound through the top of his chest. Without medical attention, the man didn't have the best of odds. James closed the trunk on the Malibu and opened the rear passenger door for Cole.

"The Suburban would make more sense," Cole said as he helped the injured man into the back.

"We can't risk it, that damn thing screams government. Same as Arthur's black dodge sedan out front," James said, waiting for the man to be laid out before he closed the door.

Cole shook his head and walked around the car to a control box by the garage door. "Speaking of Arthur, we need to get him some help."

"That's the plan," James said.

"Thought you said the plan was to head for the hills," Cole said as he pressed a button, opening the garage door.

James stopped and looked at him. "We'll get him help first. You saw the news; they have a twenty-hour curfew in place. We can only travel between 10:00 and 14:00 around the District. That gives us four hours to get him some help and get back into hiding."

Cole shot him a thumbs up and dropped into the black dodge and started the engine.

James got into the Chevy and fired it up then backed out of the garage and let Cole move the Dodge into the first bay. The man closed the garage door then checked the outside lock to make sure it was secured. A quick glance left and right, and Cole was sitting in the sedan beside him. James eased the car out of the driveway and back onto the street.

"You think anyone noticed us here?" James asked.

Cole shook his head. "If they had, they probably would have raided us." The lawman investigated the rearview mirror and waved a hand toward the street. "I don't think anyone is out making reports right now. Everyone is in their homes, afraid of terrorists and killers.

I haven't seen a single cop on patrol, not even a dog walker."

James nodded. "That'll change. People will follow the curfew for a couple days maybe three, but once the groceries and money are gone, they'll be out again. People need to work, people need to eat."

Looking side to side, Cole sighed. "So where are we going, an old girlfriend's house?"

Laughing, James said, "Someplace I probably shouldn't take you. In fact, I should blindfold your old ass before I show you how to get there."

"Oh—is this some of that shady spy shit I'm always accusing you of?" Cole grinned.

James slowed the car and turned onto a main road. He found more traffic as he left the residential area and headed into Alexandria's industrial district. Truck traffic, sedans with people in suits, and a lot of black sedans parked at intersections and in front of businesses. On the corners, he saw armed men in black standing watch. Some checking a line of people's identification before allowing them into a metro station. "You see them?" James said, keeping his eyes straight ahead.

"I see 'em," Cole grunted. "But I don't see any Alexandria police. Who the hell are these guys?"

"I don't know. Looks like the local police have all been replaced. We have new peacekeepers in town," James said as he drove past an interstate entrance. He eased into a center lane then glanced toward the interstate exit, where cars were backed up at a checkpoint manned by the men in black. "Guess we'll be staying off the highways. Looks like they are doing something as folks get off."

"Control traffic into the city. I imagine they'll let anyone leave but stop and frisk as you enter." Cole looked over the seat. Arthur hadn't said much since they'd been in the car. "You sure it's smart taking us closer to the airport? Ronald Reagan had some trouble, the security will be tighter."

James pointed ahead to a run-down-looking motel set back from the road they were traveling on. The parking lot was filled with rental cars and shuttle vans. A large sign designated the place as the Beltway Inn. Below the marquee was a neon NO VACANCY.

"Looks like they are full," Cole said, pointing at the parking lot. "Is this your plan? A shitty hotel? I could have found us another safe house."

Ignoring the comments, James drove the car into the lot and past the pull-up lane in front of the lobby. He followed the parking lot around to the back and stopped in front of a single brick structure, parking next to a white cargo van with a Beltway Inn logo painted on the side.

"You have a reservation?" Cole said. "You saw the sign, no vacancy."

James grinned and reached into his wallet, pulling out a small brass key. "Ownership has its benefits."

"You own this shit hole?" Cole asked.

James laughed. "That's not nice, and yeah a shell company of mine has this place on the books. It's registered in Delaware and can't be traced back to my legitimate businesses."

Cole looked at him then waved a hand. "I shouldn't even ask why you need an off-the-books hotel."

James smiled. "You can ask, but I won't tell you." He opened the door and stepped to the back, waiting for Cole to exit. "You help Arthur. I'll grab the bags."

Together they left the vehicle and moved toward the rear of the hotel. In the back was a narrow alley that cut through the center of the long building. Past a pair of ice machines was an elevator, and a sign pointed back toward the road that said LOBBY/DINING ROOM. James stopped at the elevator and pressed the button. Cole stepped up beside him. He was helping Arthur along, and surprisingly, the man was on his own feet, though his eyes were heavy and barely open.

The elevator dinged, and the door opened. James took them up to the third floor. It was a typical old budget hotel, floors covered with carpet, beige wallpaper, and low lighting. James turned and moved to the end of the hall, where he inserted the key and pushed the door open, letting Cole move in ahead of him. Instead of a typical hotel room, the space was decorated like a modern studio apartment. A small kitchenette in one corner, a desk in another. The rest of the room was a small living area with a trio of doors on the back wall—a bedroom on each end with a bathroom in the middle. James pointed at one of the rooms.

"Get Arthur settled," he said as he walked to the desk and lifted the phone. He looked back and could see that Cole was doing exactly that, guiding Arthur into one of the guest rooms. He pushed the zero key on the phone and waited for it to ring. After a brief pause, there was an answer and a familiar voice.

"Beltway Inn."

James knew the woman knew it was his room; she was just following the rules, giving the standard answer.

"How you are doing, Anna?" James said.

"Mr. Flynn, when did you get in?" the woman asked.

James smiled. The line was air gapped—it didn't leave the building, but you never could be too sure; anything electronic could be eavesdropped on, and he always appreciated the discretion and professionalism of Anna.

"Just got here. They canceled my flight. Listen, could you send Mr. Doolittle up to the room? I had some rodent problems."

"Doolittle." The woman waited, then replied, "He's around here somewhere. I'll ring him and see if he can stop up."

"As soon as he is available would be great."

"Anything else?" Anna asked.

James rubbed at his scalp. "If the kitchen isn't closed, some food would be great, dinner for three, maybe."

"Not a problem. See you soon, Mr. Flynn," the woman said, hanging up.

James set the phone back in the cradle and looked up to see Cole pacing near a window. He had the curtain pulled back, looking over the large parking lot and the street. He dipped his chin out toward the east. James stood and looked in the same direction. At the corner was one of the black SUVs with a pair of the men suited up in black standing in front of it, they had stopped a car and were questioning the driver. "Looks like they got eyes on this place," Cole said.

Shaking his head, James said, "Doubt it. This place is so nondescript and run-down. I'm sure they expect criminals in here, but criminals are not what those guys are hunting for."

Cole laughed. "I've heard a lot of crackheads say that just before I kicked their doors in. No place is safe if someone is looking."

There was a knock at the door. James shrugged and moved toward it. "Trust me, they aren't looking here. Not yet, anyway."

He opened the door and a heavy-set woman with thick glasses and pulled-back brown hair moved in. She stepped quickly to James and wrapped him in a tight hug. "My God, James. I talked to Maria last night—she said the police were at your house, that they wanted to arrest you."

James smiled and looked down at her. "Just a misunderstanding."

She took a step back and stared at him sideways. "It's more than that."

She turned toward the door and allowed in a tall, tan-skinned man with silver hair. The man pushed a service cart into the room. The top of the cart was lined with covered trays. Without speaking, the man pushed it through to the kitchenette and removed the covers, revealing plates of food.

Then he reached under the cart and retrieved a medical bag. The man turned to James then to Cole. His brow tightened as he looked them up and down. "Anna said you had injuries?"

"The waiter is your doctor?" Cole asked.

Smiling, James pointed to the old man. "This Andre Berisha. He happens to be Anna's husband, and also one of the best doctors in Albania."

The man scowled, not impressed with the compliment. "Do you have injured, or not? The water heater is acting up from so many guests."

Cole ignored the question. "We are a long way from Albania."

Andre went to speak again, but before he could, James stopped him. "Andre has been with my team since the Kosovo campaign. After he left the action, he married off to one of my best analysts. Somehow, he convinced Anna here to quit with him, and ever since they have been helping me run this place. He's a good doctor, and I wouldn't get on his bad side—he's also a hell of a shooter."

Cole raised his hands in surrender. "Glad to have you here then, doctor." He pointed toward the back bedroom. "If you'd follow me, I can show you the patient."

Andre grunted and followed Cole into the back bedroom. Once they were gone, James moved into the kitchen, grabbing a plate of food, and dropped into a chair at a small dining table.

Anna sat across from him. "You going to tell me what's going on, James?"

James took a heaping bite of pasta and shrugged as he chewed. He swallowed and said, "I'm pretty sure you know more than I do. So how about you give me one of those situations reports, just like the old days?"

Anna got back up from the table and went to the kitchen cupboards. She removed a bottle of scotch and two glasses. She poured several fingers into each and brought the glasses back to the table. "If you made me guess, I'd say the country is at war with itself."

James stopped eating and dropped his fork. He knew things were bad, but it wasn't the answer he was expecting. Anna was a former intelligence officer with the US Navy. She'd lived in Germany and England most of her adult life before moving back here with Andre. Even though she now fit the appearance of a hotel manager on a pension, she wasn't one to take lightly or dismiss her opinions.

James reached for a glass of scotch and took a long sip. "War?" James used his free hand to massage his forehead. "I had been thinking this was a roundup, a moment of mass arrests. I hadn't considered anything near war. Please tell me more."

"Someone is killing cops, veterans. High-level government officials are being assassinated."

"The Joint Chiefs." James nodded. "I heard about that."

Anna shook her head. "Not only them, there was an active shooter in the Senate. A lot of people across both aisles were killed. In response to that, both houses and the Whitehouse are now in full lockdown. Congress is in recess and nobody knows when they will come back. Small towns across the nation are reporting mayors and police chiefs being killed." She took a deep breath. "Someone is purging the government."

"What about the Military?"

She shook her head again. "They are all pulled into their bases and locked up tight. National Guard is AWOL. They don't have the stomach for this."

"And the President?" James asked.

Anna frowned and downed half of her glass. "The news says he's locked up in the Whitehouse bunker, but I was told he left."

"Left where?" James asked.

"Do you remember those fuel and food contracts we have with the Navy facility at Thurmont?"

James looked at her. "You're talking about Camp David—just call it Camp David."

She nodded. "That's the one. We don't have anyone on site anymore, but we do have a guy at the Marine Barracks in D.C. A lot of equipment and staff left there yesterday. All day long, they had staff and trucks moving people and equipment. My guy downtown said they were all moved to Thurmont. If I had to reason a guess, I would say the President has been moved to Camp David for safe-keeping."

"You think he is under arrest?" James asked.

She shook it off. "I don't think so. If they wanted him arrested, they would leave him here. From what I know, the military still supports the President. I think he went there as a fallback position, someplace close that could be defended against the black hats." She pointed to the window. "Those black hats can't touch him if he is surrounded by a few hundred Marines and the Secret Service."

He took another sip and slowly nodded his head in agreement. "So, who are these black hats?"

"Foreigners. Most are Spanish speakers."

"Foreign? Are you sure?"

"Positive, the ones that came through here were all Spanish."

James put his fork down and leaned back in his chair. "Why would foreign police be here?"

She grinned. "Andre thinks they were brought in because whoever did this knew the police would stand down."

"You think this was all planned?"

The woman shook her head then stared at him. "How many times have we seen this before in other countries? Of course, it was planned. All the parts of a coup d'état are right here. The only thing we haven't figured out is who is doing it and why."

"You said the men came here? Who were they looking for?" James asked.

She scowled. "We're not sure. They stop in every few hours and ask for a guest list. It seems they are looking for specific people, and so far, I've had nobody they are interested in." She smiled. "I know what you're thinking. The hotel is about eighty percent legit guests right now. The rest of the guys are unregistered or under alias. I haven't given them shit."

"Who do we have here?" James asked.

"Most of the company pilots are checked in. They closed the field and hangars at Reagan. Andrews is all locked down to anyone that isn't military. Emerson's security guys are here—"

"Emerson's team, they are here now?" James asked. "I thought they were in Kuwait."

"Nope—Ali Al Salem went into lockdown. Sent all non-military personnel home. Emerson and his boys flew into Baltimore yesterday. One of the black hats tried to pick up one of Emmerson's guys as they went through customs... and, well, you know Emmerson." She grinned. "They got away and made it here."

"Which of Emmerson's guys?"

"Wilcox," she answered. "The big guy."

James looked up at the wall then back at her. "Tiny Wilcox. He is just a kid. How they hell did he make their burn list?"

"Apparently, he was a Swick at one time and did some shady stuff."

"A Swick?" James asked, confused.

She shrugged. "Special Warfare Combat Craft Crewman. And I only know what Swick means because I asked him. He used to take SEALs to where they were going. Guess he got into some serious stuff a time or two."

"Well, must have been some interesting places if it earned him a spot on the burn list. I hired him because I was told he was an excellent driver. I guess boats are included." James said, "Who else."

Shaking her head, she said, "That's about it. The rest are yard guys—mechanics, drivers, the techs. They are all stuck here until we figure out how to get them home or we get permission to go back to work."

"Okay," James said. He reached into his shirt pocket

and pulled out the Genii device. He looked back at Anna. "Listen, I need you to talk to Emmerson. Tell him I have work for him and his team. Get him whatever he needs and tell him to stand by."

"I can do that, and what about you?"

"I need to think, and then I have a phone call to make."

CHAPTER EIGHTEEN

R aul Chavez sat in the air-conditioned cab of a black Toyota Land Cruiser. The sun had just come up, and the mercury was already rising. He squeezed his fists, looking at the scene in front of him. Eight bodies covered with sheets lying on the black asphalt. His own security team was posted up on all corners of the Route 66 Motor Lodge, securing the scene. "How did this happen?" he asked.

Matias Diaz was in the seat beside him. The young man had been a loyal friend to Raul and a high-placed lieu- tenant with La Raza de los Reyes. Serving as his primary associate back in Colombia, they had done great things together to make the Race of Kings a powerhouse. They were leaders, not only in the eyes of crime syndicates, but as well with legitimate enterprises. They had mastered the use of front companies to score leading positions in industry.

It was Diaz's idea to begin the purchase of Vortex stock once Raul had officially joined their payroll. Now, thanks to their criminal enterprise, the Kings were one of the top shareholders of legitimate global security companies. Not only had they purchased favor with Vortex, but with many sister companies, along with the very highly prized Apollo Group, which was ultimately running this show.

Vortex Corp had become an important name in Central and South America; and the same as they'd done in manipulating America's fight in the drug war, Matias and Raul had exploited that resource even further, using Vortex. When Vortex was sub-contracted to fight the war on drugs, it was Raul who led the South American branch. Unlike a state-sponsored drug war, Vortex answered to no Congress and was essential law enforcement for hire. He'd carved a path and organized the cartels in a way no one had ever done before. Raul put them behind front companies and organized the enforcers under badges of legitimacy. He was now the top employer of security men in South and Central America. So, it was only natural to go to him when Vortex pitched the idea of a massive hire up of foreign agents.

Now Vortex was being tasked to provide law enforcement assistance within the borders of the United States. Raul was perfectly placed to assist in the hiring, and with the help of Consuelo, nearly every position was filled with a Raza Reyes soldier.

"They were not our people, Raul. These were the gringos." Matias grunted disapprovingly. "Mall cops and rejected embassy security, not Kings."

Raul nodded his head slowly. "How many did we kill?"

Shaking his head side to side, Diaz said, "None."

Raul scowled. "How many men were they facing?"

"One."

"I have eight dead gringos because of one man?" Raul said, his fist now shaking. He took a deep breath, closed his eyes, and then let it out. "I guess if we have to take losses, it is best that they come from the gringos." He pressed a button, rolling down the window and allowing the dry Texas heat to enter the cab. "What do we know about the shooter?"

"Ahh, yes." Diaz reached for a tablet between the seats. "The shooter is 11069. I already requested the secured file. Target name is Alexander Winston. He is an agency asset."

"Which agency?" Raul asked.

"C.I.A, but also an Army Ranger and a veteran of several law enforcement agencies," Diaz said. "He was populated as a Mark Six and targeted for removal."

Raul frowned. "Why would the Americans want so many of their professional operators put in the ground?"

"Conflict resolution," Diaz said. "That's most of the Vortex mission on the hunter-killer teams. They want these men out of the way."

"Typical American philosophy. Use up the man until he is no longer useful then eliminate him before he can file a grievance." Raul shook his head. "No worries, we will do what we were tasked to do. Contact the Apollo techs, tell them we need a full sweep of the surrounding area. I want everything, every camera, and assign drones to this hunt."

"Already done. They are scanning records as we speak." Diaz grinned. "I tell you, boss, this Apollo Group is connected. We never had this kind of technology in Colombia."

"Careful what you praise, it's only a matter of time before they turn it on us. Let's get this job done and get home before that happens." Raul looked at a navigation map on the vehicle's display. "What way did this Winston go?"

Diaz went back to the tablet and clicked several icons, then the tablet's display went to the vehicle's. Blips overlaid the map, and Diaz pointed at several of them. "A traffic camera picked him up here, then he stopped at a convince store here." The man grinned and pointed even further east. "But his major mistake, he took one of our vehicles and a company laptop. The vehicle had a maintenance application installed. It pinged to this location," he said, pointing to a crossroad over an hour's drive to the east.

Raul's brows tightened as he looked at the display. "What is this place, and is he still there?"

Diaz grinned broadly, showing yellowed teeth. "It's a farm goods store, and the laptop began pinging the building's Wi-Fi router very late last night."

"He is trying to use their Internet?" Raul asked, confused.

"No, but the Apollo laptop he took has been passively pinging the farm store's router. Even though he has made no attempt to connect to the farm store's Internet, we have still picked up the laptop's signature. The device is designed to report in if lost." Diaz placed a finger on the map. "Yes, we are certain he is there."

Raul pointed at the man's tablet. "And drones, how long before we can get them on the target?"

"I have requested the package," Diaz said. "But as you can imagine, they are very busy. If we get lucky, they will be there by nightfall, and then we can move on the target."

Raul stared at the video display on the dashboard then rolled his window back up. "No, we can't risk a delay and the man getting away." He looked out at his personal security team. They were good men, and all of them experienced fighters brought from home. "We will go ourselves; take everyone, even the communications van. I want to be there when we kill this man."

WINSTON WOKE FROM HIS SMALL HIDE IN A COPSE OF trees between two small hills. He ran his hands through his greasy hair and rinsed his mouth with a bottle of water before returning to the old utility truck he had borrowed from the farm store. From the back, he removed the scoped rifle, closed his eyes tight, and slowly reopened them while letting out a long yawn. He looked up the hill toward the farm store when he thought he heard a vehicle's engine. It was sooner than he had expected, but he had prepared for the eventuality.

He was in the field, hundreds of meters behind the farm store building, hiding in the only tree cover he could find. It was his plan all along to lie in ambush, to kill the men hunting him. Now hearing the vehicles, he wondered if he'd made a mistake, maybe this wasn't the best time and place. The bolt-action rifle was a sniper's weapon, not really what he would want for an ambush, but he'd done more with less in the past.

Winston gripped the rifle by the handguard and climbed the rise, staying low so that he wouldn't skyline himself against the morning sun to his back. He rested at the top of the hill and put his eye to the scope. The red truck was still exactly where he had left it. He scanned further to the west and spotted a black Toyota Land Cruiser, a dust cloud just beginning to settle around it.

"Shit," he whispered to himself. "Why the hell are they way over there?"

If the vehicle didn't move closer, he'd have to move himself to engage them. The last thing he wanted was to move into the exposed terrain of the field to his front.

He scanned right, and closer to him, between the building and the hill he was resting on, wended a narrow gravel road. He watched as a black Chevy Suburban and a white Ford cargo van turned off the hardball and onto the gravel, moving along a ridge. They followed the road until they were directly behind the building, then parked with their grills facing the farm store.

The ridge gave them some cover from the building, but not from Winston's elevated position. He grinned, knowing this was the exact situation he'd hoped for; maybe his plan wasn't going to shit. He looked at the distant Toyota. He hadn't planned on a general on a hilltop to observe his activities. If he'd had a long-range

50-caliber rifle, he'd end them too. Winston frowned and focused back on the near vehicles. The men thought he was still inside.

Winston hadn't been sure about the capabilities of the Apollo laptop, so before he left the building, he placed it on the small table in the farm store and took it out of airplane mode. It was a risk, but he wanted to know if these people had the tools to track him. If they found him, he wanted it to be on his terms. Now seeing the white van with a team of six men dressed in black gathered around the back, he tried to fight back the rage.

The names he'd read the night before were stuck in his mind. Every time he closed his eyes, he saw their faces. Winston cursed himself for letting his emotions drive him. He should have ditched the laptop evidence and left before dawn. He could have been miles away before they made their empty raid. Then releasing a deep breath, he told himself it would be fine. He wanted this, he wanted them coming here, he wanted to stop them.

He scanned the surroundings again. The Toyota was still in the same spot and not moving. The Suburban and van to his front were now unloaded. Men in tactical gear were suited up and making an approach on the building. He watched as the men loaded weapons onto their vests and slapped each other's backs. They had made a grave miscalculation. They were approaching the building from the windowless back, walking in a wedge formation, and scattering from left to right. Winston eyed them through the glass; it was less than 150 meters to the nearest target. It was an easy shot on any day. The men were trapped in the open and still had to travel at least another three hundred meters to reach the building.

He glassed back down to the vehicles. Only two men had stayed behind. One was holding a pair of binoculars to his eyes and a radio to his mouth. Panning right, he saw another man at the rear doors of the van, looking into a tablet of some sort. Winston took his eye off the scope and looked at the sky, thinking drone, but he quickly shook that off. If they had a drone, they would have already spotted him. Winston closed his eyes again and reached into a cargo pocket on his right thigh. He dropped a trio of ten-round box magazines next to his shoulder. He took a deep breath and rested his eye against the scope.

The breach team was still making its way across the open field. He waited until they opened the distance another fifty meters then switched back to the man with the binoculars. He put the crosshair on the center of the man's back, caressed the trigger, and squeezed between the natural pause in his breathing. The rifle bucked; the report was louder than he expected in the quiet Texas prairie. He kept his eye to the scope, working the action, and watched the round hit just below his aim point. He shifted his rifle right and stopped at the man with the tablet. The man was stunned and crouched behind the van's open rear doors. Winston this time aimed at the base of his neck, squeezed the trigger, and shifted to the men in the field before he verified the round struck true.

The breach team was standing dumbfounded, looking at each other. None of them had seen the man with the binoculars or the tablet fall. They heard the gunshots but hadn't pinpointed the source. Winston looked to the Toyota; it hadn't moved. Quickly, he shifted back to the men in the field. The group had clustered together, still confused. One man had broken away from the pack. He had a radio to his ear, walking back toward the van.

"Thank you for identifying yourself Mr. Bigshot."

Winston put his rifle scope on the breach team's officer, this time leading the man's stride and aiming over his head. He pulled the trigger, and the .308 round struck right at his shoulder patch, throwing the man to the ground in a spin. Now the others were fully aware of what was going on. They dropped to the ground and turned toward the van, opening fire and spraying down their own vehicles with automatic weapons fire. Winston picked the most distant man and fired again, then shifted to the next. He fired again. Three men were left in the field, when one rose and sprinted for the cover of the steel building.

He allowed the man to run a bit, then a second man joined him. Winston let them go, waiting to see if the third would join in. They were fruitlessly running for a building hundreds of meters away. When the third man joining the race, Winston racked the bolt and fired. Dropping the distant runner, and then the second in rapid succession. The last man alive in the field stopped and turned back to Winston, dropped his rifle, and raised his hands in the air. The man rotated in a circle.

Winston knew there was no way the man could see him; he was positioned on a rise almost two hundred meters away with the sun to his back. Through the scope, he could see the fear on the man's face as his eyes darted left and right. He couldn't hear the words, but he knew the man would be begging for mercy.

"Sorry—this is not that kind of fight," Winston said.

He aimed and fired, watching the man drop in the field, the echo of the last shot fading away. He scanned the field for movement, counting targets as his eye moved over them. They were all down. He switched his eye back to the Toyota; the vehicle was turned around and racing to the west.

"It's time to go," he said.

CHAPTER NINETEEN

Tommy woke with a start, his eyes surveying the room, trying to remember where he was. No windows, the walls painted a battleship grey, the room furnished with only a pair of wall lockers and a twin bed. A steel case desk was against a wall with a small gun safe in a corner.

He sat up on the ragged sofa he'd been sleeping on. Tanya was asleep in the bed. Slowly he remembered he was back at the Ranch, in his team room. It really was exactly like he'd left it. He closed his eyes tight and slowly opened them again. The old man hadn't changed a thing in here. He leaned back into the sofa and listened; he could hear voices from out in the main room of the house.

The others were awake. His watch told him it was almost 0800; he must have slept through the night. He was okay with that. He needed the sleep after nearly two days on the run. He reached down and put his feet in his boots and quietly left the room, not wanting to wake Tanya.

Opening the door, he was hit with the smell of frying bacon and brewing coffee. Marcus was working the stove as Hagan had a broken-down rifle in front of him. Marcus turned and saw him as he closed the door behind him.

"Coffee?" the old Marine asked.

"You know it," Tommy said, heading straight for the kitchen lunch counter. His head suddenly spun with memories of how many meals he'd had here while training at the Ranch. He shook it off and took the cup from Marcus, inhaling the fragrance of the fresh hot coffee. "You as good a cook as you used to be?"

The Marine laughed and gave a hard stare before cracking a smile. "One of the best, kid."

Tommy pointed his chin toward the wall of team room doors. "What's up with that? Mine looks the way I left it a decade ago. You miss me so much you couldn't clean it out?"

The old man grunted. "Don't go flattering yourself. It wasn't out of any sentiment. Just wasn't my mess to deal with. I kept the place up, thinking maybe you'd come back one day. Heard about the accident, kid. Real sorry about that." Marcus looked off at a wall like he was studying something then looked back at Tommy.

Tommy held up his coffee cup in a mock toast. "Not much of an accident, brother. It was a roadside bomb, but, hey, I'm here now."

"Yeah, you're here now," Marcus said, returning the toast.

Tommy looked around at the empty walls where charts and maps used to hang. "So, what's up with this place? Is it operational or not?"

Marcus shrugged. "Something like that. One day Tyler just called me up, maybe a year or two after you dropped off the roster. Hell, once they stopped bringing on new shooters, I knew then the days for the Ranch were numbered. I knew it was coming when Tyler called and said he was closing the place down. Told me to mothball the joint."

"Mothball?" Tommy asked.

Shaking his head, Marcus said, "I don't know, Tyler never said it outright, but I got the feeling he thought this place might become useful again one day. He told me to seal up the operational side and do what I wanted with the rest of the Ranch. I wasn't about to argue with him. Hell, where was I going to go? Outside of my pension, it's not like I had anything. I was just happy I had a place to live."

Tommy nodded. "What about out there? Any news?" he said, blowing on the steaming liquid before taking another sip.

Hagan sighed, joining the conversation. "Nothing good, I'm afraid."

Tommy sipped at the coffee then set the cup down. Sol opened the main door and stepped inside, turning their heads. The man hung his long rifle on a hook and sat at the counter with the others.

"No traffic on the road, no aircraft in the sky, no foot traffic, no bears shitting in the woods," Solomon said, reporting in before accepting a coffee of his own.

"I wouldn't expect anything friendly," Marcus grunted. "The ham radio says we are on a national curfew now. Fucking A. No shitting you, martial law is now officially in effect. The news started broadcasting a 1-800 number. People are supposed to call in and give their families names and numbers so that FEMA can make meal deliveries. And, fucking shocker, you can use the same number to snitch on your friends and neighbors."

Tommy laughed. "Yeah, I'm sure you made that call, didn't ya, big guy? Ratted us all out."

"Ha, hell no. Opposite. I flipped a main switch this morning, taking us off the grid. We are 100% cut off from the outside world right now. Nothing digital or analog is going in or out of the Ranch now. We are running off solar, so even the utilities won't know anyone is here," Marcus said. "It's all happening as we speak, boys. By the way, Tommy, you don't have a phone, do you?"

Tommy reached into his jacket pocket and dropped a smartphone and the Genii device. Hagan looked at it. "That's some good tech you got there. Where'd you get it?"

"A friend," Tommy said. "Been using it to check in."

Marcus nodded then swiped up the phone and Genii device and sealed them in an anti-static bag. "I should have asked you for this yesterday. You can get them back if you leave, but for now, they're going in the steel box. We can't risk a signal leak out here."

"Is that really necessary?" Tommy asked.

Marcus shrugged. "Spence always thought so. He never thought being in the boonies was enough. He built this place to hide a heat signature from the air, but he always said radiation leaks would be enough to pinpoint us. Who knows what kind of tech the bad guys are using."

"Well, I'm going to need it back. I have to contact my handler," Tommy said.

Marcuse raised his brow. "Thought that pretty girl in the back was your handler."

"Yeah, she is." Tommy took a sip of his coffee. "It's complicated. You remember James O'Connell?"

Both Hagan and Marcus frowned. Hagan said, "The kid we lost over in Iraq."

"Syria," Tommy corrected. "But yeah, that's the one. I've been doing odd jobs for the agency. O'Connell's old man has sorta been my benefactor."

Marcus laughed and shook his head side to side. "No shit—you've been working with the Colonel? Always knew there was more to that guy than shipping beans and bullets around the globe."

"And that's only the half of it. He is my eyes and ears. I'll need to contact him to get my next assignment."

"Tomorrow then," Hagan said. "I need you to lay low today and tonight. But you wait until tomorrow and I'll open the vault, give you everything you need. You can walk the property line and make your call on the hiking trails over the old hilltop scenic overview."

"That works." Tommy nodded. "So shit is really going sideways out there? I didn't think it was possible. I mean, an actual civil war? Even as I saw it for myself out on the highway last night..." Tommy paused and looked down. "You know, there was a guy on the AM radio."

"The Mad Jack," Marcus said. "Yeah that boy sounds crazy, but he is legit. Hell, he used to work for the agency once, if you can believe that."

"He worked for the agency?" Hagan said, laughing, "I heard that fool preaching on the way down here. He sounded nutty as a fruitcake." The big man paused, looking at his now fully assembled rifle. "But hey, I tell you what, he had this shit figured out a couple days ahead of the rest of us, didn't he? Maybe he ain't that crazy."

"What's his deal?" Tommy asked.

Marcus laughed. "His name is Jackson Kennedy. He was a spook for the National Security Agency in the eighties. Spencer had me check him out a few years ago. Guess somebody picked up on his chatter and was worried about the accuracy of his messages. Sometimes the dude is spot-on over some hairy stuff. At the time, he was making daily reports about a Commie boomer off the coast of California. The dude was giving live updates on the locations of a Chinese submarine."

"Why didn't they shut him down?" Tommy asked.

Marcus shrugged, turning off the stove and bringing over two large platters filled with bacon and eggs. "Jack didn't break any laws; he just knew shit and a lot of it. I tracked him down, had a long ass talk with the man. Hell yeah, he wears a tinfoil hat and doesn't trust anyone, but the dude isn't crazy. I told Spence what I knew about that man and that was that."

Marcus sat at a bar stool. "Guess they just wanted to know who he was. I told Spence the dude wasn't getting his information from the US Government and they never bothered me about him again. I had a few chats with him over the years, bumped into him at the market in town a few times."

Tommy eyed the leathered Marine. "If he wasn't getting his info from our guys, where was it coming from?"

"That's the thing, the dude didn't reveal his sources," Marcus said.

"Now wait," Hagan said, loading a plate from the platters. "If the dude didn't give up his sources then how did they know he wasn't getting locations of the submarine from the US Government? How they know they didn't have a mole on the inside?"

"Cause the US Government didn't know shit about the Chinese boomer until they heard it from Mad Jack. The info was so detailed that they sent a Navy P-8 Poseidon out to prove the man wrong. Low and behold, they found a damn Chinese submarine right where he said it would be," Marcus said.

"You're joking." Hagan laughed.

Marcus grinned and said, "No joke, it was right there, less than a hundred miles off Los Angles. They scrambled a fleet and chased its ass off." The old man laughed again. "The cat knows things, but he isn't stealing it from us."

Hagan shook his head and pushed away an empty plate. "So, you going to tell us how then?"

"The Net tells him. The guy is a literal web genius; he's plugged in to all of it," Marcus said. "If it's online anywhere in the globe, he knows about it."

Tommy looked at his cup of coffee, then up. "You think you could find him now, contact him?"

"Why?" Marcus asked, eyeing Tommy suspiciously. "He wouldn't talk to you. Hell, with what's going on he'd probably shoot me on sight—he hates the agency."

Running a hand over the back of his neck Tommy said, "I need a plan. I need to be out there doing something to help." He paused and looked down at his empty plate. "This Mad Jack, he might be able to get me started on that."

The men turned as a door opened and Tanya stepped into the great room. She glared, having overheard the last part of the conversation. "Tommy, you aren't going anywhere or doing anything. You'll keep your ass right here until we hear from James."

Tommy smiled and stood from the bar, giving her his seat. Before he could ask, Marcus was filling her a plate. She shook her head at the men and took the offered stool. "Make nice and feed me, but I'm still not letting you go out there and get yourselves killed."

Hagan grunted then laughed. "Tommy Donovan, a kept man." He looked at Solomon and together the men laughed. "Never would have believed it if I hadn't seen it for myself."

"Yeah, we'll see about that." Tommy grinned and looked at his watch. "I bumped into some thugs on the way down here. Dressed in black, military gear, new vehicles—you know anything about them?"

Solomon nodded. "Yeah, they were running roadblocks and doing police work. It's best to avoid them."

Tanya scoffed and shook her head. "Yeah, not this guy."

Solomon looked at her. "I take you all had a run-in with them?"

"More than that," Tanya said. "He went out of his way *to not* avoid them."

"Oh yeah," Solomon said, fixing his eyes on Tommy. "I'd like to hear more about that."

Tommy shrugged. "It was nothing. I saw them running roadblocks, same as you. But when we stopped for gas a pair of them were trying to shake down some kids. I took care of it."

"Black hats, did you get any gouge on them?" Hagan asked.

Tommy grimaced. "They had Vortex identification cards. Some security firm, I guess. They were freshly minted. Big guys, young, Spanish speakers."

"Spanish?" Hagan said his eyebrows raised.

Nodding, Tommy said, "Yeah, English, but both had heavy accents. Not Mexican, probably South American."

"Colombians," Hagan said.

"How do you know that?" Tanya asked.

"I had a run-in myself." Hagan reached into a shirt pocket and dropped a Vortex ID badge on the table. On the face of the badge was the photo of an olive-skinned man and the name Mario Hernandez. "I got this off one of them up near Louisville on the way down here. I was sleeping at a freeway rest stop when he pulled up behind me in a black pickup to inform me I was breaking curfew."

"I suspect he didn't give you that badge?" Tanya said.

"Nah, he didn't give it to me, but trust me, he wasn't going to be needing it anymore." Hagan looked at Tommy. "He was Colombian. What are the odds that they are in several places and all working for Vortex?"

"Vortex is tied up with Apollo Group," Marcus said. "Bad business."

"And who are they?" Tommy asked.

Marcus rubbed his chin. "Apollo? They are like Boeing or General Dynamics, but instead of weapons, think technology. Top bidders and big shots. Few years ago, they bought Vortex dirt cheap after they screwed up that thing in Cairo."

"Cairo?" Tanya said. "That was them?"

"Oh yeah—it was a really big mess up," the old Marine said. "Cairo damn near shut them down. Department of Defense cut all ties with them, people went to jail. Pretty much bankrupted them, until Apollo Group bought it out and started picking up work with the State Department in Central and South America."

"Forget about Vortex," Tommy said. "This Apollo Group—where are they?"

"Got me. I guess they are everywhere," Marcus said. "In fact, the radio said something about them rolling out some new tech to law enforcement to help the government end all of this. Supposed to be some new wizardry to help them predict attacks before they occur."

Tommy took a step back and looked down at the floor. "We need to talk to Tyler; he would have the answers."

Marcus clenched his jaw and slowly nodded. "Yeah, he would." The old man frowned. "But how do we contact him? You go out looking for him, and you're toast. Use that phone, they'll lock on it and you're toast. Hell, all three of you boys are wanted men right now."

"We've got to do something," Tommy said.

Tanya looked at him and twisted her nose. "I know what you could do, take a shower."

Solomon belly laughed. "Friggin Tommy Donovan, a kept man."

CHAPTER TWENTY

"And you are sure everything is ready?" Mark Dorsey asked. He was in the basement server vault of the new National Geospatial-Intelligence Agency Headquarters in St. Louis. The complex took up hundreds of acres and was designated to be one of the premier combat support intelligence agencies for the Department of Defense. What most people didn't know is that Apollo Group had dug their claws in deep. There wasn't a single corner of the complex, or a person working for the agency that wasn't in some way connected with the Apollo Group.

Every contractor, every software developer, every network scientist within the GSA were on the Apollo Group payroll. Now with a flip of a simple switch, the press of a key, the Geospatial-Intelligence Agency would become the Delphi Initiative. There would be no sadness over losing the GSA; as with Delphi, the GSA would become obsolete. In fact, several agencies of the United States Government would soon become redundant.

Delphi could do it all, and with the passing of the United State Security and Monitoring Enhancement Act, it would finally be turned on. With the press of a button, the country first and eventually the world would become a safer place.

A small man with a white lab coat sat at a central console. Aaron Wright. He was the head scientist for Delphi. The man had a large stainless-steel briefcase opened and several cables strewn out and plugged into a network hub. More lab techs dressed the same were scattered around the room with handheld tablets, uploading code into mainframes and server banks.

Aaron turned to Mark and said, "Yes, sir, the logic is loaded. We can execute and begin scanning data on your word."

"And how long before it is working?" Mark asked.

The man smiled. "It will begin working immediately, but the longer it is in, the greater it becomes. It will take some time, but the system will never stop growing. Like the sun, it will rise here today, but as it passes over the country it will touch everything. Soon its code will be on every electronic device. It will be listening, interpreting, and reporting data."

"Do it," Mark said. "Turn it on."

Aaron turned to the silver case and pressed a button. With a click, a small keyboard slid out from the side, and a large monitor on the wall to their front popped to life. An Apollo Group logo locked in the center of the screen with a blue flashing cursor below it.

"Once the code is live, it cannot be removed without destroying the system." The man typed in several commands. "Everything will be processed through here, in this room, then analyzed and distributed by the collection specialist upstairs."

The Apollo logo on the screen changed to a Delphi symbol of a large cross and opposing vertical arches. Below the symbol was a flashing execute box. The man stopped his typing and turned to Mark. "Sir, would you like to do the honors?"

Mark stepped forward, looked at the keyboard, and pressed the return key. The display switched off then on and was filled with scrolling text. A progress bar popped up on the bottom and quickly shot to fifty percent.

Aaron pointed to the monitor. "This is normal; the bar will never get about fifty percent as long as the pipeline is open. It will always process data at the peak rate of ten zettabytes per second. If the processor struggles, the flow rate will reduce. If the data pipeline is cut off, Delphi will process the data in the queue, and the status bar will complete."

"Then let's make sure we keep this pipeline open," Mark said. He stood back and watched the scrolling data. "Don't delay on targeting data. I want information sent to the men in the field to be acted on as soon as it is available. We will shut all of this violence down and the country can go back to normal."

He left the room, stepped into the hall, and powered on his smartphone. Scrolling through the contacts, he dialed Victor. Mark knew that much of the plan was going as prescribed. Yes, they'd done enough damage to get Delphi through Congress but now things were beginning to spiral out of control.

On the way down to the vault, he'd watched news reports of gunfights and small skirmishes from coast to coast. It was time to change course, to stop the fighting, and allow the nation to recover under a stronger national leadership, one that he would help provide. He heard the click as Victor answered on the third ring.

"Victor, I want you to call off the attacks. Have our people stand down and wait for instructions."

He heard a sadistic laugh on the other end of the phone. "We haven't been attacking in over twenty-four hours."

"But the news," Mark said. "I just saw the most recent reports."

"Yeah, the news. Your plan, my friend, has inadvertently started a bit of a war. People are not hunkering down and waiting to be told what to do as you predicted. Many of them have already taken up arms against our agents. They are resisting. Even some police departments are actively engaged against my teams."

"This is a problem," Mark said. He frowned. "Never mind that. The system is live now. I want your people to stand by and wait for targeting information. No more open violence, no more checkpoints, do you understand? It's the fighting that is causing the problems."

"The people are angry; it won't just stop," Victor said.

"No. It will work, it's all been planned out," Mark said. "We have to let the system do its job and go after only those that Delphi deems dangerous. Delphi will calm the storm. You just wait and see."

Victor grunted. "We still have active hunts in

progress. There are still men on the original list that can hurt us. And of course, the President could still cause us problems. He is deposed, but he still has supporters in Washington."

"The President is a trapped rat. He is being dealt with," Mark said. He paused, thinking. "I said stop the hunts—the time for that is over. We need to stop turning the people against us. Let the people know that Delphi is online and that Vortex is here to help them. We must be very strategic in our targeting and let Delphi guide us now. Do you understand that?"

"Chavez won't be happy," Victor said.

Mark clenched his jaw. He'd regretted getting involved with Raul Chavez and his criminals from day one. He knew it was a mistake, but he needed their manpower. "Screw Chavez; if he wants to get paid, he will do as instructed," Mark said. "End the hunts and retire the current list. We will be building new lists shortly. Do you understand?"

"It is understood," Victor said, disconnecting the call.

Mark powered off the phone and placed it back in his jacket pocket. He turned and looked at the wall. Victor was right, the President could still cause them problems. They needed full support from the people, or this operation wouldn't work. He had Senator Shafer, but the man wasn't a leader, and he was beginning to become a liability. The Congress could call an emergency session at any moment and vote to undo Delphi as quickly as they had authorized it. He couldn't allow that to happen.

He moved back into the server room and approached

the console. Aaron looked up as he spotted him. "Was there something more?"

Mark nodded. "I want you to cut the power to Washington D.C., take them off the grid. Make the Capital a dead zone."

"Sir?" Aaron said. "Grid manipulation was not part of the Authorization Bill."

"I know what Delphi is capable of. I want the grid shut down," Mark ordered.

The tech moved to the console and entered several commands, tabbing from one credential box to another. A large map of the United States populated the screen. Several parts of the map were still covered in black grids as other sections were graphical representations of satellite images.

Aaron pointed at the map. "This is where Delphi's data load is right now in real time. It's only been minutes, but we have already infiltrated over twenty percent of the national infrastructure. The public pieces were easy. Now Delphi will have to work on the more secure areas, like banks and private industry." Aaron moved a mouse and began to zoom in on the Washington D.C. area.

On a high level, the map was fully animated, but as Aaron zoomed in, many areas became blacked out with lack of data. "We have high-level grid access, but as you can see, many of the map objects have not yet been accessed. We can cut the grid, but you do realize that if we do so now, many of these network devices will be taken offline with it, and we will be effectively creating a blind spot that Delphi cannot see in to. Delphi cannot infiltrate devices powered down and not on the grid."

"Will they know it's Delphi? Will they know it was us that shut them down?" Mark said.

Aaron bit at his lip and scratched the back of his head nervously. "Well, the original system wasn't designed to be covert; we have nothing to hide. But then again, we can do this in silence, but any power plant manager worth his salary will know it's a cyberattack. Even though, it will take some time to get the word out and even longer to confirm those suspicions, weeks maybe. But there is another risk. If plants suspect sabotage, they will disconnect from the network."

"Then what? We will lose the ability to shut them down?" Mark asked.

Aaron nodded. "Effectively, but the plant has to physically remove itself from all communications, or Delphi will find a way in. They can't just power down a device—if so, Delphi will still work passively to send communications. Only a cut cable could theoretically allow them to stay powered up and feed the grid, but then they will have no communication to the outside world."

"Do it. Shut it down all of it," Mark ordered. "I want Washington in the dark."

Aaron began hitting keys, and the map of the Capital area went black. Then in a ripple effect, much of Virginia and Maryland went dark with it.

"What was that?" Mark asked, pointing at the large areas of the map going dark, and more continuing to go black down the coast. "I didn't ask for all of that."

"Overlapping infrastructure. Taking down plants in one location will stress the grid in other areas. It's hard to predict how moving one plant offline will affect the region. I've also killed all communications and any system that tried to revert to backup power. It's all down, sir. The Capital region is effectively a dead zone."

"Very well," Mark said, looking at the map. He smiled. "Keep gathering target information, and let me know if there are any changes."

CHAPTER TWENTY-ONE

James O'Connell froze in the darkness. He was in the shower, the water still running, the lights all out. He cut off the faucet and slipped a hand from the curtain and gripped the Sig 1911 he had resting on the sink ledge. He stood listening to the sounds of dripping water and slowly pulled back the curtain. The bathroom door was still closed and locked, the way he'd left it. He could hear shouts from outside.

Grabbing a towel from the rack, he wrapped it around himself and stepped into the main room. Cole was there, looking out the window. He looked back at James. "Power just went out, and not just in the hotel; it looks like everywhere." The man pulled back the curtain and pointed to the intersection. "That black SUV with those black hats is still down there on the corner but looks like the stoplight is out. The way they are acting, I'd say they didn't know this was coming."

James walked to the phone and lifted the receiver. He held it to his ear and pressed the disconnect with his finger. "It's dead. This phone is on an internal system; it runs off the emergency power generators."

Holding up a finger then shaking his head, Cole said, "I don't think your generators came on. Unless they are really quiet." He looked at James and grinned. "Your old ass needs to get some clothes on, and then we can go check it out."

James quickly stepped to the second room and found his clothes laid out on the bed. He dressed in the dark, then reached for his jacket. Inside he had his burner phone and the Genii device. He plugged in the device and powered on the phone. Watching the display, he stood stunned then walked back into the main room. "Cell service is down too, all of it?" he said, holding the phone up toward Cole.

"You think this is all related?" Cole asked. "It has to be, right?"

Before James could answer, there were gunshots outside. They ran to the window and saw the black SUV racing away. In the center of the intersection, the black hats lay dead in the street.

"Well, that brings things up a notch, doesn't it?" James said. "Looks like the natives are getting restless."

Cole grimaced and stepped away from the window. "If the power is out, this city is going to go to shit in a hurry. I think it's time we made a run for the hills."

He pointed to a backpack by the door. It was one of the company's bugout bags. James's apartment in the Beltway Inn was equipped with several of the bags for just such an occasion, and James had given one to his friend shortly after they'd arrived. "We need to roll," Cole said.

Shooting a thumb toward the second room James said, "Can he travel?"

Shaking his head no, Cole said, "I think we should leave him here. I talked to Andre and he's agreed to take care of him."

"He's wanted same as us," James said.

Cole shrugged. "Anna seems to be good at developing cover stories."

"But those gunshot wounds are going to bring some attention," James said. "You sure about this?"

"No," Cole again shook his head. "If I'm right, gunshot wounds aren't going to be that out of the ordinary here very soon." The lawman frowned. "And if I'm wrong, Art knows the score; this place is the best chance he's got."

More gunfire outside drew their eyes to the window. A group of armed men was running up the main street. James nodded and walked back into the bedroom and returned with a heavy black backpack of his own. He strapped it on and dropped the SIG 1911 into a shoulder holster under his tan jacket. He pointed to Cole's pack by the door. "You have everything in there?"

Cole nodded and grabbed the bag by a strap and hooked it over his shoulder. "Are we leaving now?"

"I'm not sure—but with that fighting," he said pointing at the window. "I think we need to be ready." Together they stepped into the hallway. Many of the hotel room doors on the third floor were open with guests standing in the hallway, talking to each other about the sudden power outage and the shooting outside. Panic was beginning to set in.

James walked past the elevator and hit the stairwell, going all the way down to the first floor, then followed the corridor around and into the lobby. Anna was standing at a check-in counter with several patrons lined up, asking her questions. She was trying to tell them to go back to their rooms, that it wasn't safe. James noticed many of them were in airline uniforms. He frowned, knowing if there were this many legitimate guests in his dump of a hotel, then there must be a lot of stranded travelers in the city.

James walked around the check-in counter, sending Anna a quick nod and opened a manager's office door. He let Cole enter in behind him then closed the door. They moved through to a back wall. James opened a second door that led to a narrow hallway and an apartment that mirrored his up on the third floor. A hulk of a man looking out a window quickly spun around, holding a pistol carbine.

"Relax, Wilcox, it's just me," James said.

The man held a hand over his heart and dropped back against the wall before taking a step forward and sitting on a sofa. "Oh shit, Mr. O'Connell. I wasn't expecting you. There is shooting out front. People are freaking out."

"Yeah, I saw that."

James stopped as two more men walked in from an entry door that led to the rear parking lot, both sweating as if they'd been out for a run. He knew the pair, as they both worked for him. Kyle Emmerson, one of his most experienced security men, and Randolph Whittaker, his head of security for South West Asia operations. Both were broad-shouldered veterans of the War on Terror. The men wore heavy beards and were dressed in dark polo shirts and denim slacks.

"Gentleman," James said.

Emerson stepped closer and extended his hand. "Colonel, it's good to see you. Anna said you had checked in."

"Yeah, we got in earlier. Been meaning to pay you a visit. I was hoping to have a word with you," James said.

Kyle nodded and looked over James's shoulder to the man behind him. James caught the stare and paused. "Sorry, let me introduce my friend Cole Wallace. He's with the FBI—or was—who even knows anymore?"

Kyle looked at Cole and said, "Name's Kyle Emmerson. This is Randy Whittaker, and the big dummy holding down the sofa is Tony Wilcox."

Cole shrugged and walked toward a wall and leaned against it. Kyle grinned and looked back at James. "Sir, I don't know what you've got planned, but we were just about to get all of our shit together and head out. I suggest you do the same."

"You have any intel?" James asked.

Kyle went back to the door they'd just entered and flipped the bolt lock. "We were just two blocks over. There is a small stop-and-shop on the corner. I thought we could grab a few things." Kyle shook his head. "No go —it's already started, place has been looted. Now with the power out, it'll only get worse. I haven't seen a cop in almost two days, and I think you just saw what happened to those damn contractors out there. Someone killed them and took their wheels."

"Where are you planning to go?" Cole asked.

Kyle looked at him suspiciously then said, "Anna said something about the Marines reinforcing a location up in Maryland. Lot of military up there. That makes the most sense to me now that the law can't be trusted." He said that last bit, locking eyes with Cole.

"You're talking about Camp David?" James said. "They won't just let you walk in."

"But they'll let you in, and probably your security team," he said, shooting James a wink. "I figure we get up there, knock on the door, and you ask for a meeting. They know you, and you know people. We're legit State Department contractors; if anyone can get in, it's us."

"It'll be a hell of a drive," James said.

"It's only a couple hours. We leave now, I think we can do it," Kyle said.

"You been out there lately? It's not a leisurely drive. Roadblocks, checkpoints, all of it. And don't go counting on my or Cole's credentials. Turns out we are both wanted men."

"Shit." Kyle looked down. "I was planning on that, but still it's our best shot, and don't worry about the rent-a-cop roadblocks. We've got the Inka in the barn; that'll give us an edge."

James laughed. "You were planning to take my ride?"

"Wait," Cole held up a hand, "what is an Inka?"

"Well, tell him," James said, waving his hand. "It's your idea."

"It's a level six, up-armored Chevy Suburban, and

come on, Colonel, you know I wouldn't take it without asking you first," Kyle said.

James smiled. "I know you wouldn't because I've got the keys, and you aren't breaking into the Beast without destroying it."

"What do you say, Colonel? You up for this or not?" Kyle looked back toward the street. There were more gunshots. "We've already got gear packed and moved to the maintenance garage. You unlock it, and we can get it loaded up. This might be our only shot to get the hell out of here."

"Where's the rest of your team?" James asked.

Kyle pointed to the front. "Billy and Chris are out in the lobby working security."

From outside came the sounds of sirens and more gunfire, much of it fully automatic. Whittaker went to the window and began to pull back the curtain, when it exploded with gunfire. The men dropped to the floor as rounds ripped over their heads.

Wilcox turned and pressed up against the wall then peeked outside. "This ain't random, boss. Those black hats are hitting the hotel. Probably think someone in here killed those boys on the corner."

James rolled to his chest and looked at Kyle. "Okay, let's do it. Get your boys out of the lobby and meet us at the garage."

Kyle shot a thumbs up and ran to the hallway with Whittaker behind him. "Wilcox!" James shouted, "You're with us, give me some cover."

The big man grimaced and rose then leaned into the

broken window, firing in full auto. "Move, move, move!" he shouted.

James leapt for the door, spun the bolt, and moved outside with Cole right behind him. The back lot was clear, and they ran for the garage. When James reached the door, he drew his 1911, knelt, and aimed it toward the entry drive. He shouted back at the hotel for Wilcox to join them. Two large explosions boomed in the distance, shaking the ground and breaking hotel windows. The big man, in mid-sprint, fell flat then climbed back to his feet and finished the distance. James handed him a set of keys. "Get inside the garage and fire up the beast."

The big man opened the pedestrian door and disappeared inside. A roar from the entry drive turned James's head in time to see a black SUV racing in toward them. No time to guess sides, James raised his pistol and fired. Cole was posted off to his right and was doing the same. The vehicle's driver side windshield was peppered, and the SUV cut hard and smashed into a utility pole. James dropped his magazine and reached into his jacket for a reload as a man in black leapt from a rear door, holding a long rifle. The man turned in their direction and fired off a volley of rounds that went wide.

Cole returned fire, the rounds hitting the front of the vehicle. More men exited the SUV from the covered side and came up with rifles. They prepped to open fire, when Kyle and his team emerged from the back door of the hotel and sprayed down the SUV with gunfire, killing the black hats.

James got to his feet and entered the garage. It was

three cars deep and four cars wide. There were several maintenance vehicles and a large ride lawnmower, but on the end was the prize. A jet-black Suburban with dark tinted windows, what he'd called the Beast since the day he picked it up.

James had purchased the armored executive vehicle for VIP security details the year before. And being so close to the district, it had gotten plenty of work and paid for itself. The armored car had never been in a gunfight, but James was pretty sure that record would be broken today. He watched as the Suburban's brake lights flashed and the big V8 roared. With a loud click, the rear hatch opened, and Wilcox was back outside, shoveling in packs and weapons cases.

He looked at James and waved. "It's ready—let's go!"

James ran to the big door and hit a red paddle button. Nothing happened. "Shit! The power!"

He ran to the far wall and worked a lever then pulled the chains, slowly cranking the overhead door open. Gunfire again began to roar outside, and when James looked out, he could see his men were actively engaged in the fight. He ran for the Suburban and jumped in the passenger seat. "Shield them with the Beast while we pick them up."

Wilcox nodded and dropped the truck into reverse and slammed the gas, smoking the tires as he raced back. Just clearing the door, he cut the wheel hard while, at the same time, working the brakes and spinning the vehicle in a 180.

"Damn, son, I heard you could drive but I didn't know you could drive like that," James shouted.

Ignoring the comment, Wilcox slammed the brake, leaving the Beast at an angle to the hotel and giving the shooters outside cover. He opened his door and dropped his carbine between the gap and put fire on the enemy to their front. Kyle and the others saw what he was doing and peeled back. Soon the rear doors were open, and the men were dropping into the crew compartment. The vehicle was taking hits on the body and windows, but the armor was holding as designed.

"Last man in!" Whitaker shouted as he jumped into a back seat and slammed the door.

As quickly as Wilcox had stepped out, he was back in with his door closed, and his foot dropped back on the pedal. The Beast was racing out and around the hotel. In front of the lobby, a pair of black SUVs had the entry gate blocked. Black hats were leaned over the hood, firing at them. James pointed at a section of the fencing off to the right. "Hit it there; it's designed to break away."

Wilcox grunted and cut the wheel hard while laying on the gas. The tires screeched as he fought to keep the heavy vehicle on four wheels. The back of the Beast was hit and rattled with gunfire. They hit the curb at over thirty miles per hour. The Beast bounced up and crunched down on its heavy suspension, then crashed through the breakaway section of the fence. Again, Wilcox cut hard and had them headed east on an empty four-lane road.

"Anyone hit?" James said, looking back into the vehicle.

The men in the rear two bench seats were a pile of twisted bodies and gear. No time to fasten seatbelts, they'd been tossed around like rag dolls during the escape. He waited for shouts of good before he looked back to the front and hit a flat-screen display in the dash. There was a basic vehicle diagnostics app installed.

"They didn't do shit; Beast is good to go." He closed the app and opened a navigation screen. It loaded up and came alive. He looked at Wilcox. "Looks like whatever those assholes did to the lights and cell service didn't affect the satellites. Navigation is still up." James dropped in the destination and selected a route.

"Are you seeing this shit?" Kyle called from the back.

James had been distracted by the navigation display and hadn't bothered to do a sanity check on his surroundings. He looked out of his passenger window to the north as they climbed an entry ramp onto Route 7. The city was on fire, and dark plumes of black smoke were rising over Washington D.C.

"The place is on fire," one of Kyle's men called from the back—the one they called Billy. He was new to the teams, a newly discharged grunt from Georgia

James nodded. "Seems that way."

The young man leaned forward. "Try the radio."

James pressed the display and scanned stations, finding static on every one. He shook his head and looked back. "Nothing is coming through."

"That doesn't make any sense. Radios don't have shit to do with the grid being down," Billy said.

James looked at him. "You know, you're right." He reached up to a ceiling-mounted counsel and pressed a button. A Citizens Band radio dropped down from a small cabinet. James reached in, switched it over to the police bands, powered on the device, and let it scan. It sped through frequencies then stopped on a local police station. There were calls for help and units in contact. Billy went to speak, when James held up a hand, silencing him.

"They aren't fighting rioters or looting mobs," James said. "They are fighting off the black hats."

"What in the hell is going on out there?" Wilcox said, keeping his eyes glued to the road.

James looked at the radio. He reached into his pocket for his cell phone and found it still dead with no signal. Looking back in the direction of the Capital, he watched the columns of black smoke climb higher into the sky. "I don't know, but right now all that matters is that we get far away from here."

"I got that part under control, boss. Nothing is stopping us," Wilcox said.

James closed his eyes and leaned back into the leather seats. "Dear God, what is happening?"

CHAPTER TWENTY-TWO

In the pre-dawn hours, Winston stopped the truck in the center of the two-lane road. Ahead, bright lights were glowing through a low fog. He cut his own head-lights and lifted his binoculars. In the distance, at a bridge covering a gully, was another makeshift roadblock, this one more hardened like an entry control point.

He knew he was near the Arkansas border and someone was serious about controlling the movement of people. The ramp taking him from this county road and onto the interstate was blocked. He looked at the radio in the dash, considering it. Most of the stations were down, but the few channels he could find operating on the dial said the Government Security Forces had shut down interstate travel out of necessity. Only emergency vehicles and the military were allowed past the entrance and exit ramps.

Winston sat quietly in the darkness, observing the checkpoint ahead. He could see at least a dozen men and generator light sets positioned around them. Two men in black patrolled out front with long rifles clipped to their vests. Another man with a scoped rifle stood behind them in the back of a black pickup truck.

He focused on the man in the truck bed and squinted. The uniform was the same. He shook his head, recognizing the familiar outline of an AK-74 with a large mounted optic. He grimaced and took his eyes off the binoculars. American cops and military don't carry Russian battle rifles. Whoever they were, this was his enemy. He wanted to go at them head on, and right now, move up in the darkness and kill them all. Kill those on watch and slaughter the others while they slept.

He pursed his lips and looked behind him. These men had the numbers on him, with at least six vehicles behind the barriers. Winston knew they probably had three times the guard force he could see. This was their position; it wouldn't be an ambush and with the open road to his back they could pinch him in, and his fight would end here on a dark Texas highway. He cursed himself. He had to pick the fights, and this wasn't one he could win.

He looked closer, inspecting the terrain and considering his options. A large wooden barrier and steel drums blocked the road approach to the checkpoint. The roadblock was set up the same way he'd seen hundreds of times in third world toilets. There was a central lane, a bottleneck, then a pull off and inspection area where the driver would be under the muzzle of several weapons all at once while the vehicle was inspected, and the rest of the guard force waited safely in cover. And all this under the shadow of posted warning signs that any violators of instructions will be shot. This wasn't a checkpoint he could risk going through, especially after he escalated his situation at the hotel and the farm store. If they didn't have a report on his description out before, they certainly would now.

Leaving the headlights off, Winston pulled the pickup truck off the highway, and into a field of high brush, cutting a path south as he wound through it. The roads were nearly empty, travelers adhering to the curfews, so nobody was there to see him leave the road. He was alone out here in the vast expanses of open country. The radio stations he could dial in had reported wide-scale curfews and martial law. Most travel was restricted to within city limits and strictly enforced. As he navigated over the broken ground, he felt the truck lose traction and begin to slide. He cut the wheel and gunned the engine.

The back end of the truck swung down into a dry stream bed, pulling him in backward. The soft stone and sand gave way then swallowed the tire treads. Frustrated that he'd pushed the truck too far in the darkness, he cut off the engine and opened the door. The night was cold on the Texas-Arkansas border. He'd driven through the day and night, navigating around roadblocks, avoiding towns and only stopping at remote gas stations for fuel. His caution had stretched an eight-hour drive out to nearly twenty, but he knew the importance of staying hidden when on the run and letting the smoke clear from his last encounter with whoever it was hunting him.

From the bed of the truck, he grabbed his backpack

and kit. He put on his vest and strapped the MP5 to his chest. Again, he wished he'd had an M4, but the M700 would do for now. He took the long rifle and slung it over his back. Taking another scan of his surroundings, he began heading for high ground, keeping the bright lights of the roadblock off to his left. He didn't know exactly what it was the men had going on down there, but he wanted to stay clear of it.

Winston climbed a saddle up to a ridgeline and followed it around until he was in a three position to the roadblock. Ahead of him was a deep ravine, the same one the defended bridge was set up to cross.

Looking down, he could see the jagged rocks. He was certain he could get down, and probably even up the other side. But if he was spotted, he would be trapped. He would have cover, but escape routes would be limited, and the opposing forces would be able to easily block him in and cut him down, holding the high ground. Crossing east wasn't a risk he could take. He looked back north at the roadblock and could see more men moving in from the rear. He was right on his earlier assessment. The guard force consisted of at least fifteen men and all were heavily armed.

Winston was preparing to turn his attention away to flee south and away from the guard force, when he watched headlights approaching from the west. He crouched down and ran closer to take a position of cover where he could observe. "Well, son of a bitch," Winston whispered. He saw a convoy of four black Range Rovers, two in front, two in the rear, and the familiar Toyota dead in the center.

Winston watched as barriers pulled back and the vehicles were allowed through. The convoy crossed the bridge, and, to his surprise, they pulled off the road and another twelve black-clad men dismounted. He put his scope on the Toyota and watched as a pair of tall men in khakis and tanned safari shirts exited the vehicles. They were greeted by a third man from the entry control point, and they moved back toward the western end of the encampment as a group. Things were getting interesting, as the target became too much to pass up. He folded in the stock of the MP5 and stored it in his pack as he checked the action on the M700. He looked at the bridge; it was a long shot, but well within his abilities.

Winston focused on the men in tan. He knew they were a leadership element, but who the hell were they? The men were smart in the way they moved. Their protective detail kept them shielded, constantly orbiting the men in a bubble of protection. These were men used to operating in hostile environments. He was already at the maximum range of his rifle and taking a shot from his position, here on a rocky ledge, would almost certainly mean his death. He would have nowhere to run. There would be almost no way he could take a shot in the scrub brush undetected then back out. There was nothing else here.

He sat, contemplating his situation as the sun slowly broke the eastern horizon. His mind focused on the men now leaning over a table, his brain keeping occupied with differing solutions. Winston was an assassin by trade. If there was a way to kill these men in the tan shirts and slip away, he would figure it out. It wasn't about bravery; he had no fear of taking the shot and being run down. If he shot, his aim had to be true or he'd never get another chance, and he wasn't interested in dying for a miss. He switched to his more powerful binoculars and watched as the activity at the roadblock suddenly increased. He panned back to the west and watched as a pair of marked armored police vehicles slowly approached.

He recognized them as BearCats, four-wheeled armored trucks, and even though they looked a lot like their military cousins, they were far from as capable. The pair of trucks drove to within a hundred meters then stopped. Both trucks began flashing blue lights in the early shadows of dawn. Looking back to the roadblock, Winston could see that the men of the checkpoint were now on full alert. They were running forward and taking up positions behind barriers and over the hoods of their SUVs.

Winston stared down at the BearCats. "Well, looks like this isn't a friendly visit."

He dropped the binoculars and pulled the sniper rifle back into his shoulder and began estimating threats behind the barrier. The men in tan were gone. But a man in the back of a pickup was looking eager, leaning into his rifle.

A uniformed man with a Stetson took several steps away from one of the BearCats. The man walked with authority. He stopped with a right hand on the grip of a pistol then held a bull horn to his lips with his left. "This is the Texas State Police. We demand that you disperse and leave the sovereign Territory of Texas immediately."

Winston looked back to the roadblock. The men were gearing up for a fight. He shook his head. "This isn't going to end well."

CHAPTER TWENTY-THREE

R aul had barely heard the words of the uniformed officer to his front when a round snapped off behind him. He spun and saw a man in the bed of a truck holding a rifle, grinning as he lined up for another shot. Raul pointed. "Who the hell is that?" he shouted. "I ordered no one to take a shot!"

The cartel boss looked back to the road; the officer's cowboy hat lay on the blacktop as more uniformed men dragged the wounded man into cover. He shook his head, angrily waving his arms for his men to hold their fire as he began walking toward the police vehicles. He was quickly tackled from behind by Diaz as rounds cracked off the concrete to the front. The police were not standing down; these Texans came to fight. And now they were unleashing a full barrage on the roadblock.

Raul hit the ground hard and pressed his face to the concrete. His anger was building. He had enough problems with the gringo, and now he was fighting local police. They had stopped here in pursuit of the sniper, and he'd just begun to ask questions with the roadblock guard force when the police vehicles had approached. They'd had run-ins with police before, but they always complied and went away. The Vortex had orders from the highest authority, local police had orders to assist them in any way requested. So, who was this? And why had one of his own men taken that damn shot?

He turned back toward the roadblock. The armored cars now had men in top-mounted turrets, returning fire with light machine guns. "Who the hell are these guys? I was told the police had no machine guns in this country," Raul shouted to one of his men ducking for cover beside him.

A squat man who was squeezed into body armor crawled closer and pulled the black ski mask up from his face. "Texas policía—"

"I can tell they are Texas police, you fucking idiot. Why did you shoot at them?" Raul cursed, reaching out and grabbing the man, pulling him closer.

The man tried to pull away from Raul's grip, his face going flush with fear. "Sir, these men wanted trouble. They had come earlier in the last evening. They demanded we tear down this barrier and leave. When we told them no, they made threats against us. We fired on them as a warning and they fled." The man, feeling the release on his shirt, backed away. "They were just warning shots. They knew what to expect if they returned."

Raul pointed to the dead man in the street. "That was no warning shot! You killed one of their men, they won't soon forget that."

The man shrugged. "We have been killing them here." The man pointed to a mound of dirt in the distance. "I've buried several of them myself. They know better than to return."

Raul slapped the man in frustration and pulled him back closer. His face inches from the guard, he shouted. "Well, they have come back, you idiots!"

Rounds smacked closer to Raul, and the cartel boss balled his fist in frustration. "How long before we can get reinforcements up here?" he shouted to Diaz lying beside him. "Bring in men behind them, cut them off."

Diaz was lying prone, yelling into a phone. He pulled the handset away from his ear and looked at Raul. "We've got three truckloads of men headed this way. They are coming in from the east." He looked at his watch. "Ten minutes out. I can get more from the west, but it will take longer."

Raul looked up, hearing the wail of police sirens. Looking out to the west, he saw more police cars racing toward the roadblock. The armored police had reinforcements as well.

Raul seethed and snatched the phone from Diaz. "Not three trucks, bring everything. I want everything we've got, do you understand? I want everything in the region moving to my location now! Do you understand?"

He waited for a broken response from the other end of the line. There was a hesitation and then a confirmation of his orders. He tossed the phone back to Diaz then grabbed the guard beside him. "The police, they want a war. We can give them what they want." He ordered the man to follow him.

Together, they duck-walked back behind the road-block vehicles as rounds zipped overhead. He moved to a black cargo van, knowing exactly what the vehicle held. All his command teams had one. He opened the back double-doors and began violently pulling out Pelican cases onto the street until he found the one he'd been searching for.

Popping the latches, inside the case he found a pair of AT4 launchers. Raul took one and told the fighter next to him to grab the other. "Go kill that fucking armored car," he shouted, receiving a nervous reply from the guard.

Together they moved back to the front, rounds pinging off the vehicles and concrete all around them. Raul pointed out the armored car and told the fighter to move forward and take the shot. The man nodded, made a dash for a gap in the barrier, then dropped to his knees to fire. With no warning, the man's head snapped to the side in a spattering of blood and skull fragments. The man's hand squeezed the trigger in death, and the rocket fired up into the sky. The backblast covered the area in smoke and debris. Raul cursed and readied his own launcher then rose and fired it over the hood of the car he was hiding behind. There was a blast on his end as the explosive rocket raced from the tube. In the distance, the small armored police vehicle exploded in a ball of flame.

Men in police uniform writhed on the ground and pulled back from the scene as more police cars raced in, forming a defensive wall. Even with one of the armored cars destroyed, the fire from the police intensified; the lawmen were not deterred. Raul rose to his feet and tossed the empty launcher tube to the ground. He pointed to a group of men cowering in cover. "Go out there and fight."

The men nodded and leapt to their feet, breaking cover and rushing forward to the next set of barriers. Several men in their first wave were immediately cut down. Diaz ran to Raul and grabbed him by the shoulder. "Please get into cover," he said.

Raul, still angry, pushed away his arm. "We are done with this. No more rules. They want a war, they will fight by our rules now. I want everything here, and we will clean out this country. No more of this Vortex—now we will show them how the Kings fight."

Diaz took a step back. "Raul, please—Rau—"

The cartel boss turned to look at his friend. Diaz's hands were clasped to his chest, covering a spreading circle of crimson on his tan shirt. He stepped forward, blood breaking the corners of his mouth, and collapsed in Raul's arms.

"Sniper!" men shouted, running back to cover.

CHAPTER TWENTY-FOUR

The Bearcats were parked in a V-formation on the blacktop, with the armored fronts facing the road-block. With the lawman down, machine gunners popped into the turrets of the armored cars and opened fired on the roadblock. Chaos and panic ensued behind the barriers as the defenders scrambled for cover. Rounds peppered the barricades and destroyed the black vehicles. The guards were pinned under the intense fire.

Winston locked on motion, and one of the men in tan broke away from the front with another close behind him. "What the hell are they up to?" he whispered to himself, dropping the binoculars and pulling the rifle's scope back to his eye. The pair of men disappeared in the cluster of black vehicles then reemerged back toward the barricade line.

"Oh shit," he muttered, recognizing the olive-green cylindrical tubes the men were carrying. Both men were now armed with anti-tank weapons. He lost track of the man in tan, but the other man moved between the barriers and took a knee. He raised the rocket tube to his shoulder. Winston knew he had only one chance. He judged the wind and aimed accordingly, squeezing off his shot with no time to spare and watched the enemy shooter's head explode and his rocket go harmlessly over the police line.

He racked the bolt before he could take any solace in the kill, searching for the next target. A loud crack filled the air as one of the Bearcats explode in a ball of flame. He'd lost the man in tan and failed to stop him. He clenched his teeth in anger as the armored police vehicle burned. Uniformed men rolled in the street. The men in black behind the barricades were suddenly emboldened and charged forward. The policemen rebounded quickly with rifle and machine gun fire. The hasty charge was put down and men fell to the street dead and wounded.

A man in a tan shirt ran between the vehicles back at the roadblock, catching Winston's attention. He shifted his focus and leveled the rifle, dialing in the scope. The man had stopped his movement near the rear of a tall truck. Reaching out an arm, he spoke to a man in cover behind the vehicle. Winston couldn't see who he was talking to, but it didn't matter. The man was in the open, he was a leader, and that was all Winston needed. He took aim, controlled his breathing, and squeezed the trigger. The man lurched forward then took a half step before disappearing behind the truck.

He turned back toward the fight and watched the Bearcat and the remaining police continue intense fire on the roadblock. He considered putting his rifle back into the fight and joining them, when he observed more black trucks race in from the east. The men in black had reinforcements, and if the police didn't make a run for it now, they would die here.

He turned the rifle back toward the bridge. He watched men running along a guardrail and pointing in his direction. A man pointed directly at him as he watched muzzle flashes from a second armed man.

"Well that's no good," he said just before gunfire hit the rocks around him.

Winston ducked low, biting the earth and dragging his way up toward the ridge. He pulled his pack close, and dug through it, finding and tossing a smoke grenade into a cluster of dried vegetation. The grenade spewed grey smoke and flame, igniting the brush. He held his position, waiting for the smoke to overtake him and the gunfire to shift. He pulled a shemagh over his face and made a dash for the cover of the ridgeline.

He sprinted to upward as another volley of gunfire raked his position. He dove and rolled across the top, looking back in time to see more vehicles moving in from the west. The police were now sandwiched in on both sides. If he couldn't help by suppressing the enemy movement, the police would be cut down.

Winston spun, bringing his rifle back up, when more rounds rained down around him. Even though inaccurate, he could hear the zips over his head and the stone fragments on his back and pant legs. The fire was inaccurate, but inaccurate fire kills just as dead. He had no targets; the men on the bridge were in cover, and the vehicles to the west were hopelessly out of range. He watched as the machine gunner in the Bearcat took a round and slumped over his weapon.

Officers scattered and were cut down as the vehicles closed in on them. Winston took more fire from the bridge. Looking back, he could see men moving in his direction. He locked his jaw and turned his rifle, finally having a target. He passed over two men, finding one that looked like leadership and intentionally shot him through the hip. The man dropped and the assaulting men held their advance.

Winston shifted back to the bridge, where the man in tan was shouting orders and pointing toward the ridge-line. He could see men from the van pulling out a small mortar tube. "Who in the hell are these guys?"

Winston pulled the rifle tight into his shoulder and dialed in on the remaining man in tan. Before he could fire, he flinched, feeling his jacket tug away. Suddenly his left arm when limp, his elbow collapsed, and he dropped the rifle.

He fought to bring the rifle back up as a second round struck his shirt, taking off a piece of his vest above the right shoulder. He dropped the rifle and rolled to his back, pushing his body into the cover of large boulders. For the first time, he felt the pain in his left arm. He looked down at the gushing blood. Shutting out the fear and shock, he grabbed a tourniquet from his chest pockets and slapped it on just below his left armpit. He growled in agony and continued to push away from the gunfire with his boot heels. Down the saddle, a group of ten were running up at him, firing from the hip, and they charged on.

On the road below, the Bearcat was gone, and the other police vehicles were burning with several dead in the dust around them. He cursed himself as he rolled to his side and used his right arm to push himself to his feet. As he broke the crest of the ridge, the gunfire had stopped, but he could hear their shouts and the tumbling of rocks as they pursued him. Feeling the pain in his arm, he cursed his luck. He'd done nothing here but get himself shot. He didn't save the police and he didn't kill their leader, and he still didn't know who they were or what they wanted.

Winston jogged down the far side of the ridge, holding the wounded arm close to his side. He reached the bottom and tucked into a thick copse of trees. He collapsed to his knees and shrugged off the pack, clenching his eyes shut and grinding his teeth as he worked the sling over his wounded arm. Unzipping the pack, he dumped out the MP5 and reattached the sling to the D-ring on his vest. He then worked out a combat gauze and ripped it open with his teeth. Working out the white material, he pulled out the length of it and stuffed it into a large hole in his bicep. He forced himself to probe the wound, sighing in relief that the bone wasn't broken.

Shouts traveled down the terrain behind him. He looked over his shoulder where the shadows of the pursuing men bounced off the ridge. Their voices echoed in the trees; they were closing in. He stuffed the bandage wrapper into his pack and got back to his feet. He flexed his left arm. It hurt like hell but still worked for the moment. He forced his feet to move and ran deeper into the woods.

CHAPTER TWENTY-FIVE

The Inka pulled to a stopped in the center of the two-lane highway. James, alerted by the lack of motion, was startled awake. Through the windshield he could see they were on a narrow country highway; the sun was low in the sky, still hours from dusk. There were trees on both sides, and the road was empty—no traffic, no homes, not even an animal.

He turned Wilcox. "Why'd you stop?"

Wilcox dipped his head and pointed in the distance. "You don't see them?"

James squinted. He saw nothing but blurred shapes. "Humor me, son. As you can see, I don't have my glasses."

"There's a military roadblock ahead, and it's not like those black hats. It's real green stuff; they look like Marines."

Kyle and Cole leaned up and looked out ahead. "You think they are friendly?" Kyle asked.

James shrugged and smacked the dash. "Well, that's

what we drove all this way to find out, isn't it?" He pointed to the driver then the roadblock. "Onward."

Wilcox smiled out of the side of his mouth and eased the vehicle back into gear. James investigated the back. The men were all awake now. They had rifles tucked between their knees and tactical vests on their bodies.

He turned back to Kyle. "Maybe we should store the kit?"

Kyle shook his head no. "I reckon it's best to let them know right off who we are."

Cole laughed and looked at that man. "And who exactly are we?"

"We're a bunch of badasses that just fought our way out of DC. And now we are here to help them all out," Kyle said. "Save the world all that good shit."

James turned his head to the side then nodded. "I like it." He laughed and looked up, seeing a HUMVEE with a mounted .50-cal in the top turret bearing down on them. "At least if we die, it'll be quick."

Marines stood up from behind sandbag barricades. A trio appeared from behind another vehicle and patrolled forward with their rifles up. James reached out his left hand and put it on Wilcox's arm. "Okay, that's good. Shut the engine, keep your hands in view, and let them come to you."

The young man did as he was told and placed his hands in plain sight on the top of the steering wheel as the armed Marines approached. As they neared, two of them moved off to the right while the third circled to the driver's door. He shouted at them to lower the windows.

Wilcox pressed a button and all the vehicle's windows dropped down two-thirds.

"All the way," the Marine shouted. "All the windows —down all the way."

Wilcox put a hand on the top of the glass. Then locked eyes with the Marine. "Brother, this stuff is almost four inches thick. This is all the way down."

The Marine's eyes got big as he stepped forward and scanned the vehicle. "Damn, you all are shot to shit."

Wilcox laughed. "Yeah, we had some trouble in the city."

The Marine shook his head, his eyes still examining the bullet marks on the body and windows of the big SUV. He looked back up at Wilcox. "Sorry, sir, but we have to turn you around. This highway is closed. No traffic is allowed in."

James went to speak, but when he leaned forward, the Marines on the other side stepped in closer with their weapons up. The Marine on the driver's side raised his hand. "Sorry about that, sir, but please no sudden movements."

Smiling, James nodded his head and said, "We are actually here to see your boss." James showed the man his empty hands. "I have identification in my jacket pocket."

The Marine nodded, and James reached into his jacket and pulled out his wallet. Inside, he had several cards, two of them credentialing him for the White House and the Capitol Building. The third was his retired Military ID card. He handed them to Wilcox, who passed them to the Marine. The man took steps back and inspected them. He scowled. "Sorry, Colonel O'Connell, I'm not familiar with this identification. I'll have to call it up to the captain."

James nodded. "Go ahead, son—and while you are at it, mention that I am friends with the President."

The Marine nodded and walked back toward the sandbag barriers. The two remaining Marines stepped back, dropping their rifles to the low ready.

"That true?" Wilcox asked. "Are you friends with the President?"

James shrugged. "I'd say we all should be his friend, for as many special projects we do for the man."

"Special projects?" Wilcox nodded, "Like what? Anything I've been in on?"

Laughing, James pointed a thumb toward Cole. "We probably shouldn't talk business in front of the Fed."

Cole grunted and threw James a middle finger then pointed toward the barriers. "Looks like someone is trying to get your attention."

The Marine who had walked off with the ID cards was now pulling back a barrier and waving the vehicle forward. Wilcox started the truck and eased it toward the sandbag wall. When they were right beside it, the Marine approached the driver's window and passed back the ID cards. "Sorry for the delay, Colonel. The Hummer will escort you through the checkpoints and into the facility. Director Spence is eager to speak with you."

James leaned in. "Tyler Spence is here?"

The Marine nodded. "Yes, sir. You should hurry; they said it's important that we send you right through."

James nodded and pointed to the lead vehicle. Wilcox did as told and followed the Hummer through more barricades and onto a heavily guarded side road.

Kyle had his eyes glued to the side window. "Damn, they got more Marines up here than at Iwo Jima." He leaned back in his seat. "So, James, who is this Tyler Spence guy?"

James sighed and said, "He's a spook, top guy over at the CIA."

Cole laughed and shook his head. "He's a hell of a lot more than that. He leads the clandestine services branch. He's the number two at the CIA, and if you buy into the legends, he'd been involved in some real shady shit."

James looked at Wilcox and again shot his thumb at Cole. "See? This is why we don't speak in front of the Fed." James grunted. "'Shady,' if that's what you call keeping us safe."

Kyle leaned in between the seats. "So how is it you know him?"

Cole held up a hand. "Clandestine services, son. It's no secret that's what you and your boss are up to your elbows in."

"I like it." Kyle smiled and settled back into his seat. "I knew we were into some cool shit, but I had no idea I was the CIA's top cover man." He looked at Cole. "And sanctioned by the President, no less."

Cole laughed. "You aren't nothing—a nobody. Thomas Donovan is their boy."

"The hell, Cole?" James said, looking back at his old friend. "You just dumping cover on people left and right now?"

"What does it matter now? Donovan is probably dead, and the President is on the run," Cole rebutted.

"Wait," Kyle said. "Donovan, the guy from the Syria thing?"

James sighed. "How do you know about Syria?"

Kyle laughed. "Hell, everyone knows about the Syria thing. I didn't know Donovan was on our books. Where is he at? We could certainly use him now."

"No idea," James said. "I wish I did."

As the vehicles stopped, more barriers were moved out of the way and they were waved through. As they traveled on the road, the military presence increased and became more diverse. Along with the Marines, James saw several soldiers, and even a group of Navy Seabees setting up HESCO bags filled with rock.

"They are setting up for something big," Kyle said.

Wilcox swerved through a set of serpentine obstacles then stopped behind the HUMVEE. A group of men in dark suits walked down a path toward them. As they neared, the group dispersed, and from the middle, stepped a man in dark khakis and a pressed white shirt. He held a handgun in a leather shoulder holster. James smiled, recognizing him, and opened his door.

"Holy hell," Tyler Spence said. "Damn, James O'Connell. It's good to see you, my friend." He moved closer, extending his hand.

James closed the distance and accepted the handshake. "Wasn't easy, but we made it."

Tyler looked at the SUV. "Tell me you brought some of your top guys with you."

Nodding his head, James said, "This is one of my

security teams." He turned back, pointing to the truck. "Wish I had more to offer you."

Cupping his hands and looking at the truck, Tyler pursed his lips. "Well, I can set your friends up with food and a place to rest. But I'd like to get a debrief from you, if I could."

Cole walked around the back of the SUV. "Sir, we were actually hoping to get information from you." He stopped and waved his arms. "Like what the hell is going on around here?"

Tyler eyed the man suspiciously until Cole flipped out his FBI credentials and said, "I know this doesn't carry much weight anymore, but I'm Cole Wallace. I'm with the Bureau."

"FBI?" Tyler said. "Damn, we haven't heard from you all in a while."

The lawman nodded. "And that is another thing I wanted to talk to you about."

Holding up a hand, Tyler silenced him. He looked at one of the suited men next to him, a tall black man wearing a suit jacket at least one size too small. "Eric, can we do something to get this vehicle in the barn?" He paused, looking at the team of men. "And let's get these guys settled in and fed."

The man dipped his chin, then Tyler turned to James. "Let's go."

Without waiting for an answer, he turned back to the path headed toward the buildings.

James grinned and slapped Cole on the back. "You heard the man, let's go."

The walking path wound through the well-groomed

property. James looked left and right; there was activity in every corner. Trucks were being unloaded, and lines were formed as uniformed men received equipment. Tyler stopped and stepped to the side as they were passed by armed Marines on golf carts.

On the lawn, James saw the defenses were serious; there were trenches dug into gardens and sandbag bunkers placed between trees. The military had been busy fortifying the President's retreat.

Tyler didn't wait, and James moved quickly to keep up. At the end of the path, they left the woods. In what looked like a large field, there were military helicopters. Right off, James identified a trio of Sikorsky Sea Kings, the President's personal fleet of helicopters, as well as several other green Black Hawks and a pair of Apaches.

Tyler stopped short of a large building and turned around. He pointed at the far end of the field filled with military tents. "On the tennis courts and sporting range, we've got two partial Marine battalions set up." He pointed to the aircraft. "We've got POTUS's bird over there as well as some boys from the 160th that made it in from Campbell. On another field, we have Ospreys and a Chinooks."

"You expecting a fight?" Cole asked.

Tyler winked. "Why don't we save those questions for the briefing."

James went to speak, but before he could, Tyler held up his hand, silencing him. Then he continued to the building. James looked to Cole; the lawman shrugged and followed Spence on the path. The building's doors were opened before Tyler reached them, and he passed inside. James saw a pair of armed men who looked at him hard but made no effort to stop him. He passed into the building and down brightly lit hallways.

The walls of the hall were stacked with cases of MREs and water. Cole looked at James and whispered, "They're stockpiling for a siege. You sure it was a good idea coming here?"

James sighed as they reached the end of the hallway and another open door. He whispered back, "I'm not sure of anything anymore."

The men followed Spence through the open door, and it was closed behind them. The lights dimmed. James found himself standing at the end of a nearly filled conference table. James's eyes searched the seats, and he stammered back when he saw President MacLeod and his staff at the far end of the table. He froze and stood at attention out of years of habit.

"Relax, James, I think we are beyond all of that," the President said. "I was happy to hear you'd found your way here. Your skills might come in handy."

James rolled his shoulders and took a pair of steps forward, moving to the end of the table. "Mr. President, it's good to see you."

MacLeod bit his lower lip and slowly shook his head. "You seem to have arrived at a good time. I was about to be briefed on the current situation in the Capital District. Those Marines on the perimeter tell me you've just come from that way."

James nodded. "Yes, sir, we did."

Tyler walked to a flat-panel display mounted on a wall. Using a remote, he clicked it on then walked around the table. He motioned for Cole and James to be seated then took a seat of his own behind a laptop. He looked at James. "Before we begin, what did you see there?"

"Excuse me?" James said. "There was a lot to see. Where would you like me to start."

"That's fair enough. How about we start with some images, and you can attempt to clue us in?" Tyler nodded and clicked the laptop keys. The display switched from black to a large overhead view of the Capital. Much of the metro area was concealed in black smoke.

"Dear God," James gasped.

Tyler ignored the comment and hit a key, switching the view to thermal, revealing several hot spots overtop of government buildings. "It's far worse than that. The city is burning in multiple areas. You and your team are the ones with the most recent experience in the district..." He paused and turned to face the Colonel. "Sir, do you know what happened?"

James stared at the monitor and shook his head no. "We were in Alexandria. As of the time we left, there were no fires—none that we could see, anyway. The power went out, and we were attacked at nearly the same time. We egressed out, and as we hit the highway traveling north, that was when we saw the fires."

"And who attacked you?" Tyler asked.

Cole smirked. "Your hired thugs attacked us. The ones they are calling the black hats, the same scumbags killing my FBI agents, the same ones that targeted Mr. O'Connell and myself."

Tyler paused and looked at the President then back

at Cole. "Vortex? You're saying it was Vortex men that attacked you?"

"And tried to kill us. They took down at least one of our FBI field offices, also."

"You're sure it was vortex?" Tyler asked.

Cole, now noticeably irritated, said, "I have no clue who this Vortex is, but men in black have been trying to scratch names off the DOJ burn list, and they have been killing cops and FBI agents right along with them."

"What burn list?" the President asked.

Cole shook his head and looked down. "Of course, now nobody knows about the list." He rubbed his hand and took in a deep breath. "Nearly a week ago, a list was published at Justice and went out to select agents in the field. The directive was to target anyone on the list. There was an emphasis in the instructions that the targets were dangerous, and that making a live arrest was not the priority. These people needed to be taken out before they could strike at the heartland."

"A list?" the President asked again. He looked at his intelligence man and said, "Spence, pull up the Terror Watch List we received."

Spence clacked at keys, and the list of suspect names for attacks across the country populated on the screen. "Cole, is this the same list?" the President asked.

Cole studied the screen. There were four columns of twenty names stretched across it. He nodded his head and said, "I recognize several of them, but there are more than that." He looked at James then back to Spence. "I had received multiple updates to the list. The first had a known asset on it, a Thomas Donovan."

"Yes, we know about the attack in Saint Thomas," the President said.

Cole shook his head and smiled. "No, you don't. I tipped Colonel O'Connell off about the burn list—and Tommy Donovan. He had Donovan pulled off the island as the attack was commencing."

"Thomas had nothing to do with it," James said. "He was as big a target in the island attack as the embassy was."

Tyler sat down. He stared at the laptop screen then looked across to James. "Donovan isn't dead then?"

James shook his head. "No, sir. My team was able to pull him out, along with an agency asset."

"Tanya Delgado?" the President said.

"Yes, sir," Cole said. "But the point is, Thomas Donovan was set up, and even after pulling him out, he was convicted and listed as dead in the assault." The FBI man looked back at James. "And the following day, James and many others were added to the list, including me."

"You said the list came from Justice?" Tyler asked. "Why would Justice target you, or even James?"

Cole shrugged. "The assumption was Justice, my boss, briefed our team on it. Said they were all imminent threats. But as you know, the AG has been absent."

"Yes, we know about the AG. What about the rest of your team? What is their status? "Tyler asked.

"I'm pretty sure they are all dead," Cole answered.

A man stood at the end of the table. James recognized him as Charles Carson, the President's Chief of Staff. He pointed at the list. "With this new information, I think we have to assume that all of these names are setups. We need to try and figure out how they are all related, and why they were targeted."

Tyler laughed. "That's not all that hard to do, these men were killed and targeted to get them out of the way."

James nodded. "If Tommy wasn't responsible for the attack in the islands, someone was."

"Vortex," the President said.

Tyler shook his head. "I think it's bigger than that."

"Then who?" Charles asked.

Scowling, Tyler said, "Dorsey, Senator Shafer, and the Apollo Group."

Charles went to speak again, when the President placed his hand on his shoulder. "And what about the Capital? The fires?"

"EMP," one of the staffers at the table said. "It explains the grid failure and the fires."

Tyler looked at James. "Did you see any evidence of that? Was there an EMP strike?"

"Jesus," James said. "Who the hell do you think is attacking us? You think these Apollo guys have nukes?"

The President held a finger up. "We still don't know who is attacking us. We all have obvious suspicions, but burning the city isn't something we had foreseen." Mac paused and pointed at the TV that had flipped back to the overhead maps of the district. "So, I have to ask again, did you see any evidence of an EMP?"

James shook his head. "We didn't see a nuke, if that's what you're asking. But if it was high orbit, I'm not sure I would see it anyway." James looked down at his hands. "We were able to use the GPS in the vehicle on the way here; a high orbit nuke should have killed that."

Cole interrupted. "I don't think it was an EMP. Grid failure, yes. Maybe people stayed home from work at the powerplant and collapsed the grid... Who knows?"

The young staffer scoffed. "Do you have any evidence to back that up?"

Grinning, Cole leaned in. "Let me ask you, son— what is your evidence of an EMP?"

Not deterred the staffer scowled. "We have power outages all down the East Coast. Everything is out— computers, phones, power plants are all down. We are seeing fires everywhere we can fly a drone." The man hardened his eyes and locked on Cole. "Is that enough for you?"

Cole shook his head. "No, not really."

"Okay, enough," Tyler said. He flipped back to a map of the US with a large chunk of the country shaded in black. He pointed to the staffer. "As Mr. Collins has said, there does seem to be significant evidence of an EMP— but with that, I agree, right now, we shouldn't make assumptions on what caused it. Currently, it does appear to have been triggered intentionally. We lost everything from the Capital to as far west as Nashville and down southeast to the coastline. We have no communications with anyone in that direction, including Fort Benning and Fort Bragg. We have been able to fly drone missions as far south as Benning."

"Why do we have power here?" James asked.

Tyler sighed. "We have buried utilities and our own power plant."

James looked at the man as if he had more to say. "And?"

The man nodded and flipped to a new slide. "Just as we lost power, the IT guys were hammered with cyber intrusions. They made a hard cut on the fiberoptic line headed into the facility, but the intrusions continued. We cut Wi-Fi, and for the moment, we are secure."

"This was a cyber-attack?" Cole asked. "Could that explain the blackouts?"

"It's a theory," Collins, the young staffer, answered. "We haven't been able to reach any other sites to confirm."

The President spoke again. "James, is there anything else you can tell us? You're the only one that has come out of the dead zone."

"I'm afraid not," James said. "We were a bit selfish with our time in the city, more focused on dodging bullets than with recon."

There was a knock at the door. All eyes turned toward the entrance as it opened. A young woman with her hair pulled back entered. She moved quickly to Tyler's side and whispered in his ear.

He pulled back and looked at her. "Are you sure?"

She quickly nodded her head.

Tyler looked at the President. "Sir, we seem to have a quickly developing issue."

He pointed a remote at the display and it flipped to a news broadcast out of New York. A man in a dark blue suit was sitting at an anchor desk while over his shoulder images of a burning White House billowed black smoke. James didn't need to know what the man was saying; the blue ribbon at the bottom of the screen said it all: *BREAKING NEWS: President Frederick MacLeod orders nuclear strike on Capital district in retaliation for forced removal from office.*

On his feet, the President shouted, "What in the hell is this? Turn up the damn volume!"

Tyler adjusted the volume as told, and the broadcaster read the prepared words. "It appears President MacLeod's staff was evacuated from the White House sometime in the last ninety-six hours. Then, in what can only be described at a pre-mediated strike, a short-range ballistic missile struck somewhere high above the Capital region. What has been described as an air blast has caused massive reports of causalities, destruction, and wide-ranging power outages, reaching as far south as the Florida coast.

"Survivors are currently being assisted by security contractors arranged by the Department of State. Citizens affected by the disaster are advised to remain indoors if possible and to vacate to assigned staging areas for evacuation to safe zones. The President has reportedly fled north to Camp David; law enforcement and military personnel are being dispatched immediately to apprehend him. Civilians in the area of Catoctin Mountain Park, are advised to vacate immediately."

The news then switched to a somber-looking Senator Charles Shafer. He was standing in front of the Capitol Building. Over the image, the broadcaster said, "This video was just transported back to us by courier. Cell phone and all power is out in the region in what scientists are describing as an EMP event."

The audio then flipped to the senator mid-sentence. "... moments after the United State Security and Monitoring Enhancement Act passed a bipartisan vote in the House and Senate, the President made direct threats against the Legislature. He considered the passing of the bill a direct threat against his administration. Shortly after..."

The senator looked off in the distance and then shook his head slowly side to side.

The microphone went back to the reporter and the man asked, "Sir, we have heard reports that the President may also be responsible for the shooting on the Senate floor and the strike against the Joint Chiefs."

Shafer tried to look shocked then pursed his lips. "I hate to speculate, but sometimes there are no coincidences."

"Enough!" MacLeod shouted. "Turn that shit off."

The President looked hard at James. "I have a question. Can you get Tommy Donovan here?"

James reached into his pocket, removing the mobile phone. The signal bars were all back and full. "Yes, sir, that is something I might be able to help you with. But Donovan isn't a politician; he won't be able to fix this."

"No, but he is an assassin and a fixer." President MacLeod looked at Tyler then pointed at the TV. "And I want that traitorous son of a bitch removed from office."

The Chief of Staff stood. "Sir, if we do that, we will be playing right into their hands."

MacLeod scowled. "Did I stutter? That man is a terrorist—I want him gone and dealt with." The President then looked back at James. "Now, is that something Tommy can do?"

James turned his head to the side then said, "That is pretty much exactly what the man does."

Tyler flipped to another overlay on the screen. "Sir, we can hit them, but we may have other problems." The screen flipped from the live news to a satellite image of Camp David. Tyler scrolled out, showing a wide image then zoomed in on an interstate highway. There were columns of vehicles headed toward them.

"What is that?" MacLeod asked.

"This is a live drone pass. It appears the news wasn't all fake." He clicked several keys and another set of images appeared. Zooming in, they could make out armored vehicles and troop trucks. "Something is headed our way, and they aren't ours."

MacLeod grunted. "We have two Battalions of Marines dug in around this place, is it enough?"

Tyler stared at the screen. "It might be. But we should make plans to leave just in case."

The President waved off the comment. "Can you reach General Cartwright?"

Tyler shook his head. "The General is at Bragg, in the dead zone."

"Then the Marines will have to be enough," the President said. He looked at James. "Let me know as soon as you contact Donovan. I want him here." He looked at Tyler and pointed at the troop column on the display. "Find out who that is."

CHAPTER TWENTY-SIX

Tommy followed behind the point man as they patrolled the perimeter fence. Hagan led the way, a short-barreled carbine tucked into his side, his eyes out scanning the dark trees to their front. It had been a full day since he'd arrived at the Ranch and Tommy was growing restless. Marcus had equipped him with clean clothes and new weapons, but what he really wanted was information.

Most of the airways were dead now—even the Mad Jack radio broadcasts had ended sometime the night before. There was sporadic news from the Northeast. Marcus had been able to pick up an NBC broadcast out of New York on one of his antenna arrays, but it was broken, and what they did receive seemed dire. Areas in Atlanta and to the east had all lost power in some sort of massive blackout. Areas to the west were under martial law in a nationwide crackdown on lawlessness.

Tommy knew he had to get out and make his call, and reluctantly the rest of the team finally agreed.

Holing up was the safe bet, but it also felt cowardly for men of the Ground Division, who had been bred to fight. And now here he was out on the late afternoon perimeter walk. Hagan would take him all the way to the southwest road then set up an observation post while Tommy continued across the rural highway. It would only be a short hike south and up a neighboring hill. Marcus had said there was a large cell tower over that way; he would be able to see it once he traversed the hilltop.

It was critical that he was on the western slope when he made the call. If his phone pinged the western tower and had a blocked signal to the east, it would be difficult for anyone looking to triangulate on his position. Impossible, in fact, as a single tower ping would just put in him the range of the western tower and no other. It was above standard precautions, but Marcus had pounded into him the importance of securing the Ranch from radiation leaks and anything a drone or satellite could use to detect their presence. Nobody knew they were there, and Marcus wanted to keep it that way.

The big man up front took a knee then looked back at Tommy. He put two fingers to his eyes then waved him forward. Tommy made a quick rotation, checking their back trail then moved ahead, squatting beside the other man. Hagan pointed between tall pines and through thick brush. Tommy squinted, but in the late afternoon sun, he could see the grey tint of the asphalt. He went to step off when Hagan grabbed his shoulder. The man pulled up a sleeve and revealed a cheap Timex watch. "You got one hour, to get there and back, or I'll come after you."

Tommy shook his head. "Just stay put and cover this trail. I'll make it back."

Without waiting for a response, Tommy stalked through the trees to the road. Then after crossing, he took off at a brisk jog. He was dressed like a hunter in dark-brown canvas pants, a black-and-grey flannel with a black watch cap. If he was caught, he would claim to be a poacher, just looking to fill the family pot.

He cleared the open terrain and dropped back into the cover of trees and slowed back to a walk. His cover would only work at a distance. If anyone got close to him, or if he was captured, it would all fall apart. If his real identity was found out, anyone targeting him would eventually look for the Ranch. He looked at his well-equipped suppressed rifle. It was a bit more than a typical lower Alabama hunter would carry, and he knew his backpack had enough goodies to make a special operator cry with envy. "Just don't get caught then," he whispered to himself.

He checked a cheap compass he'd taped to the stock of his rifle. He wanted to fire up a GPS, but Marcus had warned him against using any electronics until he'd gotten far from the property lines. In the distance, he could see the hilltop and the worn game trail the wended its way around rough terrain. He stopped and took a knee, scanning the high ground, looking for any movement. The air was still. He could hear birds chirping, and the longer he waited, small game began to rustle the leaves. He slowly rose back to his feet and continued on the trail. Hell, maybe he would see a deer. It wasn't in the mission cards, but nobody except Marcus would bitch about fresh venison.

Tommy stuck to the trail and, as he neared the summit, he could tell the area was well-traveled. He began to find more and more signs of human presence. Food wrappers, water bottles, painted rocks, all the typical signs of nature lovers out doing their damage. He stopped again just before the top of the hill and listened intently. The hilltop was barren except for the tall golden grass that covered it. There was a breeze blowing now, and he could hear the dry vegetation rustling.

The top of the hill, aside from the road, would be the most dangerous position he needed to cross. Tommy looked around, surveying the terrain, debating on just circling to the other side. But he didn't want to waste time and risk not locating the cell tower. No, over the top would be the best course. He knew he would be sky lining himself in every direction to anyone else in the area. It was okay—he was just a poacher out on a hunt. He would get to the top, locate the tower, and move out to a position of cover to make his phone call. If necessary, he could always move in a different direction for a few miles to break off anyone who may pursue him.

Staying low, he duck-walked on his approach to the hilltop, keeping the top of the grass at his shoulders. The trail ended on a flattened circle of earth, where hikers had probably picnicked. He moved along the outer edges of the cut then focused his eyes to the west. Keeping his eyes just above the level of the vegetation, he scanned left to right and spotted the tower. It was hard to judge the distance by eye, but it appeared to be at least two miles

away. He looked down the hill, where the trail continued. Unlike the eastern slope covered in woods, this side
was grass covered.

At the bottom of the slope, he could see where the
trail wound around and through another field before it
met a flattened patch of terrain next to a two-lane highway. There were several cars parked in the lot, and
Tommy instinctively ducked lower. Even though he was
on the look out for strangers, he hadn't expected to find
any. There was no good cover, so he stuck to the high
ground and moved a hundred feet down the slope,
staying in line with the cell tower. He found a natural
depression on the slope and settled into it.

He unzipped his black vest and reached inside, grabbing the anti-static bag. He opened the bag's ziplock
closure and dumped the phone and Genii device into his
palm. He looked at his watch; it was far past time for the
Colonel's phone call. He would have to break protocol
and dial the number himself. He pressed the power
button on the top of the burner phone and put in an
earbud as he waited for it to connect. He saw the phone's
display light up and the signal bars go to full.

Tommy inserted the Genii device then opened an
encrypted file, revealing a single number. He tapped the
digits and the call button popped up. He hit it, knowing
he wouldn't get an immediate response. As with everything else O'Connell did, even this had a process. He let
the phone ring twice then disconnected the call. Now
was the hard part—was James there or not? He leaned
back into his hide, watching the road below. It moved in
from the west then curved toward the south at its closest

point to the hill then curved by the car park at the bottom. There were farms on the east-west road.

In the distance, he could see a convoy of black vehicles moving in from the west. He recognized them as Vortex security; the trucks looked identical to the ones that belonged to the men who had harassed the kids at the gas station.

"You thugs still out here?" he whispered as he shrugged off his pack and removed a pair of binoculars. He focused in on the lead vehicle. "Well, I'll be damned," he said.

The Tahoe leading the way had obvious signs of battle damage. The front fenders were pockmarked with bullet holes and part of the windshield was broken. Just as the trucks pulled off the road and into the driveway of a farmhouse, his phone chirped. Tommy took his eyes off the binoculars and looked at the display. *"Sorry new phone, who is this?"*

Tommy tapped the reply icon and wrote, *"We've been trying to reach you regarding your vehicle's extended warranty."*

"But I don't own a car," came the reply.

Tommy smiled now. Within moments, the phone vibrated, and he tapped the earpiece.

O'Connell's heavily modulated voice through the Genii device. "Damn, Tommy, where the hell are you? You've missed two calls."

"Been busy, but aren't you the one that hung up on me? What the hell happened?"

There was a pause at the end of the line, then the Colonel came back. "We had trouble in the city and had to move close to friends." Another pause. "What about you, are you settled?"

Tommy sighed, knowing there was no way he would get a straight answer over a mobile phone, encrypted or not. "Same here, I am afraid. We are staying with family —a bunch of the cousins. We're all checked in, but I need to know what to do. They would love to see you."

"We're with Tanya's uncle," James said.

Tommy froze; he'd used her real name on the open line, and he knew that "uncle" could only be one person. She worked directly for the President as a liaison to Tommy. He took in a breath and said, "Where?"

"At the summer camp. There is a lot of work, can you get here?"

Camp David. Tommy knew of the place; he'd done security sweeps on the location years before when he was still learning the ropes of countersurveillance. "It'll be a day's drive."

There was hesitation on the other end of the line, and Tommy realized many ears were listening in. James suddenly loosed the reins and said, "Where are you?"

Tommy thought, *If James is really at Camp David with the President, then Tyler Spence would be close by.* "Like I said, I'm with my cousins. Everyone that could make it is at the ranch."

Another long pause and then James came back on. "Understood. Stay where you are, pack a bag, and we'll come get you in a bus. It'll be faster that way."

Tommy looked down the hill and noticed that the vehicle convoy was moving again. It had rounded the bend and was now stopped at the car park at the bottom of the hill. Doors were opening and men were getting out, searching the cars at the bottom of the hill. For the first time, Tommy put his binoculars on the abandoned cars at the bottom. One looked like it had been there for years, but the other was a dark-blue sedan with bullet holes to match the black convoy. And it was the sedan that had the convoy's attention.

"Shit," he whispered.

"What was that?" James said. Even through modulation, Tommy could hear the concern.

"I have something going on here."

Tommy watched as the men went to the backs of the black Vortex vehicles and suited up in vests and helmets. He put his eyes back on the sedan. From this distance, he couldn't tell what or who they were after.

"Okay, see you tomorrow morning at the bus garage," James said as the call disconnected.

Tommy pulled out the Genii device and powered down the phone as he stuffed it back into the anti-static bag, then pushed it into his jacket. He lay in the prone position and watched as the men at the car park fanned out and began to walk toward the trailhead. There was a bright flash of light, a black cloud of smoke, and the car park was filled with dust and debris. Somewhere off to the left was a report of gunfire. Men in black fled back to the vehicles, some taking cover behind the blue car moments before it exploded in an orange-yellow fireball.

His instinct and training told him to beat feet, but someone was running a hell of an ambush in his backyard, and he knew it might be important to find out who. The smoke was clearing around the car park. Several of the men were still on their feet with twice as many down in the gravel. Tommy stowed the binoculars and went to his rifle. He raised it in time to see one of the men in black take a burst of rifle fire to his vest.

Tommy shifted his stance, looking for the source. He followed the terrain. There were several places to form a bottleneck ambush like what was being executed below. Tommy hadn't noticed the rolls in the sloping hill before. Near the bottom, the hilly terrain had several fingers where depressions had been formed by running water. There was a depression just like the one he was currently sitting in, then others with knuckle-shaped mounds of earth dividing them. Maybe a hundred yards to his front, the rim of a center-facing hole lay covered in high vegetation. The shooter would have been invisible from the ground until he opened fire, and if the shooter had been there long enough, he could have dug a hell of a foxhole.

The position was hidden from Tommy and would also be difficult to see from the car park. There were several other places a trained shooter could hide, but there was only one place where Tommy would go. He listened to another burst of gunfire. Another man in the car park screamed, taking hits to the pelvis. Now looking at the dip, he knew the shooter was just on the other side, raising hell on the Vortex men below.

The black-armored men around the SUVs began to organize. He could see eight shooters left on their feet. Four men leapt into cover then sprayed suppressing fire in the unknown shooter's direction, as the other half sprinted for the fingers of the hill. They were slowly getting their shit together. The suppressive fire was keeping the shooter's head down. Four of the eight crossed over the finger-like ridge and rolled into Tommy's view. They were attempting to flank the depression from Tommy's side of the slope.

This puzzled Tommy. The men moved like they were experienced in combat, but they crossed the finger, not even bothering to look in his direction. They were after a lone gunman. The men leopard-crawled along the ridge while the shooter exchanged fire with the men below. There was another high-pitched scream, and Tommy looked on as a shooter in the park's head snapped back. Whoever was giving these guys hell was good, and Tommy wasn't about to let the man be ambushed by thugs.

He raised his rifle and waited for the leopard-crawling men to get into cover, then he let loose with a three-round burst into the lead man's body. The crawling attacker shuddered and collapsed to the ground. The three men following froze in confusion. Tommy took advantage of the chaos and focused on the next man in the column. He fired and as the rounds left his barrel. He watched two more rise and fire in his direction. Rounds impacted the earth to his front and dirt pelted his face.

"Oh, it's on like Donkey Kong now," Tommy shouted at them.

He drained the rest of his magazine then stood, hitting the release, letting an empty fall to the ground as he slapped a fresh one home. He had the rifle at eye level, laying down precision fire as he moved down the slope. Two more black-clad men were down; one was returning fire and a fourth seemed to contemplate making a run for it. Tommy focused on the fighter then killed the fleeing man. He'd expended another six rounds before turning toward the car park, planning to deliver more hate, when he saw the fight was over.

The remaining three men were lying in the dirt. The gunfire had stopped. He scanned the terrain; over a dozen men were dead. He lowered his rifle and looked in the direction of the shooter's position.

Now the hard part, he thought to himself.

He should probably beat feat and let this be an anonymous gesture of goodwill, but his curiosity wouldn't let him. He moved into the open, letting his rifle hang at the low ready as he walked forward.

"I'm a friendly, I'm coming across, don't shoot me," he shouted.

Tommy heard no reply. He wondered if the shooter had taken rounds, maybe he was hit and bleeding out in the grass. He increased his pace, repeating the challenge as he moved. "I'm a friend. If you're hurt, I can help you."

He crossed the remaining distance, moving onto the high ground, looking down into the depression. On the ground at the back of the hole, lay the man, his face covered in grime, his eyes closed, his left arm in a sling and heavily taped in blood-soaked bandages.

The shooter looked up at Tommy and smiled. "Damn, Donovan," the man grunted, trying to roll to his side. "How did you know?" Between labored breaths, the man said, "What the hell are you doing out here?"

Tommy took another step forward. "Winston? Is that you?"

"Why? Were you expecting someone else?" The man groaned, trying to get to his feet. "Hell, yeah it's me—unless you know any other badass just hanging out on hills, stacking bodies."

Tommy moved quickly to help Winston to his feet and out of the hole. Then he guided him back and out of the depression. Tommy dropped his pack and dug out the first aid kit. While he worked, he pointed at the distant cell tower. "I was only out here to make a phone call. Marcus has the Ranch unplugged."

Winston went to nod but instead took an unsteady step backward. Tommy grabbed him and lowered him back to the ground. He looked at the bloodied arm and said, "You got a bad wing, what happened?"

Winston looked at the arm and let out an exhausted sigh. "I took a round through it somewhere around Texarkana. These assholes have been following me ever since. I stop every few hours to kill some, but they won't stop hunting me." He looked down at the ground then his head suddenly snapped back up like he'd forgotten an important fact. He looked hard at Tommy. "You're dead."

"Not so much, brother. Come on, we need to keep moving."

Winston grunted and looked at the western road. "There'll be more. A lot more."

Tommy nodded in agreement. "They'll see your little ambush site down there." He looked at the exploded Malibu and the bodies surrounding it. "But you intended for them to find that, didn't you?"

Now smiling, Winston said, "You like that? I stopped

at that farm and told them if those cartel boys come looking for me to be sure and point them in this direction. Then I parked that car so it could easily be seen from the road."

"Cartel?" Tommy asked.

"Yeah," Winston said. "Believe it or not. I had the pleasure of conversing with one of them. Like most cowards, he talked a lot as he died. Let's just say these boys aren't locals. They are officially credentialed up, but they aren't from here."

Tommy looked at the road in the distance and saw a long snaking convoy coming into view. The lead vehicles were all black, but behind them were serval irregular vehicles, including a pair of busses. He pointed at the horizon. "Looks like your friends are coming; we need to head out."

Winston grabbed Tommy's arm. "I didn't know anyone would be at the Ranch." He closed his eyes and leaned his head back. "I wouldn't have come this way. I wouldn't have led them here if I knew. I thought you all were dead."

Tommy grinned as he got to his feet then yanked the wounded man up. "It's not just me, we got Hagan, Kidd, and Marcus."

Shaking his head, no, Winston said, "Four, even five of us against them—Tommy it isn't enough. Leave me here. I'll end it and you can stay undiscovered."

Tommy looked out at the approaching convoy. "Hell, from here it hardly looks like a fair fight. You sure they ain't got more? I thought this was supposed to be hard."

"Fuck off, just go," Winston said.

Looking down at the man, Tommy could tell he was in no mood for gallows humor. "Sorry, brother, I can't let you die a hero and steal all the glory." He laughed walking up the hill, pulling Winston behind. "You know I'm the only hero in Ground Division."

Winston attempted to laugh; instead, it came out as a wet cough. He tried to hold his head up as he mumbled, "Yeah, you're right. You were always the attention whore of the team." The wounded man stopped and fell to a knee then looked up at Tommy. "Hey, brother, it really is good to see you," he said before collapsing to the grass.

CHAPTER TWENTY-SEVEN

In a cold, brightly lit room Mark Dorsey sat at an empty conference table. Every inch of the space was white, the table surface, the chairs, even the speakerphone sitting in the center of the table. Mark couldn't complain about the decorating; he had designed this room. Hell, Mark had designed the entire building, the entire complex. Mark and his Apollo Group were the technical developers and master architects of the United States National Intelligence Survey Administration, the newest and most developed technology and intelligence asset within the US Government.

Apollo Group and Mark Dorsey had been brought in early in the concept phase of the center and the complex. It was Mark's vision and procurement talents that truly brought the ideas to reality. Mark knew the best people, he had access to the best developers, and he had the capital and investors to make it all happen. The US Government had deep pockets, but even the Treasury would have sticker shock if they knew the extent of what was going on in the basements of this facility, if they knew the salaries Mark had approved to the world's top application developers.

The USNISA was intentioned to be the hub of all the American intelligence agencies. He had grand plans for the organization. With him at the helm, he would revolutionize intelligence gathering in the world. He would reduce redundancy, streamline investigations, and close the gap on keeping American's truly safe from their enemies. He developed the Delphi Initiative to ensure it. The United State Security and Monitoring Enhancement Act would make people safe; it would stop crimes before they happened. Mark wasn't a philanthropist or a patriot. He didn't take on this project out of any civil duty. From the start, he had intended to one day run the complex, but he had never planned to take it over by force.

All he needed was for Delphi to go live. But the President and his administration fought him every step of the way. His Justice Department scored the program unconstitutional, and when Dorsey's name had been floated around to lead the new agency, President MacLeod soundly rejected the idea. Mark made a fist, thinking of the idea of surrendering everything he had built here. Just the thought of having to hand this facility over to some bureaucrat made him physically ill. He grinned and looked around the room. "Nobody is taking this from me," he whispered.

If the government wouldn't turn the USNISA over to Apollo Group, then Mark would find a way to move the US Government under the control of Apollo Group.

Things were not going according to plan. After Delphi passed the House and Senate, the President was supposed to resign. Then his friends in the Senate would move to the next phase to put place Mark Dorsey at the top of the USNISA, then he would bring Delphi to its full potential. He made another fist, this time hitting the table. He winced at the pain in his wrist.

The President had refused to resign, and Senator Shafer was losing his backbone. Instead of rallying Congress to support him, there were rumors they may vote to take Delphi down before it could prove its value. The President had more friends in the Congress than Mark had given him credit for, friends that needed to be silenced. Mark had ordered the blackout on the Capital District. He wanted to temporarily shut down the government. But he didn't realize the extent of the risk of cutting the grid cold.

The fires and the spread of the blackout down the East Coast had angered a nation already in turmoil. But Mark wasn't worried. He controlled the media, and they were working to sell his message. The people were believing his propaganda campaign to blame MacLeod for using an EMP device against his own nation's capital. He laughed, thinking of the ridiculousness of the idea, but it was the journalists themselves who originally sold the idea of an EMP strike. All Mark had to do was use the power of Delphi to point a finger, and now DC was a dead zone, and Apollo Group has escaped all blame. But there was one other loose end he needed to contain.

The phone to his front rang. Mark held his breath and exhaled slowly before hitting the connect button on the base of the phone. "Hope you have good news for me," he said.

On the other end of the line was Senator Shafer. He was supposed to be closing a deal with Chris Michaels, the Vice President, to end the stalemate, to convince MacLeod to resign, to leave his stronghold in Maryland and let the country return to normalcy.

"The news isn't good, I am afraid," Shafer said.

Mark scowled. "So Chris isn't cooperating?"

"It's a bit worse than that. He is threatening to go public; he's scheduling a national address. He says he has direct evidence that Delphi, not MacLeod, is responsible for burning the White House."

"That's impossible," Mark said. "The evidence on our side is unquestionable."

"You don't have to convince me, Mark." The line went silent for a moment then Shafer came back. "Chris says they have gathered intelligence from several locations that show a cyber intrusion against the power plants and other pieces of government infrastructure. He has techs at his location now. They are presenting evidence captured in the seconds before the power went out. He says he can prove it was Delphi and not a high-orbit nuclear device that took down the Capital." Another pause. "And, Mark, there are a lot of experts already doubting the idea that it was a nuclear weapon. The Israelis are ready to state that their satellites detected no atmospheric detonations. There are teams on the ground telling us they've found no evidence of fallout."

"Are you fucking serious right now?" Mark shouted,

suddenly losing his temper. "MacLeod did this! Why are you even humoring this guy?"

"This guy?" Shaffer shouted back. "This guy is the Vice President of the United States! Even people who want to believe the President is capable of such a thing are starting to doubt it. He's going to go public, and then we will lose the Senate's support."

"You have to stop him," Mark said, bringing his voice back down. "We need more time to prove our case."

"The media is accusing the President of the United States of using a nuclear weapon against his own people. Mark, the Vice President is not going to stay quiet on this."

"Where is he?" Mark asked. "Still in Chicago?"

"Yes, he's staying at the naval base north of the city. There is no getting to him, if that's what you are thinking," Shafer said.

Mark laughed, and said, "Senator, what exactly do you take me for? I told you, this was MacLeod's doing. All I want to do is help put this country back together again. Listen, we are not talking about this anymore; I am sending Victor to retrieve you and bring you back here. It's time we reestablished control of the situation."

Before Shafer could reply, Mark hit the end button, disconnecting the call. He then ran his hand over the surface of the white table. A digital keyboard illuminated on the surface. He punched in several commands, and the wall to his front transformed into a bank of computer displays.

Opening the main interface with Delphi, he dug deep into the inner workings of the network. From the main hub in the USNISA complex, he had access to every working system in the United States' arsenal. He stopped at a login panel for the United States Strategic Command. He clicked a Delphi seal on the bottom corner of his display and let the artificial intelligence do its work. In moments, he was inside the secure network. He clicked a button, launching the AI module and took his hands off the virtual keyboard.

"Delphi, give me missile launch sites."

Four of the smaller displays converted into one, then a map of the United States with red dots populated the map.

"Show Iowa," Mark said.

The map zoomed in on the state, then switched to satellite images. Fifteen locations populated. Mark looked at the sites.

"Display low yield."

All but one vanished. Echo Thirty, a Minuteman VII site northeast of Waterloo. He dialed in on the warhead type, a $W78$ with variable yield. Mark grimaced and ran his hand over the table, illuminating the keyboard again. He pulled up the device nomenclature then nodded. He stared at the map. It was big; this would be devastating.

"Delphi, give me the terminal," Mark said.

This time all eight screens on the wall transformed into the command center of the Minuteman Silo. Mark could see all the red blocks on the screen, the failsafes and safeties that would prevent just this sort of launch. There were manual safeties to prevent a rogue operator from making a launch, but all of those could be circumvented by a system capable of firing the circuits on its own. He looked at the map of four silos, all missiles fueled and ready for launch.

He would love to send all four silos at the President at Camp David, but he had the majority of his ground forces surrounding the base there. He couldn't risk killing his own people. No, and this was better. He could kill off the Vice President and make it look like retaliation. For what, it didn't matter; the media would report whatever he said. And if the armed forces thought the President was dropping nukes on his own people, they would defect.

"Delphi, select Silo 1."

"Selection, confirmed."

"Delphi, set yield to five kilotons."

"Selection, confirmed."

"Delphi, target Great Lakes Naval Station, Illinois."

"Selection, confirmed."

The screen transformed. The terminal went live. An active target list populated then was scrubbed with the grid coordinates of the naval base locked into the right of silo one. His screen changed, and the display locked. He knew that the silo operators were trying to override his command. "Delphi, lock all internal command center doors, and shut down all internal monitors, shutdown all internal systems and communications. Delphi, disable bunker life support."

"Selection, confirmed."

He waited and watched as the screen returned to its previous settings. "Delphi, proceed with immediate launch."

"Selection, confirmed."

Mark leaned back in his chair and looked at the display. Two digital timers populated the center of the screen. The first was time to launch, the second time to target.

He watched the launch timer. Five minutes, he would have thought such a thing would be hastier. In the case of nuclear war, he'd always assumed things would be quick. "I mean, they are called Minuteman, not Five Minuteman." He laughed sadistically at his own joke.

There was a loud knock at the door. "Enter," he shouted.

The door behind him opened and he spun around in his chair. Victor Kesson stood before him. "Sir, there has been a development, actionable intelligence from Delphi," the man said.

He was talking to Mark, but his eyes were fixed on the launch terminal. Mark smiled, knowing the muscle-bound Russian would have no idea what he was looking at.

"Yes, that is what the system is designed for. What do you have?"

Victor scowled; his eyes were still fixed on the display. "There was a captured communication from a call to the facility at Camp David. The call was made using a rudimentary encryption device. Delphi easily cracked the security and gave us information on the call. Whoever was calling is important to the facility, and they will be sending transportation."

"Who was the caller?" Mark asked.

Victor shook his head. "That we couldn't discern. The voices had analog modulation."

"The location?"

"Lower Alabama."

Mark looked back at the timer then back to Victor. "That is near Raul's sector. Give him the call location and have him check it out. Have him capture whoever made the communication and deliver the information to us."

"All due respect, I think my team should go. Raul is more of a hammer than a scalpel."

Mark looked up at the ceiling with his fingers interlocked, twirling his thumbs. "No, Raul can handle this. Make it his priority."

Victor, obviously not happy, nodded his head in submission. "I will see that it happens. Still, I think at least I should also fly to the location; this person was using encryption technology placing a call to the President. He may be of great value to us."

Mark shook his head. "No, I have something else for you."

"Sir?"

"Take your people, your best people, and go to Washington. Find Senator Shafer and return him here."

"You want me to go to Washington now?" the man asked. "We have no control there; the city is in meltdown."

"Yes, take your Spetsnaz buddies. The mercenary friends that you claim to not have."

Victor grinned. "Yes, sir, we will leave right away."

Mark shook his head. "Not right away—make the call to Raul first."

CHAPTER TWENTY-EIGHT

He walked across the dusty parking lot, crushing gravel beneath his boots. No longer dressed in the tan khakis and shirt, he was now in the same black utility uniform as the rest of his men. Diaz had paid for that lesson; it was bad to stand out in a group when there were snipers in the area. He looked down at the dead men, several scattered and maimed around a destroyed automobile, another cluster of dead around a muddy crater where an IED had been planted.

Raul kept his eyes locked on the carnage as he spoke. "How many?"

"How many?" an officer said in Spanish-accented English. "How many what, my captain?"

Raul stopped and looked the man in the eyes. He missed Diaz, his right-hand man. Diaz would have already given him critical stat. With this idiot, every tidbit of information had to be painstakingly extracted, every question exact, and then contradicting information poured out when he didn't want it. He glared at the man, wanting to pull his pistol now and shoot the idiot in the face. "How many men did we fucking lose?" he said, his voice hard and cold. "And I am not your fucking captain."

"Eighteen."

Raul turned away, walking toward a row of stacked bodies. Other men of his unit were gathering weapons and removing equipment from the dead. He looked back at the road. There were five vehicles heavily damaged with bullet holes. Beyond them, further back on the highway, was his own convoy of twenty plus vehicles.

"Five vehicles and eighteen men from one gringo," Raul said under his breath.

"My captain," the officer said. "That was just here—he has killed fifty from our force in total. And we are also taking heavy losses from the Texans west of the Mississippi."

Raul locked his jaw in anger. He turned, drew his sidearm, and shot the officer in the side of the face. "Now it is fifty-one! Would anyone else care to recount the gringo's numbers?"

The men around the ambush scene had frozen in place. Slowly their heads shook side to side, then they went back to the task of piling up the dead. One of the men, instead of cowering, returned his hard stare. The man was short, wide-shouldered, his beard well-trimmed, but his boots worn. The man wore his sidearm high on his right hip in a retention holster instead of in a drop holster like the rest of his men.

Raul pointed at the man. "You—what is your name?"

"Jose Gonzalez, senor," the man said, not looking away.

He pointed to the man's pistol. "Why do you wear your sidearm like that? Were you not issued the correct holster?"

"These holsters are shit; I prefer my own." the man answered.

Raul smirked; he knew the man was right—the drop holsters were shit. They'd been bought cheap from an online supplier and shipped to an address in EL Paso, all distributed in the days before the attacks. "And where did you get that one?"

"I was a sergeant in the Grupo de Operaciones Espe-ciale," the man said. "Mexican Federal Police."

"Ahh." Raul grinned. "A real killer in my presence." He stepped closer to the man and asked him, "Why are you here if you are a cop?"

The man didn't waver. "Money, senor, why else?"

Raul smiled and slapped the man's arm. "Well, Jose, you are now my right-hand man. Follow me." He stepped off then stopped and turned back at Jose. "And if you call me captain, you know what happens."

Jose stood upright. He looked at the dead officer on the ground. "You will shoot me in the face, senor?"

Raul smiled. "That is correct. I will shoot you in the face." He turned toward the hill and began walking a trail that led to the top. He already had his trackers and scouts working the scene. They were clustered around a hole about a third of the way up. Raul moved to them and looked down. The grass had been torn away and a small cut dug out.

He moved into the hole and looked down. One of his scouts was standing to the side of the position. The scout pointed his arms out straight like holding a rifle, he then moved them left and right. "This man chose his position well; he had a perfect view of the park. He would have triggered the explosive devices as our men examined the vehicle, then gunned down the rest."

Raul nodded his head in agreement. "Every time, he lays an ambush and every time, we walk right into it. Every time, he predicts where we will be."

Jose looked up the hill and pointed. "He wasn't alone."

Raul turned quickly and looked at Jose, whose arm was extended, pointing up the hill.

"There is only one shooter," the scout said.

Raul moved to his side and focused on the vegetation where Jose was pointing, seeing nothing. "I don't see it."

"No, there was another," Jose said again. He took two steps then stopped and looked to his left. He pointed. Four black-clad bodies were lying five meters away. "These men attempted to flank this position. It was a good intention, the shooter in the hole would not have seen them coming." He then pointed again back to the hillside. "Someone in that location cut them down."

Jose began walking up the hill as Raul stayed just behind him. The man stopped on the lip of a second depression. The grass here was trampled. Jose knelt and sifted through the grass then held up three rifle casings. "We are looking for two men, senor."

Raul took the rifle casing and examined then. He turned to his scouts and tossed the brass in their direction. Before he could admonish them, his phone rang. He held up a finger and stepped away from Jose. He removed the phone from his jacket pocket and scowled. It was Victor. He didn't have time for this.

He swiped the green icon and held the phone to his ear. "Yes."

"Where are you?" he heard the voice of Victor.

Raul scowled. "Alabama."

"Your sector is the southwest. Why are you in Alabama? We have heard that you lost Texas. Please tell me I heard wrong."

"I am actively tracking a target," Raul said, ignoring the rest of the man's comments. He was already feeling the anger grow at being questioned. "Why are you calling?"

"The hunts have been canceled," Victor said. "We need you for something else."

He was seething now and considering ending the phone call. "Again, I ask, why are you calling?"

Victor sighed audibly. "It is good that you are in Alabama; we have a lead that you need to track down."

Raul shook his head. He wasn't in the mood to be chasing leads while he was in pursuit of a killer. "It will have to keep—I am already occupied."

There was a long pause. Raul could hear Victor's heavy breathing, and he knew the man was as frustrated as he was. "This is a priority, Raul," Victor said. "We have a target that is in direct communications with the President. He made a phone call. We captured the call and the caller's location; we need you to get there and investigate as soon as possible."

Raul shook his head and reached into his pocket for a small handheld GPS. There was no way he would give up on the task at hand for this errand, but it was easier to agree than to keep arguing. "I assume you have a location for me then."

"Yes, of course," Victor said then quickly read off several grid coordinates.

After punching the numbers into his device, Raul smirked. "Very funny. I know my location—where is the target?"

"I just gave you the location," Victor said.

Raul took a step back and looked around the area. "How long ago was this phone call made?"

After a beat, Victor came back. "One hour ago."

Raul put his hand over the phone and looked at the scouts. "When was the attack?"

The man looked down and shrugged. "Maybe one hour, if not less."

Smiling, Raul looked around again, then out at the ambush site. He put the phone back to his mouth. "We are hunting the same man. What information can you give me about him?"

"I am sending satellite images of the area to your phone now. We don't know who it was."

"Where was he going?" Raul asked, happy at the prospect of being able to get ahead of the gringo, the possibility to hit him in a place of their choosing this time.

"He mentioned a ranch. We have checked the over-head maps and found nothing. But there is a farm very close to you. It is the only one set of structures in the area, over the hill and a mile to the northeast. From the satellite, we see a large farmhouse and a barn."

"Vehicles?" Raul asked.

"No vehicles, but they could have hidden them in the barn. We believe your target is there or headed that way."

"No, he will be just over this hill waiting to ambush my men again as we pursue him," Raul said.

Victor waited then said, "Wherever you think he may be, you must move soon. The details from the phone call indicated the target will be moving out tomorrow morning, and it is impossible to know the size of the pickup team."

Raul frowned. "This help—how will they travel?"

"They stated a bus but given the circumstances, we would expect a helicopter."

Raul smiled and looked back at his men then back to the small GPS device in his hand. "Send me the coordinates of this farm, and I will handle the rest."

"It would be good if you could capture the man alive; he may have good intelligence value," Victor added.

"That will not be possible, please send the farm's coordinates."

"These men could be important to the President. We need them alive for leverage."

Raul laughed. "I will kill this man for you, then after this last request, you should consider our association over. I am done working for you and Apollo Group."

CHAPTER TWENTY-NINE

The sky had turned a dark purple, there was thunder in the distance, and the heavens began to pour. Rain pounded on the steel roof of the barn. Winston was back in the main room of the Ranch, laid out on the kitchen counter. Marcus had him lightly sedated but awake as he probed his arm, cleaning the wound of bullet fragments and infected tissue.

"How old is this injury? It looks like shit," Marcus said, dragging a gauze over the dead tissue, scrubbing it clean.

Through clenched teeth, Winston gasped. "Day, maybe two. I sort of lost track."

Tommy was standing behind them; the rest of the team were downstairs in the bunker, grabbing weapons and equipment. He'd already explained the best he could that they were being hunted. That there were many of them and even though the pursuers were on the far side of the hill, it wouldn't take them long to figure this place out and begin the trek over. He also happened to mention that they would be getting picked up the next morning and transported to a new location.

Marcus pulled the wounded man's arm straight then wrapped it tightly in bandages. He dropped everything on the table then reached back into the medical pack, removing a tiny glass vial. He pulled liquid from it with a syringe and stuck Winston in the hip.

Winston man barely flinched. "Morphine?"

"No," Marcus said. "Antibiotics. I need you on your feet."

Winston scoffed. "You know I've fought jacked up before, just give me something to take the edge off."

Smiling, Marcus shook his head and zipped up the aid bag. "You said you've been walking around with this for a couple days; you should be used to it by now."

A door closed and Hagan walked in, pushing a cart. Behind him were Kidd and Tanya carrying heavy canvas bags. The cart was pushed to the center of the room, then the bags dropped on the floor beside it. Marcus walked around the counter and washed his hands in a large basin. "This is the best of what we got." He looked at Winston. "You think they'll come in the daylight or at night?"

Winston shrugged and forced himself up into a seated position. "All the attacks have been in daylight thus far, but then again, I have planned everything up until now." He scowled and looked at a clock on the wall. "If they are hunting me, they'll probably come right over the hill. They won't wait longer than it takes to get reinforcements. They have confidence in numbers, and from what I have seen, they have unlimited numbers of shooters. I imagine they'll move over that hill and spot the road. Probably call the convoy around and meet up with it out front, then move in to check out the farmhouse.

"Will they fight in the dark?"

Winston shook his head. "I don't know, but they seem to be too stupid to be afraid of the dark."

Tommy raised his brows as he walked toward the cart filled with weapons and ammo cases. "If they are rolling up on us, thinking we are unaware, what's one more ambush to guys that can't take a hint?"

"How are they on night vision?" Marcus asked, still considering the tactics of the situation.

Again, Winston shrugged. "I haven't seen any of. But I'd imagine they've got some; they've been well equipped."

"Crew served?" Marcus asked. "Heavy machine guns?"

Winston shook his head. "No heavy machine guns, but they do have anti-tank rockets, and back in Texas they had mortars."

"Damn, they are like a small army." Marcus moved to a wall cabinet and opened it with a key. He pulled out a long drawer and grabbed a pair of M79 grenade launchers and added them to the cart, then squatted and opened a pair of doors on the cabinet below, exposing cases of 40mm ammunition. He pulled the cases out, and behind them were two pre-loaded grenade bandoliers. Marcus took them as well and placed them on the cart.

Tanya moved around and tossed one of the heavy canvas bags to the floor. "I found these uniforms in the basement. I thought maybe you might want them."

Tommy reached for the bag and unzipped it, pulling out a camouflage jacket. He held it up, seeing it was adorned with a Ground Division patch on the right shoulder. "It's been a while since I have seen these. What do you say, fellas? For the old days. Should we roll out in Ground Division tuxedos and really give these clowns a show?"

Winston, still struggling to sit up, said, "Save me a set —if they aren't all taken up by you fat guys."

Tanya moved closer and looked at the jacket Tommy had removed from the bag, pointing to a patch on the right shoulder. The patch was of a skull wearing a bonnie cap and skeleton fists gripping trench knives. "Does it represent anything, or is it just supposed to look cool?"

Tommy laughed. "Rule number one, always look cool." He could see she wasn't amused, so he turned the sleeve over and pointed at the patch. "Papa once told me the bonnie cap represented those clandestine warfighters that came before us, and that the trench knives meant we were able to get up close and shed blood."

He said the words and looked at Tanya. She had drawn back from him. He paused then looked back to the bags, fishing out trousers and boots.

She said, "I knew what you did, but I never really thought about it."

Tommy nodded. "It's okay; it's not something guys like me talk about on a date."

"But it's real, isn't it?" she said. "Like in the movies, you do go out and do the things that we don't want to know about. You guys kill people, don't you?"

Tommy stopped what he was doing. He could see

that she was bothered by it. Even after what they had been through over the last week, she was still in shock from all of it.

"Yeah, I kill things. Lots of things, but they are all bad things." He took a breath and looked at the bag of uniforms before him. "You know this doesn't change who I am, right? This is just a job. Some people put boxes on a shelf, I make assholes disappear." He stopped and looked back at her; he could see that her expression had softened.

Marcus had moved back to a panel near the main door. He was flipping switches that looked like circuit breakers. "I know it sounds odd, but after all the money we put into this place, all the defensive measures in the yard, all the weapons lockers, the cameras, the bunkers..." He moved to the corner and opened another door and flipped open another panel, swiping his hand down activating more switches. "Still, even with all of that, we never truly expected to be attacked here."

He took his hand off a bank of switches then turned to face them. With his hands on his hips, he gave them a massive grin. "Do you all have any idea how excited I am right now? All the time and effort I put into this place, and there is finally someone dumb enough to let me test all of this shit out."

"What does it all do?" Tanya asked the old Marine.

He looked back at the panel then walked to another cabinet under the bar. "Cameras, spotlights, sirens, laser motion sensors, old-school trip flares, all kinds of fun shit." From under the cabinet, he pulled a Glock 17 and an MP5. He looked back at Tanya. "Can you handle these?"

"I've been through the basic combat course," she said, standing straighter.

Marcus looked at her and frowned. "Well, I'm going to give these weapons to you anyway. Just don't hurt yourself, okay?" He looked at Tommy. "What are you thinking about all this?"

Tommy moved to the cart and grabbed one of the M79 grenade launchers. He looked it over, opened the breech, then snapped it back shut. He snatched a small bandoleer of mixed 40mm rounds and hung it off his shoulder. There was a suppressed reaper AR10 rifle on the table and he grabbed that too. "Marcus, I know this is your place and you have a plan for its defense, but you also know how I fight—I'm no good in here; I need to get out there and throw punches, ambush them on that trail, and slow them down."

Marcus pursed his lips and nodded. "I expected that."

The older man looked at the other faces in the room, then back at Tommy. "Go ahead and do your thing, hit them across the road and reduce their numbers. Stay on comms and report back to us on what you are doing, then lead them back this way."

He stepped closer to Tommy and the old Marine grabbed him behind the neck and pulled him close. "Tommy, you fuck them up, do you understand? Only after you are sure that they are broken and desperate, will you fall back here."

Marcus looked to the right. "When you fall back,

they'll think you're on the run. They'll rush the farm-house. They don't know this place; they'll assume that's where you are and go there first. They can't see the barn from the drive."

Tommy nodded his head and grimaced. This wasn't his first rodeo, and ambush science didn't compare to building rockets. "And you'll have the rest of the guys set up to eat them in the crossfire."

He grabbed a tactical vest and dropped it over his body. On the cart were already magazines loaded with .308 ammunition. He stuffed six into the front of his vest and three more on each side.

Hagan was beside him with Kidd on the other side. Tommy was ready to ask them where they would be during all his fighting, when Marcus filled him in.

"They don't know about this place; they'll be targeting the farmhouse. Tanya and Winston will stay back here to defend the Ranch. I'll put Kidd on the roof of the barn with a long rifle and thermal scope for over-watch. Hagan will be in a dugout on the corner of the driveway with a Browning machinegun. He'll be able to cover any vehicles that move on the road or driveway while you are out probing. I'll be in the farmhouse, waiting for you. Once you get there, we will all bound back here to the Ranch together and kill anything that's left."

"Wait," Tommy said, ignoring most of what Marcus had just said. "We have a Browning? When did you get an M2?"

Marcus looked at him like he was completely daft. "You do know what the fuck we do here, right? We kill people. Is an M2 .50-cal machine gun that far of a reach?"

Donovan held his gaze and put his hands up. "No judgment, bro." He looked at Hagan. "Just make sure you know where you shoot that thing if I'm going to be down-range. They tend to mess things up."

Hagan shrugged. "I'll manage. How long you think we got?"

Tommy grabbed the rifle and used a clip on the sling to attach it to his vest. Then he snapped the M79 under the apron on his chest armor. The last bit of gear was a throat mic and earpiece already sewn into the collar of his armor. "Those guys seemed pretty amped up. I suspect they would roll to the top of that hill then, after a good look around, start moving this way." Tommy checked his watch. He squinted and looked back at Hagan. "I should get moving."

CHAPTER THIRTY

The top of the hill was muddy in the pouring rain. Raul stood back from the trail as a large group of men stood around him, waiting for the order to move out. They checked weapons and smoked cigarettes. These were his soldiers, Kings, real killers from the streets of Colombia. They had no fear of a pair of wet rats hiding in the woods below them. Unlike the men he'd sent before, the ones that lay dead in the mud at the bottom of the hill, these men would fight. This wouldn't end like the rest of the hunts. This time he knew where the gringo was.

Raul scowled. This time, his numbers had doubled, and he knew the terrain in advance. Every day since the first encounter with this killer, the assassin would shoot then move on, only to ambush his men again. Every encounter with the killer, he had dealt them a deadly blow. Under normal circumstances, Raul would respect such a killer, admire him even. And even now, he might have a soft spot for the warrior if the man hadn't made the mistake of killing Diaz. For that, he would have to pay, and this is where it would end for him. Raul had called in everything he had left. Drivers, shooters, the thugs held in reserve—he had called all of them to this point.

Looking down the hill at the car park behind him, he could see three large flatbed trucks filled with troops. Beyond them, the remainder of the men he'd brought from home waited in their black SUVs. To his front, the hill sloped down steeply, following a trail that led into the woods. That is where they suspected the gringo and his new friend would be hiding. Just lying in wait, tucked into the dark woods, looking to ambush the cartel men as they chased him down the trail. But not today, this time Raul was planning the attack.

To the northeast, he knew from Victor's map overlays, was an old farm where they suspected the gringo would go next to catch a ride on a helicopter. But he will never make it there. Today this all ends, this distraction that had pulled him from the responsibilities of his sector. This obstruction, this challenge to his machismo, this embarrassment to a long career, today it would all end.

He seethed, thinking about the last week. All he was supposed to do was move into Texas and patrol some streets. To keep the peace and track down a few dangerous men. Instead, he had occupied himself with a single man, and because of this man he had managed to lose control of his entire operation, lose a sector, and one of his best friends.

Raul had called up the remaining forces of his Southwest Sector Vortex force. He'd strayed far from his area, crossing the Mississippi River. The Texans were pushing on his heels. The neighboring Vortex forces patrolling the Southeast were already occupied in the fighting in Atlanta. Raul had already called his friends in the east for more help and been turned down. He had allies south of the border moving here, but it would be days, if not weeks before they could join him. And still, this was one man, maybe two. He clenched his teeth; this was not the assignment he'd been contracted for.

He moved to a large rain-soaked stone and sat heavily. This fight was already lost. Apollo wouldn't win what they had started here, but that didn't mean he had nothing to gain himself. He wouldn't pursue any Apollo Group mission after this. Every move he made after the killing of the gringo would be in the name of La Raza de los Reyes. Apollo had no loyalty to his cause, and he had no loyalty to theirs.

He was done with Victor and Apollo Group. The Americans were in chaos, and he would take advantage of that. There was a vacuum. He had seen it with his own eyes traveling the country. His friends in the south would travel here and, together, they would move in reinforcements. Sure, Texas would be a problem, but they had routes to move around them and into the heartland. Soon this immediate task would be over, and he would focus on taking a foothold of his own in America.

But first, the gringo had to be dealt with. He knew the man wasn't already at the farmhouse; this gringo had a penchant for ambushes and there was a high possibility he was waiting in the woods below, waiting for his men to move in so that he could gun them down. He would plan to kill them, then run away again. Jose expected this and was already down the hill, leading a recon element.

Once Jose located the gringo, he would hold back and radio his position. Raul would then move down the hill with his group, attempting a flanking move, giving the gringo confidence that his plan was working. They would stop short of the man forcing him to come out of hiding, then pin him in a gunfight. All of this as the trucks would ferry in a secondary force to the gringo's rear. If the trucks moved in too early, the man would just disappear and wait until he had the right time to hit them. They had to corner him first. They had to pin him so that the reaction force could move in behind, crushing any plan of escape.

Raul smiled and, looking down at the woods, he whispered, "Not this time. If you run today, you will just find more of us behind you. Today we will kill you like a rat."

His radio beeped, and Raul grabbed it from a clip on his chest. "Go for lead."

"This is Spear," the man said. Raul never used call signs and code words, but Jose had demanded it. "I am at the bottom of the hill. There is a road here. We have seen no sign of the combatant. He may have already slipped across the road."

Raul stared at the radio. "He must be there, search the woods and proceed with caution until you find him."

There was a pause, then Jose said, "We are set up here on the low ground; we have a good spot. You should move your forces forward to this position and hold it while we begin a search.",

He considered the recommendation; he held the radio and as he prepared to order his men down the hill, he heard a pair of booms and gunfire from below. He took a startled step back. More booms and smoke began to fill the terrain below him. Jose had missed the target, but this plan could still succeed. He had to get his people behind the gringo. He put the radio to his mouth and yelled, "Move the trucks to the farm!"

CHAPTER THIRTY-ONE

Tommy was in the prone, his body buried in the leaves to the left of a large tree stump. To his front was the trail he'd traveled earlier in the day. The trail rolled up less than fifty meters from his hide then down and away from him before it twisted off in the distance toward the large hill. He couldn't see the hill through a heavy mist, and, in the downpouring rain, he couldn't hear any movement in the woods. This worried him. He wouldn't see or hear any attackers until they were right on top of him. But the same would prove true for the men hunting him.

The rifle was propped up to his front. The M79 was by his side with his left hand on the stock, the weapon already loaded with a buckshot round filled with hundreds of ball bearings. The rest of the bandoleer was positioned next to it. He tapped the earpiece, turning on the radio device sewn into his collar of his vest. "Tommy is ready," he whispered.

"Hagan set."

"Kidd locked and cocked."

"Marcus is a go."

"Winston is up."

A snapping of a branch caused him to hold his breath and freeze. The largest part of not being detected was not moving. He held completely still, only allowing his eyes to scan the terrain to his front. A man was breaking out of the mist, walking slowly. Crouched down, he carried a rifle in his right hand as his left moved tree limbs out of the way. The man was moving on a line that ran parallel the trail. If Tommy held his position, the man would pass less than twelve meters to his front. But that wasn't going to happen; that wasn't why he'd set up here in the rain.

Tommy watched as the man took three more steps then knelt. He held his rifle up to his eyes as two more men patrolled forward. They stopped on the left and right side of him. The man to the left pulled up a rifle, looking out. The man on the right did the same. Moments later, another pair of men appeared at the rise of the trail further to his right. "Shit," Tommy whispered.

"What is it?" Hagan came back. He was the closest to Tommy's position, being just across the road in a hidden position by the driveway gate.

Tommy had forgotten the line was open. He blinked away the rain and said, "They are moving in a line formation, spread out across my front. They are searching. I got five targets; I'm about to go hot."

"Good hunting," Hagan replied.

Tommy tightened his grip on the M79 single-shot grenade launcher and pulled it toward him as he brought his right arm across his body to help brace the recoil. He looked out and could see the three men in the woods. One of them now had his rifle down and a handheld radio to his mouth. Tommy couldn't hear the words, but it didn't matter. He adjusted the aim of the Thumper and pulled the trigger.

A loud blast overcame all other sounds in the forest as a 40mm shotgun round ate a path to his front, plowing through vegetation and leaving a wake of white smoke. Rifles began firing from his right, and Tommy buried his head in the wet leaves as he loaded another buckshot round. Not taking time to aim, he pointed in the same direction then fired again. Another loud boom, and the breaking of tree limbs filled the forest floor. He grabbed the last three blue-tipped rounds in the bandoleer. He knew they were all tear gas, and exactly what he wanted.

He loaded the first, this time aimed at the rise in the trail and thumped it out. He loaded the second and fired in the same spot, only higher. On the third round, a man came over the rise on the hill. He spotted Tommy and raised his rifle. Tommy rolled hard to the left and leveled the M79 and put a tear gas canister right into the man's face. It did the job, and the enemy shooter tumbled back down the far side of the trail as the round bounded into the brush and began spewing its smoke.

Tommy grabbed the rifle and sprinted back to a downed log he'd spotted on the walk in. He dove behind it just as rounds kicked up the earth around him. He cursed, knowing there were a hell of a lot more men in the element than he'd expected.

"How are you doing over there?" He recognized Marcus's voice.

"Busy," Tommy said.

He crawled to the left of the log and peeked out. A man with an AK47 was on the trail's highpoint, firing into the vicinity of his last location. Tommy stayed low and brought up his rifle, firing two rounds, both finding their target. The man's rifle flew into the brush as his body collapsed to the trail.

"Trucks on the road, trucks on the road!" Hagan shouted over the radio. "You need to pull back or you're going to get cut off."

Tommy peeked over the log again and could see that the tear gas was doing its job to slow the enemy advance. The trail area to his front was obscured in smoke. He looked to the spot where the trio of men had been. The vegetation was torn up. He saw a pair of boots, but the other two men were gone. He rose to a knee, keeping the rifle at his ready, then bounded back the remaining distance to the shoulder of the road.

He heard rounds zip past him from the hill; they'd already spotted him. He dove into more cover and turned back to see a group of men who were coughing and running on the trail. They were firing from the hip as they searched for cover. Tommy turned his weapon on them and opened fire. The men jumped to the ground, rolling into the thick brush on the sides of the packed earth.

He leaned forward and fired several rounds to keep their heads down then went to move again, immediately drawing more fire and forcing him back to the ground. He thought of the M79's high explosive rounds then cursed himself for leaving the weapon in his last position. "Shit, they are trying to pin me," Tommy said.

"These trucks are getting closer," Hagan said. "You've got to move, or we'll be cut off from each other."

Tommy rose again, taking intense fire. He rolled away and could hear more gunfire coming from his left. "They planned this," Tommy said. "They want those trucks to bracket me in."

"I'll open up with the machine gun and stop them," Hagan shouted. "Then I'll turn in your way and you can run in under the rounds."

Peeking over the rise, he could see them now. A group of five men off to his left in the cover of the heavy trees, coughing and gagging from the gas. To the right, others were crawling forward along the trail. He looked back behind him; the road was less than a fifteen-meter sprint but, looking out to the south, he could already see the glint of the trucks.

"Wait," Tommy said. "If you fire now, they'll know we have people across the road. They'll just dismount and hit us from the back."

Tommy again rose and fired rounds into the group of the trees to try to slow the enemy approach. He watched them immediately pull back. "They aren't moving at me, Hagan; this was the plan all along. They wanted to surround me and cut me off from the road. They don't know there is anyone else. Let's let them box me in."

"How does that help you right now?" Hagan asked. "Getting killed or captured doesn't do us any good."

"Let them set up on the road. I'll give the word, then you light them up." Tommy popped off another burst of rounds at the trail, keeping the men's heads down. He then said, "I'll get out of here in the chaos, meet you at the dugout."

Tommy put his head into the earth. He could feel the sting in his eyes as the tear gas settled into the woods, covering the wet ground like a blanket. He'd had plenty of experience with the riot gas and it hardly fazed him anymore. The men to his front were not fairing as well. He could see them rubbing their eyes and firing wildly in his direction. Tommy hugged the earth and crawled into a low spot, clawing the ground to pull himself forward.

He could hear the trucks roll up on the road behind him. Men in the backs were shouting in Spanish. A door opened. He dared a look to his left and could see three large flatbed trucks filled with men. It was a lot more than he had expected to see. Tommy looked back to his right. Emboldened by the sight of the reinforcements, the men in the woods were moving again.

"Now or never," Hagan said.

Tommy pulled his head down, trying to become one with the forest floor. "Get after it, brother."

The heavy machine gun raised hell as a response. Loud and thundering through the woods, there was no other sound in a fight like a fifty-caliber machine gun going cyclic. Tommy pressed up and looked right. The men in the woods were gone—they'd all dived to cover. He didn't even bother looking left; instead, he took off in a leopard-crawl, moving through the vegetation as quickly as he could. He made it fifty meters without drawing fire then cut left and ran to the shoulder of the road.

Squatting, he could see Hagan's position in the low light, flame spouting from the barrel of his machine gun. Behind him were the destroyed trucks, bodies lying in the street. Other men had escaped the carnage and were hiding in a depression at the side of the road. Tommy took advantage of the suppressive fire and sprinted to the ranch side of the road, diving into cover far behind the dugout.

"I'm across," he gasped.

There was no response. Tommy knew Hagan's hearing would be trashed from firing the machine gun. There was a break in the fire.

Hagan shouted into the radio, "Reloading."

Tommy spun back with his rifle in the direction of the now burning trucks lying on the shoulder of the road. He pointed his rifle toward the vehicles. With the lull in the firing, men rose from the ditch. They were shouting through the smoke. There was confusion among the group, not having expected the second attack. A pair of men attempted to sprint across the road to take on the machine gun. Tommy snapped off quick shots, hitting one, who faceplanted to the gravel road. He missed the other.

"One got by me," Tommy said. "He's moving up the driveway."

"Target down," Kidd said. The man was hundreds of meters away in the attic of the barn; he had wide fields of fire.

Tommy looked back to the road. Beyond the three burning flatbed trucks, five more of the regular black SUVs were in the road. Men were dismounting and moving to the shoulder. "We got problems. I see at least twenty crossing the road on the southwest."

He raised his rifle and looked through the scope. Too many to stop from his range. He opened fire, anyway, hitting one and forcing the rest to dive to the ground. It was time for him to move. "Hagan, you up? I could use some cover."

"Gotcha covered," Hagan said as the machine gun roared again.

The already destroyed and burning trucks were raked with more fire. Then the gun swiveled out and fired on a line of the black SUVs, the men thinking they were out of range. Tommy rolled out of his cover and ran onto the Ranch property, cutting through trees until finally hitting the tall grass, where he dove. Rounds were flying overhead; he could hear them buzz past, as men in the woods fired blindly in his direction. He was crawling along the ground, following an unmarked path that would zigzag him through the property's sensors. He broke out of the grass at the corner of the driveway just behind the dugout where Hagan was working the heavy machine gun.

The weapon stopped firing again, and the enemy fire increased. Kidd's rifle picked up the slack, sniping at men bold enough to rush the machine gun position. Tommy ran to the dugout.

"Moving to you, Hagan, from your six," he shouted just as he reached the back of the small poured-concrete square. It was essentially a bunker, but for a casual observer, it would look like a place to stack garbage cans. Hagan was down behind the weapon, trying to load another belt of ammo. The Browning was white-hot, the barrel sizzling as the rainwater hit it.

Tommy moved in beside him with his rifle up. He fired into the road at targets as they exposed themselves.

A voice came through Tommy's earpiece. "You boys need to fall back." This time it was Marcus in the farmhouse. "Your element of surprise is gone; they are all over the fields to the south of the farmhouse. You need to get in here so I can cover the back."

"Come on, bro, we've got to bounce," Tommy said to Hagan.

Hagan scowled; he'd nearly had the weapon back up. He tossed the ammo can into the thick grass behind him. Using a heavy glove, he pulled the weapon into cover and removed the barrel and trigger assembly then tossed them behind him, as well. The big man reached down below and grabbed his carbine. He put a hand on Tommy's back, letting him know he was ready to move.

"We're headed to the house; give us cover," Tommy said on the comms.

"Go," Kidd said, his rifle barking.

"Moving," Tommy shouted back as he ducked low and sprinted for the farmhouse. The barn would have been a shorter distance, but they needed the bad guys to focus on the house. To stay away from Kidd in the attic. And the closer they got to the barn, the odds of them finding the Ranch in the northern woods grew. He ran up the driveway then cut over a split-rail fence, jumping across a set of ancient planters and finally running up the porch, taking the stairs two at a time. He didn't even bother using the knob. He led with his shoulder and exploded through the front door.

Tommy hit the ground hard, but as he went to get up, he was blasted from behind as Hagan flew in and landed on top of him. Together they crawled across the wood floor as rounds peppered the doorframe and walls. Then the firing stopped. All of it.

Tommy moved to the center of the family room and collapsed on his back, exhausted. "What's going on out there?" he asked.

Tommy blinked his eyes then rolled back to his belly and crawled deeper into the living room of the old farmhouse, stopping next to a red-brick fireplace. The home was empty of furniture, every surface covered with a thin coating of dust.

There was a large family room and a hall down the center that led to a large kitchen. On the back wall was an open staircase that led to three bedrooms. Tommy knew the layout from running drills in the house. He knew that the home's walls up to the windowsills were made of fieldstone.

Kidd's voice came through the comms. "They're backing off, running back across the road to hide in the trees. Looks like someone is trying to regroup and rally them."

"No, they are just pussies, afraid to run through all of that open grass while we shoot at them," Marcus said, his voice coming across as a hoarse whisper.

Tommy looked around the room, searching for the old Marine. "Marcus, where the hell are you?"

"Upstairs bedroom watching the back approach. What's your status?"

Tommy looked at his arms and legs then looked over at Hagan squatting at a window across the room from him. The man shot Tommy a thumbs up. "We're good, boss. What's the play?" Tommy said as he fished a drinking tube from his gear and began gulping water. He looked at his watch. It was growing late; the sun would be setting soon.

There was a long pause before the Marine answered. "I suspect they'll be waiting for dark."

"How you think we did?" Hagan asked.

Tommy shook his head. "I couldn't see much. I know I hit a few of them. You put a hurting on those troop trucks." He leaned out and tried to look through the window. He could see the tree line but no movement. "I can't see anything. Kidd, what do you see?"

"Don't go distracting Kidd," Marcus said. "Winston, what's on the security monitors?"

There was a long delay then the man back in the Ranch answered. "Like you all suspected, the sensors all along the tree line are blipping. Nothing on the cameras. System is saying thirty unique ground targets." There was a sigh. "If the plan was to get outnumbered and pinned down, mission accomplished."

Marcus laughed. "Hell, we ain't pinned down. We got them all in a line—just setting up a traditional shooting gallery. I suggest you all get comfy, cause as soon as the sun comes down, they'll move in for the kill."

CHAPTER THIRTY-TWO

R aul walked behind the burnt-out trucks, still feeling the heat from their fires. Snot was running from his nose as his eyes watered. Jose walked up beside him. The man was carrying an AK47, and he was wearing a tan chest rig loaded with magazines. The man looked at Raul then handed him a towel. The senior cartel man took the rag and wiped his face. He took a step and nearly tripped over the body of a fallen soldier.

"It's just the gas. Its effect will fade," Jose said.

Raul's eyes swept the dark terrain, dead men lay all over the ground, illuminated by the flames of the vehicles. He coughed again. "What happened?"

"Most of them never got out of the trucks," Jose said. "The other teams are in position up the road. We can hit the house with close to thirty men as soon as it is dark."

Raul shook his head. "That son of a bitch, Victor. He set me up. All of this was him—this list they created, this man they sent us after, all of it was Victor."

Shrugging, Jose said, "Maybe, or just a clever

counter-ambush on their part. These things happen in combat."

Raul seethed and went to pull his weapon, but Jose was faster. He caught the cartel man on the draw and grabbed the slide of the CZ pistol. "Oh no, senor, I mean no disrespect," Jose said, his cold eyes locked on Raul's. "Yes, we were outplayed, but I don't think this was set up; nobody knew our plan. These moves couldn't have been predicted."

The cartel man was stunned but impressed with the man's aggressiveness. He nodded and re-holstered the weapon. "What do we do now? We have no more men in reserve. Our friends from the south are days away, and anyone else loyal to La Raza de los Reyes is busy fighting in the east."

Jose looked down and then stepped closer to Raul, lowering his voice. "You should leave."

"Leave?" Raul said, his voice not covering the surprise. "And just let them go?"

Nodding, Jose said, "Yes, leave. You are a general, not a captain." Jose said the words, looking at Raul for recognition that he instantly received. "You said earlier that the Americans were moving in a team to recover this man. If you stay, you risk being killed or captured. I suggest you leave tonight. I will stay behind to coordinate this attack; you go and plan our next move." He paused and put a hand on Raul's shoulder, squeezing it. "Is this man truly your mission? Is this why you came to America?"

Raul shook his head; despair was filling his gut. This man, a foot soldier in his ranks, could see clearly what he had been ignoring for days. His entire mission had been lost in the pursuit of a single man. "No, this is not what we came here for, Jose." He whispered, "We came to gain a foothold, but all I have done is lose men."

"Then what do you want to do, senor? The choice is yours. The soldiers will follow you."

Raul sighed and walked toward a tree and leaned back against it. He could see the outline of the farmhouse in the reflections of the flames. He wanted nothing more than to kill the man inside. But he considered the phone call. This man worked for someone, he had connections to the President, that was his true enemy, not some fighter.

He nodded. "Jose, we will leave the men here to continue the assault. Have my vehicle brought up; we will travel to Atlanta to join our comrades there."

Jose smiled. "Very well, senor. I will prepare a plan for the men's assault against the farm. I can lead them myself."

"No," Raul said. He looked at the younger man and grabbed his forearm. "I will need your guidance in the war to come. Brief the men and ready our vehicle."

CHAPTER THIRTY-THREE

The burning trucks cast an eerie glow over the fields to the front of the farmhouse. Tommy had moved to a window that overlooked the front lawn. Hagan was on the side of the house, looking out over the right side of the approach. Marcus up top had the back, and Kidd in the barn could see over the left side and road. There had been no movement since the enemy shooters had pulled back. No demands, no messengers with white flags. It was as if they had all vanished.

"I got something," Kidd said. The man was in the attic of the barn, holding a high-powered rifle equipped with a thermal scope.

"I see it too," Hagan called out. "Vehicle on the road. It's moving really slow with the headlights off."

"Vehicle has one driver, no other packs; you want me to kill it?" Kidd asked.

"No, watch and wait," Marcus ordered.

Tommy held his position, looking out over the field to his front. As the vehicle continued, it moved into his view. It slowed as it neared the burning trucks, moving closer to the near side of the road to avoid them. The billowing fires exposed the profile of the vehicle and the single driver.

"Looks like a Toyota Land Cruiser," Tommy said. "I confirm a single driver."

"I got two more targets. They are leaving the woods, entering the vehicle," Kidd said.

Before anyone else could speak, Tommy watched as the vehicle raced away on the road headed east.

"Well, that was fucking weird," Kidd said.

"Maybe they are headed out for a beer run?" Hagan said.

"I could really use a beer right now," Tommy added.

Tommy shifted his position and looked out over the field with his night-vision goggles down over his eyes. Far to his right, a bloom of bright light erupted, then a high-pitched whistle and a klaxon siren. Strobe lights illuminated in the trees. Tommy pushed up the washed-out NODs from his eyes and looked out over the sights of his rifle.

"Here they come boys!" Hagan said moments before Tommy heard the man's rifle fire. Tommy looked out as his position was raked with gunfire, forcing him back into the cover of the house.

Kidd's radio erupted; Tommy could hear the firing of the man's rifle over the comms. "I see two groups of ten. One north and south and a third group right down the middle. Aww, hell, they spotted me; I'm going to have to re-position."

The bad guys had wised up. The men were coming

at them from two corners of the field, supporting each element with fire as they moved. In the center directly to Tommy's front, a third line of concealed gunners was firing on the windows of the house. Tommy looked across the room and could see that Hagan had also been forced to duck inside. "We got to get off this wall," Hagan shouted from across the room. "We can't stop them from rushing if we are pinned."

The men outside were fighting and moving as a unit now. They were blasting the front of the farmhouse. Tommy hugged the floor and crawled toward the kitchen. He heard footfalls on the porch outside. "Breach, breach, breach, main entrance!" Hagan yelled.

Tommy rolled hard and watched as the first man ran through the open doorway with his weapon up. He was scanning left to right when he was cut down with three shots from Hagan's rifle. Tommy rolled to his back. With his feet pointed toward the door, he did a sit-up, holding his rifle out in front, and rapid-fired into a stack of men pouring through the front door. As men rushed into the house, the fire continued blasting at the walls.

Hagan was separated on the far side of the room, trapped by the incoming fire. He raised his rifle and fired over the windowsill, doing nothing to slow the assault. Tommy heard more steps on the porch. This time, instead of an assault, a grenade rolled in and bounced off a back wall. "Frag!" Tommy screamed. He contorted his body, leapt for the grenade, and slapped it back out of the open door. He curled into a ball and the grenade exploded just as it landed on the porch.

His ears were ringing now and his eyes watering

from the caustic smoke. He held his rifle up one-handed and fired a burst at a flash of movement. The bolt locked back, and he tossed the rifle to the side, drawing his sidearm with his right hand and using his left to rise to a squat. A gunshot from behind hit his backplate and spun him around. He rolled with the motion and again found himself lying on the floor, looking into the face of a charging man. Tommy leveled his pistol. The man to his front was peppered with gunfire from Hagan. The enemy soldier took a final step then fell past Tommy, colliding with the wall.

Tommy rolled to his side and focused on the hallway to the kitchen, where the man had entered. There was movement and he fired a volley of rounds to slow them down.

"They're inside," he shouted over the radio.

He looked across the room and could see Hagan was already moving to the back of the house, so Tommy turned again to cover the front door.

He heard them outside again. He raised his pistol and shot high on the wall, where he assumed the men would be stacking up. He heard a scream and a man ran into the entrance. Tommy fired twice more, hitting him. Then they were on him, the stack charging in. They moved in fast, no time to reload, he leapt at the attackers.

He collided with the first one, grabbing the man in a bear hug around his hips, and lifted him up and charged toward a third man. Together, they tumbled out onto the porch. Tommy hit the ground, landing on top of the man he'd hugged. The man wasn't moving—probably unconscious from the hard fall. Tommy pulled a knife from his chest rig and plunged it deep into the side of the man's neck, not waiting for him to recover.

He rolled off, finding himself in the high grass in front of the porch. He was on his knees, a knife in his hands with his arms covered in blood. The enemy had lost sight of him. He could see the enemy soldiers in the yard, but they were all focused on the house. They didn't know he'd gone outside. With the vehicle fires to his back, he could see the shadowy movements on the porch, the muzzle flashes from inside the house.

He couldn't find his pistol; he'd dropped it somewhere. Tommy pushed aside any fear he had left in his body and charged up the steps at the remaining men. A soldier at the door waiting to enter turned as he approached. Tommy slashed out with the blade, catching the man under the chin, ripping out the man's throat. He bounded past the bleeding man and collided with another stacked immediately behind him, pinning the man to the wall. The soldier held an AK47. Tommy pressed it against the wall with his left hand as he plunged the blade into the man's stomach with his right. He snatched the weapon away from the man's weakening grip and dropped back onto the porch, leaning against the wall.

A column of men, thinking they had taken control of the farmhouse were sprinting up the driveway. Tommy leveled on the center of the group with the Russian rifle and fired in full auto. He watched the men fall from hits as others searched for cover. He stood and ran forward, jumping over the porch rail. He ran into the yard, firing into the bodies from the hip. When his rifle ran dry, he tossed it to the side and grabbed another from the dead.

He was in the yard now, behind the clusters of approaching men. He was looking into the backs of the advancing soldiers. His brain had pushed all other thoughts aside and was focused on the fight. He could see their shadowy forms moving through the field in the dark. He stood with the rifle to his eye as he walked from left to right across the front yard, taking careful shots, dropping men where they stood.

Again, his rifle emptied, and he recovered another from the dead. Looking out now, he couldn't find a target. He took a step forward and felt weak. His hands were shaking, and his legs were heavy. He staggered another two steps toward the house and took a knee. The gunfire had lessened, there were still muzzle flashes and booms from inside the house, but the yard was clear. He had lost contact with his team and had been fighting alone.

"Somebody talk to me," he shouted. Not hearing any response, he put his bloodied hand to his ear and realized the earpiece had fallen out; it was hanging from the coiled cord.

As soon as it was in, he heard Marcus, shout, "Back-yard is clear."

"This is Kidd, I had to bail out of the barn, I'm clear."

Tommy looked toward the barn but couldn't see anything in the darkness. He pushed back up to his feet and staggered to the porch steps still holding the AK47. The front of the home was destroyed. The porch covered with mangled bodies. Tommy stepped over them. There were more dead in the entrance. He saw his pistol. He knelt and picked it up then holstered it. His AR10 was in the corner, the stock destroyed. He saw movement at the back of the room and raised his rifle then quickly lowered it as he stared into the smiling face of Hagan.

Something was wrong. The man sat with his knees bent, his back against the hallway wall. His rifle was beside him. Tommy took another step, and he could see that Hagan had his hand held against the left side of his rib cage.

"You okay, brother?" Tommy said.

Hagan frowned and held up his right hand covered in blood.

"Aww, hell, Hagan is hit," Tommy said before rushing forward.

He knelt beside his friend. Immediately he could see that there was a lot of blood. He heard boots pounding down the stairs, and quickly, Marcus was over them, holding a flashlight.

Tommy rolled Hagan to his side, pushing his right arm out of the way. The side of his Kevlar vest was torn where a round had passed through just below the man's armpit. Tommy pulled his knife and cut away the fabric, rewarded with a ripped T-shirt soaked in blood.

"Get the light closer," he said.

He found where the round had caught Hagan. It hit the flesh and tore away the meat then deflected off his ribs, pulling out the back side. He probed the wound as Hagan howled. It was a nasty gouge, but he'd live. Tommy grabbed Hagan by the face and looked at him closely.

"It just bounced off your ribs, you lucky bastard."

Hagan shook his head with clenched teeth. "Funny, I don't feel so lucky."

"Get out of the way, son," Marcus said, moving Tommy aside. The older Marine already had a kit opened and a field dressing in his hand.

Tommy did as he was told and scooted away from the wall and walked back into the main room. Making his way over the dead, he stepped onto the porch. He scanned the field, seeing the destruction and death. Tommy shook his head, wondering what it was all for. All this killing, and he still had no idea why. He looked at his watch. The flight would be there soon, and he was determined to get answers.

CHAPTER THIRTY-FOUR

The dark-green MV-22 Osprey circled over the Ranch then dropped in altitude and came in from the north, landing on a wide-open field at the back of the property. Tommy immediately recognized it as one of the President's escort aircraft. He looked at Marcus and shrugged.

"You know shit has hit the fan when the old man sends his personal ride down here for you," Marcus said. "Hope you're ready for this, son."

Tommy kept his eyes on the Osprey as the back ramp dropped. His pack was to his side, a rifle strapped to the top, while Tanya and Winston stood just behind him.

Marcus put a hand on his shoulder. "You sure you don't want to take Solomon?" the old Marine asked.

He shook his head no. "We should stay in pairs, and Hagan is banged up. He'll need some downtime before he can fight again." Tommy stared at the aircraft as four armed men ran out, securing the ground around the back ramp. Two more men began walking in his direction.

"Kidd will take care of Hagan. If we need something, I'll send word."

Marcus nodded and squinted. Then he laughed and said, "Well, hell, look what the cat dragged in." He stepped toward the approaching men.

One was obviously part of a security detail, but the other man Tommy knew. The man leading the pack, headed in his direction, was Tyler Spence. Tommy grinned and stood his ground. Marcus continued forward, greeting the man. Tanya was by his side now. He looked at her. "You could stay here; it might be safer than whatever it is we are getting into."

Tanya looked at him and twisted her face. "Yeah, the last thing I want to do is stay here." She turned and looked at him. "Listen, Tommy, I think—"

Tommy smiled. "Let me guess: 'It's not you, it's me.' Right?"

She shook her head. "Oh no, Tommy, this is all you." She frowned and touched his cheek then walked toward the aircraft.

Winston laughed. "I don't think anyone wants to stay here after the landscaping job you boys did last night." Winston reached down and grabbed his pack and started walking toward the Osprey.

Tanya looked back at Tommy. "Are you coming?"

He nodded and told her to go on ahead. Tommy stayed where he was until Tyler stopped in front of him. The man hadn't aged a day since the last time he'd seen him over a decade ago. That was back when he was still running the Ground Division.

"You look like shit, Tommy," the man said. "You do

know you are going to the President's retreat, right?"

Tommy looked at his uniform... the bloodstains on the rolled-up sleeves, the mud and dirt on his pant legs... he shrugged. "Guess I missed laundry day. Should we reschedule?"

The man smiled. "It's good to see you. I saw Winston —where are the other guys?"

Shaking his head, Tommy said, "Hagan took a round last night. Kidd is going to stay back with him."

Tyler looked down at the ground. He bit at his lower lip then nodded his agreement. "Yeah, that's probably a good plan. Marcus will take care of them, make sure they stay operational."

Tyler stepped to the side and lifted Tommy's rifle off his bag and handed it to him. Then he took Tommy's bag. "Come on, we've got to move; I can brief you on the flight back."

Tommy followed the man to the back of the aircraft and up the ramp. Tanya and Winston were already seated partway up, in black fabric jump seats attached to the aircraft's walls. Tyler took a seat and pointed to an empty one across from him. As Tommy sat, he watched the Marine guards run up the rear ramp, and the aircraft began to climb as the ramp closed.

Tommy fastened a waist belt then accepted a pair of headphones from Tyler. He was ready to suggest passing a headset back to Winston, but he could tell the man had already fallen asleep. Tommy grinned and donned the headgear and pulled the microphone close to his lips. He looked at the man across from him and said, "So what do you want me to do at Camp David?"

"You're not going to David—you're not staying there, anyway."

Smirking, Tommy said, "Okay, then, where am I going?"

This time it was Tyler who smirked. He pointed to Tommy's sleeve and the Ground Division patch. "You planning to get the band back together?"

"I figured that was why you called."

"Not sure what you know about the situation, Donovan," Tyler said. "Things are happing fast and even we are struggling to keep up."

"Can you give me the high-level brief, and then tell me what you want me to kill?" Tommy said.

"Well, there have been rumors that someone dropped an EMP over Washington D.C. The entire East Coast from Maryland to Florida is without power or communications, with no estimate on when we can get them back up. The national media and some high-placed government officials are accusing the President of launching a high-orbit nuclear device on his own White House." Tyler paused to look at Tommy for recognition.

Tommy's face remained hard. He nodded. "Sounds like a pretty shitty thing to do. So, what really happened?"

Tyler grimaced. "We think it was a cyber intrusion. As the President left the White House and positioned himself at Camp David, we believe an outside source attacked the D.C. area power plants. Those plants went down hard, the grid was quickly overloaded, and the ripple effect blew lines and transformers down the East Coast." Tyler sighed. "Along with it, cell tower, telecommunication hubs, Internet service providers, and anything running electronics was scrammed. We don't know how, but most of the Capital District is a dead zone now."

"So, you know who did it, and you want me to go kill them and get the lights back on," Tommy said, his expression still fixed. "I'm not much with electronics, but that other thing I can help with."

Tyler shook his head. "I wish it was that simple. Yesterday afternoon the Vice President was in Chicago at a naval base north of the city. He was prepared to present evidence to the nation in a national address that the EMP was a false flag and that the perpetrators are executing a coup d'état."

"How did that work out?" Tommy asked.

"Tommy, Vice President Christopher Michaels is dead, along with millions of others. Chicago is gone..."

This time Tommy's jaw dropped, and he felt his stomach begin to turn. His poker face was gone. "How?"

"There was a nuclear detonation on the naval base. We know that it came from one of our Minuteman VII silos in North Dakota. The media is again blaming the President. We have reached out to US Strategic Command, but they don't know how it happened; the silo crew was found dead outside the launch facility late last night. They assure us that there is no way the crew could have fired the missile on their own. We have managed to save the remainder of the arsenal, but the damage is done. Half the population thinks that the President of the United States has escalated a civil war."

"Where does the military stand in all of this?" Tommy asked.

Tyler frowned. "As you can imagine, the reaction is mixed. We are facing wide numbers of desertions and Reserve and National Guard personnel are at incapable numbers. The people that have shown up have no stomach to fight a war against our own population. For the time being, the President has ordered them to shelter inside their bases."

"I don't understand. Where I do fall into all of this? What exactly do you expect me to do?"

"We believe we know who is responsible for all of this. He is still in the Capital. We have assets on the ground there that have tracked him to an office structure south of the city."

"Who are the assets?" Tommy asked.

"A couple of O'Connell's men. We flew them in last night. They have made contact via satellite phone. Kyle Emmerson and Randolph Whittaker. Do you know them?"

"I've heard the names," Tommy said. "Who is the target?"

"Charles Shafer," Tyler said quickly.

Tommy raised his eyebrows. "Charles Shafer, the United States Senator?"

"This isn't the first time we've had to clean house at home," Tyler said.

"You want me to kill a senator?" Tommy asked. "Those are my orders?"

Tyler shook his head. "No, that can't happen. We need him alive to clear the President. If Shafer dies, it's going to be all-out war." He sighed and looked back at Tommy. "When we land at Camp David, you'll be met with another team. They have a Black Hawk already spinning up. You'll move with them and be dropped near the Washington Navy Yard. You'll move in with the team, take custody of the Senator, then call for extraction, and return here."

Tommy looked at the man with a sideways glare. "Sounds super easy, and I imagine this guy is really excited to come with me. What else should I know?"

Tyler looked out at the front of the aircraft then back. "Well, Camp David is under direct contact and under serious threat of being overrun. We are currently under evacuation orders as the base defense holds the lines." The intel man looked up at the ceiling like he was searching for something. "Let' see, what else? Oh yeah, we think criminal elements of a drug cartel are operating on US soil and there is risk of foreign nations getting involved."

"Anything else?" Tommy asked.

"Kyle called in this morning and said another team may be protecting Shafer."

"Cool," Tommy said.

Tyler smirked. "Yeah, it's pretty cool." His face turned serious. "If you can't pull this off, we're screwed, you know that, right?"

Tommy didn't answer; he just put his head back in the seat, not lifting it back up until he felt the aircraft bank hard and begin to corkscrew in for a combat landing. He looked back into the crew compartment and saw Tanya. Her eyes were fixed straight ahead. She was

ignoring him, and he was okay with that. She was probably better off not being connected to him; he knew
Tyler would make sure she stayed safe. The MV-22
bucked and changed direction again. Winston opened
his eyes and looked back at him. The man shot a thumbs
up with his tightly taped arm.

The bird landed, and the back ramp began to drop.
The Marine guards were quickly on their feet and
running out. Tommy grabbed his pack and got in the line
exiting the aircraft. As he walked out, he could see crews
rushing in to refuel the Osprey. Outside, he saw that the
camp really was under assault. Marines were running
back and forth, ferrying ammunition out to the perimeter. There were sandbag walls built up along a walkway
with civilians lined up, sheltering against them, holding
small backpacks. He could hear distant gunfire and
explosions.

Tommy looked at the civilians and pointed as Tyler
moved up beside him. "What the hell are they doing out
here?"

Tyler frowned and pointed at the Osprey they'd just
exited. "They were waiting for that; we're evacuating the
camp."

Ahead Tommy saw a group of six men with dark
green helmets. Tyler pointed at them and said, "The
grunts are from Campbell, they came with the UH-60.
That's your team now, grab Winston and move out.
They'll give you the details in route." Before Tommy
could say anything, else Tyler was gone. Winston had
moved up beside him, he went to look for Tanya but
before he could find her, she had grabbed him in a tight

hug. She pulled back, looked him in the eye then kissed him on the cheek, then ran off after Tyler without speaking.

Tommy looked at Winston who just shrugged and said, "I think she's pissed at you Bro."

They walked together to the end of the sandbag wall, at the end there were more civilians gathered waiting to join the evacuation lines.

"This is going to be a shit show," Tommy said.

Winston grunted and moved closer, "I hear they are all headed to Dover." The man shook his head, "I doubt they'll find anything better out there."

Tommy grimaced and looked at the soldiers in the dark green helmets, they were suddenly distracted, their eyes had turned to a tree line. One of them pointed and another raised his rifle and fired.

Tommy searched out to the tree line and saw it too. A half dozen men in black body armor were running at the airfield with weapons blazing. He heard a woman scream to his front as rounds impacted the ground all around her and a young boy. Men began dragging the woman and boy toward the awaiting Helicopters when the boy broke free.

"Aww hell," Tommy said to himself. He lunged forward, firing at the attackers as he ran after the boy. He closed on the little man fast and scooped him up with his free hand tucking the struggling boy in close to his side. He turned sideways shielding the kid with his body as he fired, and shuffle stepped back to the wall.

Reaching the sandbag barrier, he scanned and could see the attacker's bodies lying in the grass. Tommy turned back, the woman and other civilians were gone, the Marines had them near the waiting Helicopters. Tommy located the panicked mother frantic to get away from a Marine holding her back. The boy was kicking and squirming, Tommy tightened his grip and quick stepped in the direction of the evac birds. He was ready to scold the boy, but when he sat him on the deck of the waiting helo he could see the fear in the kid's eyes.

Looking at the boy Tommy gulped and asked. "Are you okay?"

The boy nodded his head and said. "Can you help me find my dad?"

"Your Dad?" Tommy said.

The Mother moved up and took her son in a tight hug from behind. "I'm sorry, his father is a Marine out on the line, he doesn't understand why he isn't going with us."

Tommy nodded, then he removed the Velcro Ground Division patch from his shoulder. "What's your name?"

The boy looked at his mother who nodded, he said "Andrew Mason."

"Listen Andrew, your Dad is out there protecting people, just like I am protecting people here." He handed Andrew the unit patch, "I'm giving you this, and that means that now you will be responsible for protecting your mom okay. Make sure she gets on one of those helicopters, do you understand me?"

The boy took the patch and squeezed it in his hand, and even though his eyes welled up with tears he said, "okay." Tommy nodded and stood. The Dark Green helmets were now waving impatiently for him to move.

CHAPTER THIRTY-FIVE

Tommy climbed into the Black Hawk with the others piling into the compartment, all of them sitting against the walls with packs in the middle.

A soldier wearing Sergeant First Class rank on his collar extended a hand. "I'm Wyatt."

Tommy extended his hand and noticed the soldier's fatigues were as torn and bloody as his own. Tommy scanned the crew compartment. Everyone in it was beat to shit. He gripped the sergeant's hand and said, "I'm Donovan. Looks like you've had some trouble."

The man grinned. "Been a long day for all of us."

"Who are they fighting down there?" Tommy asked.

"Mostly Vortex, but some scumbag National Guard guys have switched sides as well. There is a Colonel Price leading the way. Last I heard, he had a battalion of turncoats out of Maryland, and he's picking up more volunteers as he travels. Guess his dad is some big shot, and the dickhead thinks this is his destiny. You know, to relive some Civil War bullshit."

"Sounds like a real asshole," Tommy said.

"Oh, he is." Wyatt reached into a hip pocket and pulled out a map case and unfolded it. "I suppose you'd like to know what kind of shit we are getting into?"

He pointed to Winston and tossed him a headset. The man slapped it on and slid in closer. "Anything you can tell us will help."

Wyatt nodded. "The target is holed up in a building on the south side of the district. It's an office complex but nothing fancy. Elevator in the middle and stairs on both sides. We expect the elevator to be down, although it may be running. Some of these older buildings had generators that are still functional."

Tommy nodded. "Security?"

"That's a grey area. The ground assets have said the target has at least four of his regular security detail. The asset on scene said there was a late addition of another eight that arrived early this morning. They are outsiders but our guy on the ground says they are good."

"Are they willing to die for their principle?" Winston asked.

Wyatt pursed his lips and nodded. "I guess you can make that call for them. We are weapons hot, the gloves are off on everyone except the target."

"Where are we going in?" Tommy asked.

Wyatt shrugged. "We'll get dropped in on a parking lot one building over. We move down the street, move right in the front doors, disable the elevator—if running —then split into two teams, move up the stairwells, secure the package, and the helo picks us up on the roof."

Tommy smiled. "You know it's not going to work like that, right?"

Smiling, the man said, "This is just what they told me." He looked at Tommy. "Spence said you are in charge. Whatever you say goes."

"I like your style, Sergeant," Tommy said. "Let's just breach and go from there. You know that no plan survives first contact."

The crew chief looked back at them and flashed five fingers. Tommy leaned into Wyatt again. "And the assets, where are they?"

"Building across the street. They got eyes on and rifles up."

Tommy gave the sergeant a thumbs up then sat back with his eyes closed, steeling himself for what was ahead.

Minutes later, they were on the ground and running to the front building, 326 as it was identified on their tactical map. Tommy had his earpiece in, and he called for the assets, which he'd seen on the map key code was named "Looking glass." Not very creative but code names never were. His own call sign on this op was Haymaker, and the troops were Anvil. He tapped the earbud in his right ear and opened the channel. "Looking Glass, this is Haymaker. What are we walking into?"

"Welcome to the party, Haymaker."

The voice came back far clearer than Tommy had expected it to. He reached the front edge of Building 326 and pressed in next to it, taking a knee. Winston pulled in behind him and the six soldiers stacked up last.

"Lobby unlocked; we probed the entrance earlier. Lobby is clear, but from that point on, we can't guarantee anything. Looks like most movement is on the third floor."

"Do you have eyes on Jism?" He heard laughter on the line. Tommy looked back at Wyatt and said, "Seriously? 'Jism'? Who picked these call signs?"

Wyatt smiled. "It was 'Snake,' but Spence changed it last minute. He said you'd get a kick out of it."

The call came back. "We saw him earlier this morning, but nothing since the new guys came on scene."

"How did the new guys arrive?" Tommy asked.

"Came in on foot. Haven't seen any sign of transport."

Tommy squatted and looked down the wall then back at his team. He spoke in a normal voice, knowing his microphone was on and they would all be listening. "Two ways to do this: stealthy or fuck shit up." Before anyone could key in, he added, "I have a feeling they will have security on the doors beyond the lobby. We all know that, so more than likely, fuck shit up will just lead to a prolonged gunfight we can't win without support."

"It's your call," Wyatt said.

Tommy nodded. "We move in, secure the lobby. You all follow close and kick some ass while Winston and I sweep the building. We take and secure the floors top to bottom, one at a time. We get into trouble, and you guys bail us out."

Wyatt didn't say a word and instead shot him a mock salute. Tommy looked at Winston, who just winked at him and said, "I like it when you talk sexy."

Tommy looked at the man's bandaged arm. "How is the wing?"

"Bit late to be worried about that, ain't it?" Winston said.

Tommy grinned and said, "Good talk." Then he was back up and moving to the lobby doors.

Minutes later, they were marching forward in a single-file line, Tommy leading the way with his suppressed M4 at eye level. He turned the corner and pushed at the lobby door. They swung easily, and he stepped inside, sweeping in all directions as the team swept in behind him. There was a camera up on the wall. He pointed at it.

One of the troops, Tommy thought his name was DeBello, ran a hand across his neck. "Lights are out. Cameras are dead," he said.

Immediately, Tommy heard footfalls through a door leading left on a first-floor hallway. He crouched low and moved toward it with his weapon up. Without looking, he knew that half the men would be stacked up behind him as the other half moved to the hallway door, going to the right. When he got closer, he could see that the door had been propped open.

Again, he pointed, and, again, DeBello responded. "Maglocks, power is out, so they are braced open."

Tommy moved wide and positioned himself in front of the door as Winston grabbed the handle. He looked at Tommy and said, "Three, two, one," and slowly pushed the door in.

On the far side was a guard with a submachine gun in his right hand. The man was turned away from Tommy, pacing the hall. Halfway down, another man was sleeping in a chair. Sentries on a patrol. Tommy raised his rifle and put a series of suppressed rounds into the guard's back and into the side of the sleeping man. He heard a *clack, clack, clack* and without looking, he knew the Anvil team going to the right had just killed a second set of guards.

Tommy moved through the door with three men behind him and made his way to the stairwell. *So far so good*, he thought to himself. He checked the door and found it unlocked. And stepped into the stairwell and moved up to the second-floor landing. Then the Anvil team moved on either side and would defend the stairwell as Haymaker cleared the floor. He looked at Winston.

The man blinked his eyes and said, "Now the fun part."

They moved through the open door together, traveling right down the hallway, swinging open doors and clearing offices as they moved. Most were unlocked with obvious signs of forced entry. Someone had already cleared this building. It took less than ten minutes to reach the opposite stairwell and again they moved up one flight with the D-Boys moving in, securing it.

Tommy checked with Winston, and again they stepped off. This floor was different right off, and the difference was immediate. It was dark. Someone had moved through the floor and closed all the blinds.

They stepped off quickly, their boots hardly making a sound on the tile floor. They swung barrels into empty offices. When Tommy heard a man cough, he froze and pressed against the wall. Two men stepped out only two doors ahead of him. Tommy fired once and switched to the next man, firing again. Both bodies hit the floor with rounds to the face.

Winston moved in beside him, and they cut into the room. A man was sitting at a desk, shirtless with a half-eaten burrito in front of him. There was a pistol on a side table next to him. The man looked like he wanted to reach for it. Winston popped him twice in the chest then circled around the desk and removed the man's ID from his back pocket. "Ken Bründle? Is this our Jism?" Winston said.

Tommy shook his head no. "And good thing, too, because we're supposed to take him alive."

"Yikes," Winston said, tossing the wallet on the desk. "My bad."

They moved back into the hallway as two big men from further down burst out, firing with unsuppressed rifles. Tommy dove to the floor, firing back, while Winston ducked back into the room. "Anvil, east side, back us up," he shouted.

Quickly, two soldiers appeared from the stairwell door behind the shooters and shot them in the back. "Secure the top deck!" Tommy shouted over the comms.

The silence had been broken, and there was only one floor left above them. He heard the Anvil unit call back that they were on the top of each stairwell. They could hear people inside. Tommy and Winston continued running to the east side then moved up to the third-floor door, where DeBello and another man were guarding it.

DeBello pulled a mirror from his pocket attached to a telescoping rod. He leaned out and flashed it around the door. The mirror was immediately shot off the rod.

"I could bang it," the trooper said, pointing to a pair of flashbangs on his chest.

Tommy shook his head and moved around the man, sliding to a wall beside the door. Tommy readied his rifle and called on the radio, "Hey, Wyatt, I need you to poke your barrel out and make some noise in three, two, one."

On the last count, Tommy heard the gunfire, and he popped out low to the ground. A man was standing directly to his front with an AK47 rifle pointed at the door, but his head was turned to the stairwell door behind him. Tommy fired three times at an up-angle, striking the man in the chest and face, knocking him back.

Not trying to stop his momentum, Tommy moved through the hallway and into an office on the other side, moments before rounds tore into the walls. "I'm in," he said. "Wyatt, draw fire."

More gunfire boomed, followed up by a fully automatic blast of what Tommy knew was an RPK74. He held his breath, then rolled out into the hallway.

He quickly found he wasn't being shot at. Up the hall, three doors away, a man in grey body armor was leaning into the hallway, firing at Wyatt's position. The defender looked back to check his six, and his eyes went huge when he spotted Tommy with a rifle pointed at him. Tommy fired a quick volley, knocking the man back into the room. Without giving a command, Winston was in the hallway standing next to him.

"Anvil, we are in the hall; don't shoot us," Tommy said.

Near the middle on the right-hand side was the last

office. Tommy could hear scurrying inside then a man's shouts. Tommy slipped into a room across the hall, where he would have an angle on the office door.

He did the math in his head. "Looking Glass, you were sure the security detail was twelve men?"

"Roger that, four of his own plus eight. Been watching them all day."

"Only one guard left," Winston said.

"Anvil hallway is clear."

Tommy fired on the base of the doorway in full auto, the suppressed weapon still loud in the confined space. Wood splintered and he could hear a man whimpering from inside the room and another man telling him to shut up. Tommy calmly reloaded his rifle and focused on the office door. He looked toward the stairwells and could see that the Anvil team was now moving along the walls and stacking up for a breach.

"It's over, Senator, you can come with us now, or we'll burn you out."

A man went to speak, and there was a loud slap. "Shit—who says I won't kill him myself?" a man said from inside the office.

"I have a better deal for you. Walk out now, and we'll let you go; give us the senator, and then we can kill him," Tommy said.

"How do I know you won't kill me if I come out?" the man said.

Tommy looked at Winston, who shrugged. "Listen," Tommy said. "I don't care if you come out. Just send Shafer out, and we'll be on our way. Then you can do whatever the hell you want in there."

There was a long pause before the man said, "Okay."

Moments later, Shafer walked into the hallway with his arms up. When he saw Tommy, he said, "Thank God! You're with the military."

Tommy didn't speak. Instead, he grabbed the man behind the head and front tripped him down to the floor. Within seconds he was gagged and his hands zip-tied behind his back. Anvil had Jism secured and were moving to the stairwell as Wyatt already placed the call for the pickup. Winston was still standing by the edge of the door. "What about this guy?"

Tommy shrugged. "Deal's a deal. I imagine we'll have another opportunity to kill him."

Together, they egressed back to the stairwell and up to the roof, where the Black Hawk was already moving in on approach. Tommy looked out over the city. He'd been here several times and never seen it like this. The streets were empty of traffic, in the far distance he could see a fire burning in the Capitol Dome. He looked down at the man sitting cross-legged, his hands zip-tied behind his back, and black bag over his head. Tommy moved closer to the troopers as they waited for the helicopter to land.

He shook his head again, looking at the bound man, wondering if it would just be better to end him right now. He could tell there was no stopping what this man had started. There was a war in progress and no confession was going to end it. There was nothing this guy could say to put the madness back in its box.

There is no happy ending.

Mark was led down a long dark hallway and into the executive elevator. Guards stepped aside and allowed him to enter the small box then filed in around him on all sides. Aaron Wright the head scientist for Delphi followed the group in, his white lab coat and jeans replaced with a dark suit. He walked into the elevator and hit a button for the level two floors below the basement server bunker.

"Has Victor Checked in yet." Mark Dorsey asked.

Aaron turned and looked at Mark with surprise then at the guards surrounding his boss.

Mark laughed, "Don't worry about my security team, I trust them more than I trust you."

Tucking his top lip Aaron nodded and said, "No, there has been no word from Victor or his team."

"And Senator Shafer?"

Aaron shook his head, "Sorry, we lost contact with him. His satellite phone has gone offline. As there was no report from Victor we must assume he has been picked up by the opposition or fled."

Mark scowled and went to speak again, as the elevator stopped, and the doors opened. Aaron stepped back and let his boss move into the hallway first. This floor unlike the others in the building was only partially finished. The floor and walls were shaped of smooth concrete still awaiting tile and paint. Lights and cables were exposed from the ceiling, metal grids suspended empty of the fiberglass panels that would eventually be hung there. This floor was to become the true temple where the Oracle of Delphi would exist and function. The spaces above it a new Alexandria would be born.

The CEO of Apollo group made a quick scan of the space then began walking the hallway. "How is the second phase going?" Mark asked.

Clearing his throat Aaron increased his pace and fell in alongside his boss. The nuclear strikes against Chicago and Washington D.C. have put fear into the Cog–."

Mark stopped and held up his hand and said, "Wait–, what the hell is the Cog?"

Aaron gulped nervously, "Sorry, Sir, the Continuity of Government group. They have seen what The President is capable of and they are ready to cooperate with us, if we win over the Cog, the States will come on board."

Rubbing his chin Mark tightened his brow, he stepped off toward the door saying, "And the President?"

"He's gone Sir, our man on the ground Agent Gray says The President was evacuated to an unknown shelter."

"Gray. Yes of course Anthony Gray, he is still on the inside?" Mark asked.

"Yes Sir, for the time being, he has been very diligent working in his consultant role, making regular check ins. He will stay close to the opposition until you make the call to pull him out." Aaron said.

Mark acknowledged the comment with a sly smile, "Yeah–, get him here, I knew Anthony would be a good fit on the team. Make sure he gets a nice office on the third floor."

He opened the door at the end of the hallway. His guards posted up on the left and right side and he stepped in followed only by Aaron. There was a long wood conference table with dark leather chairs surrounding it. The far corner of the space was furnished in elaborate leather sofas and overstuffed chairs. Unlike the rest of the floor, this room was complete. At the end of the room stood a stunning bronze skinned woman with long black hair. She wore a white suit with her hands clasped in front of her.

"Mark, it is so good to see you again." She said smiling.

"Shravya, I was hoping you'd already arrived" Mark answered, his face lighting up. "How was your flight in?"

The woman grinned and moved closer to Mark taking his hand, "It was fine, but I feel better now that I am here with you." She said.

"Of course, of course," Mark said. "Anthony was just catching me up on the current situation."

Shravya pointed to one of the overstuffed chairs and Mark gratefully took a seat and Aaron moved to stand against a back wall. She stepped to the counter and opened a bottle of scotch and poured Mark three fingers in a lead tumbler. She handed it to him with a seductive smile "Your plan is going splendidly."

"Really?" Mark said sarcastically, "Aaron had me thinking the sky was falling." He said taking the glass.

Shravya took a small remote from a table and pressed a button. Suddenly the wall was replaced with a large map of the United States. Most of the East Coast in dark red, The Saint Louis area in blue, and the rest of the nation was flashing in orange except for a black circle over Chicago.

Mark sipped at the scotch, savoring the burn then said. "You are sure the Government is with us?"

The woman shrugged, "There isn't much we can be sure of now. Fighting has gotten worse across the nation. The California National Guard units have engaged in combat with Nevada Guard units. There are riots nationwide. There are regional food outages and there is a lack of leadership across most of the nation. Yet most of the Active Military still stands ready to deploy."

"Deploy, deploy against who?" Mark asked.

Shravya looked at the screen then back at Mark with a half-smile. "The President still controls most of the active forces, he could call them against us at any time."

"Then why hasn't he?" Mark asked.

"Our mis-information campaigns are working, and mostly because of Shafer. I suspect that he is the missing piece in their intelligence. They just need his confirmation to tell the American people who is really behind all of this." She said, then looked at Mark biting at her lower lip, she leaned closer and said, "That and your nuke strike against the Vice President was genius, it has made them really jumpy."

Mark grimaced, "I see, so if they have Shafer none of this works. What are your suggestions?"

"Leverage," Shravya said. "There is no point in lying to them anymore. If Victor fails, and Shafer speaks, the people will eventually learn what we have done here, if we do nothing they will come after us."

Mark sipped the drink, his eyes still fixed on the map, "What sort of leverage are you talking about?"

"We will take their power away, take their tech away. And only give it back if and as long as they cooperate." Shravya said.

"In D.C. I tried that, Delphi destroyed their grid. If I promise to get the power back on and hold it against them, then Delphi better be able to deliver."

Shravya laughed and walked back to the counter pouring herself a drink, then looked at the animation on the far wall. "Delphi will get the power back on if you ask." she took a step closer and dropped into one of the empty chairs. "Delphi learned a lot from its actions in D.C., it is smarter now, the AI will perform."

"But what if Shafer tells them." Mark said. "The people will still turn on us."

"Tells them what?" Shravya asked. "Tell them that we have taken control of their lives and that now we are in charge. Follow us or we will send them back to the stone age?" She leaned into Mark took a sip from her own glass and sighed. "It's too late for all of that. We already have the power; they just don't know it yet."

Mark hardened his jaw and looked at the screen, he sipped from his glass, then smiled. He looked at Shravya. "Make it happen then, inform the remaining leadership that we are now in charge. They will fall in line, or we will shut them down."

ABOUT WJ LUNDY

Join the WJ Lundy mailing list for news, updates and contest giveaways.

W. J. Lundy is a still serving Veteran of the U.S. Military with service in Afghanistan. He has over 16 years of combined service with the Army and Navy in Europe, the Balkans and Southwest Asia. W.J. is a USA Today Best-Selling Author, backpacker and shooting enthusiast. He currently resides with his wife and daughter in Central Michigan.

Find WJ Lundy on facebook:

For more from the expanding world of Tommy Donovan check out The Creed Series.

Matthew Hagan is one of the last holdouts from a society lost. Embedded deep inside Alexandria, he is an operative and vigilante-for-hire. Wherever he goes, a path of destruction follows, making him one of the most wanted men by the despotic government of the small nation-state.

As Hagan loses hope that he'll be able to carry out his original objective, he obtains a list of names. Names of the people involved with the attack on his village two years ago. Names that will pay for their crimes against his family. But as he tracks down his targets, Hagan discovers that one of Alexandria's most elite soldiers is hot on his heels, threatening his quest for retribution.

Will Hagan succeed in bringing justice to the unjust? Or will he fall into the hands of the brutal dictatorship of Alexandria?
The hunt is on in this post-apocalyptic military thriller written by AJ Powers and W.J. Lundy.

Whiskey Tango Foxtrot Series.
Whiskey Tango Foxtrot is an introduction into the apocalyptic world of Staff Sergeant Brad Thompson.   A series with over 1,500 five-star reviews on Amazon.

Alone in a foreign land. The radio goes quiet while on convoy in Afghanistan, a lost patrol alone in the desert. With his unit and his home base destroyed, Staff Sergeant Brad Thompson suddenly finds himself isolated and in command of a small group of men trying to survive in the Afghan wasteland.

Every turn leads to danger. The local population has been afflicted with an illness that turns them into rabid animals. They pursue him and his men at every corner and stop. Struggling to hold his team together and unite survivors, he must fight and evade his way to safety.

A fast paced zombie war story like no other.

Escaping The Dead
  Tales of The Forgotten
  Only The Dead Live Forever
  Walking In The Shadow Of Death
  Something To Fight For
  Divided We Fall
  Bound By Honor

Praise for Whiskey Tango Foxtrot:

"The beginning of a fantastic story. Action packed and full of likeable characters. If you want military authenticity, look no further. You won't be sorry."
-Owen Baillie, Author of Best-selling series, Invasion of the Dead.

"A brilliantly entertaining post-apocalyptic thriller. You'll find it hard to putdown"
-Darren Wearmouth, Best-selling author of First Activation, Critical Dawn, Sixth Cycle

"W.J. Lundy captured two things I love in one novel-- military and zombies!"
-Terri King, Editor Death Throes Webzine

"War is horror and having a horror set during wartime works well in this story. Highly recommended!"
-Allen Gamboa, Author of Dead Island: Operation Zulu

"There are good books in this genre, and then there are the ones that stand out from the rest-- the ones that make me want to purchase all the books in the series in one shot and keep reading. W.J. Lundy's Whiskey Tango Foxtrot falls into the latter category."
-Under the Oaks reviews

"The author's unique skills set this one apart from the masses of other zombie novels making it one of the most exciting that I have read so far."
-HJ Harry, of Author Splinter

The Invasion Trilogy
The Darkness is a fast-paced story of survival that brings the apocalypse to Main Street USA.

While the world falls apart, Jacob Anderson barricades his family behind locked doors. News reports tell of civil unrest in the streets, murders, and disappearances; citizens are warned to remain behind locked doors. When Jacob becomes witness to horrible events and the alarming actions of his neighbors, he and his family realize everything is far worse than being reported.

Every father's nightmare comes true as Jacob's normal life--and a promise to protect his family--is torn apart.

From the Best-Selling Author of **Whiskey Tango Foxtrot comes a new telling of Armageddon.**

The Darkness
The Shadows
The Light

Praise for the Invasion Trilogy:

"The Darkness is like an air raid siren that won't shut off; thrilling and downright horrifying!" ***Nicholas Sansbury Smith, Best Selling Author of Orbs and The Extinction Cycle.***

"Absolutely amazing. This story hooked me from the first page and didn't let up. I read the story in one sitting and now I am desperate for more. ...Mr. Lundy has definitely broken new ground with this tale of humanity, sacrifice and love of family ... In short, read this book." ***William Allen, Author of Walking in the Rain.***

"First book I've pre-ordered before it was published. Well done story of survival with a relentless pace, great action, and characters I cared about! Some scenes are still in my head!" ***Stephen A. North, Author of Dead Tide and The Drifter.***

From the expanding world of Whiskey Tango Foxtrot.

The Soldier Series

From the War on Terror a world crippling Bio-Weapon is released. The United States scrambles teams of scientists from the Centers For Disease Control. America's top field agent are tasked with collecting samples and developing a cure. In a national laboratory scientists race against the clock searching for a cure. Borders are closed, martial law and soldiers deployed across the homeland.

Torment

Sanctuary

Made in the USA
Monee, IL
06 September 2020